I0563112

GOOD KIND OF GONE

A HEARTHSTONE NOVEL
BOOK 5

SARAH KADES

STARK
PUBLISHING

Copyright © 2023 by Sarah Graham

All rights reserved. No part of this publication may be reproduced, distributed or transmitted in any form or by any means, without prior written permission of the publisher.

Stark Publishing, Waterloo, ON

www.starkpublishing.ca

Publisher's Note: This is a work of fiction. Names, characters, places, and incidents are a product of the author's imagination. Real locales and names may sometimes be used for atmospheric purposes. Any resemblance to actual people, living or dead, or to businesses, companies, events, institutions, or locales is either completely coincidental or is used in a completely fictional manner.

We acknowledge the support of the Canada Council for the Arts

Conseil des Arts du Canada   **Canada Council for the Arts**

The Canada Council for the Arts contributes to the vibrancy of a creative and diverse arts and literary scene and supports its presence across Canada and around the world. The Council is Canada's public arts funder, with a mandate to "foster and promote the study and enjoyment of, and the production of works in, the arts." The Council's grants, services, initiatives, prizes, and payments support Canadian artists, authors, and arts groups and organizations. This support allows them to pursue artistic expression, create works of art, and promote and disseminate the arts and literature.

Good Kind of Gone / Sarah Kades – 1st ed.

Trade Paperback ISBN: 978-1-7390474-2-9

eBook ISBN: 978-1-7390474-3-6

To Lorie,
Happy Mabon

CHAPTER ONE

C *anada*
"I watched him die." Tanner Stone was unable to fabricate remorse. His biological father's treachery had been unconscionable. The diabolical ripples from the man's lethal scheming were still being felt—shudders felt worldwide. Watching the man overdose hadn't been a pleasure nor brought pain.

Stone would have settled for relief.

It was Christmas Day, and he was sitting next to Tucker, one of his recently-found Canadian half-brothers. They sat on Becca's wrap-around porch. His half-sister had recently opened an eco-inn in the foothills of the Rocky Mountains, naming it *Hearth-stone Ranch*. An apt name, to be sure. Though she didn't realize it, his half-sister was the heart and soul of the Tanner Family, and her home a nurturing oasis.

A Chinook had blown in. Stone had been raised in Australia and experienced foehns, but the warm Alberta mountain wind was as eerie as it was welcome. Melting snow and ice dripped everywhere.

Becca and her fiancé Jason were hosting the Christmas holidays for family and friends, found and otherwise. The eclectic bunch made Stone feel oddly at home. It had been the best Christmas Stone could remember in a very long time. After more than a decade with ASIS, Australia's Security Intelligence Service, he wasn't sure he was built for such things. Nor was he confident that jumping into the Tanner clan's orbit was a good idea. Yet, the way Tucker looked at him, so expectant and open, Stone almost wanted to try.

At the very least, the man deserved to know the truth about his father.

"When I got there—his apartment, he had just injected. I watched him pull the needle out. He quickly tossed it aside like I wouldn't notice." Stone braced himself. The next part was ugly. "I had a Naloxone kit with me."

The admission hung in the air between them; a line in the sand Stone had crossed. They were both in law enforcement—Tucker was a police detective, but Stone was pretty sure their do-not-cross lines came in at different angles.

He looked across the ranch yard. If he walked away, his footprints wouldn't last in the melting snow. He should go. He'd answer Tucker's questions and then get the fuck out.

"What happened?" Tucker's voice was low but not accusatory.

It tripped him up. Everything from that awful day came screeching back. "I couldn't use it. I couldn't try to save his life—not after what he'd done. He shot and tried to torch our sister and the man she loves, even his own wife. He knowingly provided intel to ambush Gabe while on a CSIS mission. And you. His partner pumped three bullets into your back at point-blank range."

"The bullets were meant for another," Tucker reminded him, fair as always.

"Were they?"

Tucker stilled, and helpless anger ignited within Stone. He flung his hands up, pissed on behalf of his half-siblings. "What kind of father does that?"

The kind that never claimed you.

Stone shoved the pointless reminder down. He had made peace with the circumstances of his birth years ago. "Omran and I found more intel. Carl, the bank manager, was on Bruce's payroll, and Bruce was broke."

"As in no cash, broke?"

Stone nodded.

Tucker looked thoughtful. "Do you think that's why he married Meredith?"

"Yeah. And her connections. She's still loaded." Stone laughed. "Like filthy rich, loaded, and knows *everyone*." Connected and loaded—she would have been a conman's wet dream.

His half-brother quietly added, "And she's kind."

Stone stared at him, surprised. It was no secret that the Tanner siblings had not welcomed Meredith—the *other* woman who finally broke Bruce and Samantha's marriage apart. Stone had never had the option to accept or dismiss any of Bruce's wives. Stone's mother had never gotten past the mistress stage. Doris had no connections or wealth but had been young and beautiful. Bruce's interest in Stone's mom had been base, nothing more, whereas Doris's interest in Bruce had been the woeful naïveté of untested passion.

It was different with Meredith. Bruce had pursued a romance with Meredith for her money and political connections. Meredith had thought she had finally fallen in love.

Tucker ignored Stone's curious stare and asked, "Any idea on the leak?"

Stone crossed his arms. Tucker wouldn't like what he was about to say. "Omran and I've done some discreet digging. Up until two months ago, Detective Jones was heavily mortgaged and carrying substantial credit card debt. Now he's not."

"That doesn't sound like Jones."

His little brother didn't quite bleed blue, but close enough. Detective Jones had been the first colleague to visit Tucker in the hospital. Tucker would be hesitant to jump to conclusions or believe anything bad about the guy.

"His son was an addict. Looks like Jones and his wife tried scores of private rehab facilities when their son got kicked out of the public ones."

Tucker was frowning.

"It'll probably take a few days to unpack where the money came from," Stone assuaged. "Jones's record is spotless. My guess is Bruce threatened or blackmailed Jones into cooperating."

Tucker's eyes turned bleak. "Jones is a good man, a dedicated father. Bruce would have been able to find the man's pressure points."

Stone agreed, but all he added was, "The monster's dead."

He had spent the first half of his life ignoring the fact the man he called *Dad* wasn't his biological one, and the second half unraveling just how dangerous Bruce Tanner was and trying to protect the world from his machinations in global politics and power plays, let alone trying to murder his own family.

Tucker looked at Stone. "He never claimed you as his son. That was pretty shitty."

Stone scrubbed his face with his hands. "That's water under the bridge."

"It is?" Tucker sounded genuinely curious.

Stone shrugged. "My stepdad adored my mom and accepted me as his own. He was everything Bruce Tanner wasn't. I didn't have to grow up with the monster. Knowing now what we do, I honestly don't know how you guys did it." It was close enough to the truth. His stepdad would have liked it a hell of a lot more if Stone had cut his mom more slack.

His half-brother sat back. "We didn't know then. I mean, none of us saw this coming. He was narcissistic and cruel, but none of us realized what he had become. Growing up, we had each other. And Clint. Our mom is fucked in her own way. Actually, I think she did the best she knew how." Tucker blew out a heavy breath, and Stone wondered what house of cards had just crumbled. Family realizations were like that.

Both men sat, quiet, staring out across the ranch yard. The midday winter light was weak but growing. Every day since the winter solstice, the days were getting longer again.

"What's next for you?" Tucker asked.

"Becca insists I'm here through New Years."

"She's like that."

Stone's smile was real. "I like it." His smile threatened to slip as he thought of his mom unbidden. She had been the only woman he had let care for him, and Stone hadn't let her in, in a long time. Not since he had asked questions with answers better left unsaid. Their relationship had been a strained shell since.

Tucker clapped him on the back. "You are so going to eat your words. Between Becca, Grace, and Lillian, you don't stand a chance. I'm sure Savannah would mother hen you just as much, but with them living across the country, we barely see them."

"I doubt that."

Tucker leveled him with a long stare. "What's that supposed to mean?"

"Come on. It's not like it's a secret anymore. Gabe knew I existed and never said a damn thing. It's not like he and Savannah are cool with me."

"He was a child," Tucker reasoned.

"Who grew up. I understand why he never said anything as a kid, but at some point in the last decade, he could have mentioned I existed. He chose to keep quiet." Obviously, to Gabe, Stone was nothing more than a dark secret, a mistake his father made, and something to remain banished to the shadows.

"He's a good guy. Family is ... complicated."

Stone wasn't so sure. Gabe had done the one thing he could to keep Stone out of their perfect little sibling group. Gabe considered Stone a bastard. What stung was that he was right.

Stone kept his voice even when he asked, "What about you,

Colt, Gabe, and Jason? Are you guys okay if I stay through New Years?"

"We're good." Tucker sounded like he meant it. "I know you and Gabe have some shit to work out. Maybe you guys will have a chance to."

"Maybe." Stone doubted it. "Look, I have to ask—"

Tucker cut him off. "I'm glad you told me how Bruce died. It doesn't change how I feel about you. I want you as my brother."

The massive heaviness that had settled in Stone since that fateful day shifted.

Before he had a chance to speak, Tucker spoke again, "I don't know what I would have done if I had found him first." His bleak gaze met Stone's. "That's haunted me since the fire."

Fresh anger rose within Stone; even dead, Bruce Tanner tormented his children. "You'll never have to. I consider that a win."

"Teague Alans is still out there."

Stone briefly clapped his hand over Tucker's shoulder. "I've got this one, little brother."

There was no way Stone would let that fucker Teague Alans end what their murderous father had started.

Stone would stop Teague Alans before anyone else got hurt or die trying.

CHAPTER TWO

"Paris is always a good idea." Savannah MacIntyre exclaimed, following Maggie Monroe into Becca Tanner's eco-inn's kitchen.

"Is it?" Maggie asked her best friend before heading to the side counter to refill the empty plate of brownies.

"Are you kidding me? Yes!"

Becca Tanner walked in after them, carrying an empty teapot. She gave a gentler endorsement. "It is truly magical."

It was Christmas Day. The entire holiday season had been filled with the love and laughter of dear friends and the enchanting magic of new ones. Maggie couldn't remember the last time she had felt so relaxed and happy. Just the thought of leaving the happy cocoon the extended family and friends had created at Becca's inn had left Maggie feeling something close to despair.

Much as she tried to hide it, life wasn't usually so happy.

Here, it felt like Maggie was in a different world. A beautiful, accepting, safe world. *Hearthstone Ranch* routinely entertained high-ranking international officials and was outfitted accordingly. In the next room, a roomful of women Maggie had just met were planning a baby shower, and Maggie was already invited.

Becca grinned, leaning against the counter and waiting for the kettle to boil. "She's right. I popped over to the City of Lights at least a dozen times while working in Germany. The history, the culture, the food, the *energy* of the place—I love it over there."

Another wave of restlessness washed over Maggie. How she wished she was the type of person that could just breeze off to Paris. She had longed to go for years but had never made the trip. "It's always sounded rather magical."

"It is." Becca was beaming, and Maggie turned to see what had caught her attention.

Becca's fiancé, Jason Chasseur, strode into the dining room. He dropped a kiss on Becca's lips before snagging a brownie. "Hi, honey."

Maggie turned to Savannah, smiling. "Are they for real?"

That got a cackle out of Becca. "Please. My brother and Savannah can't keep their hands off each other."

"Fair point," Maggie conceded. Gabe and Savannah were not shy about being crazy about each other. Was there something in the water here? Every time Maggie turned, another friend was pairing off.

"What about Paris?" Jason asked before biting the brownie he had snagged from the plate.

"We're trying to talk Maggie into going."

Jason smiled. "Sounds fun."

Maggie looked around the table. Everyone was smiling at her, encouraging her adventures. It was a beautiful moment. "Thank you all for including me. This truly has been the best Christmas ever."

"It's our pleasure. You're welcome here anytime." Becca wrapped her hand in Jason's, and they both smiled warmly at her.

This beautiful couple had no idea how their warm acceptance had meant the world to Maggie.

Becca suddenly jumped up. "I forgot about the coffee!"

Savannah laughed. "I'll bring Gabe his."

Maggie snorted. "Is that what the kids are calling it these days?"

Savannah threw a miniature candy cane at her. Maggie laughed, easily catching it, before asking Becca, "Need help? I think Tucker and Stone are on the porch. I can bring them theirs."

Becca gave her a grateful smile. "That would be lovely, thank you. I don't want to leave Samantha and Meredith for too long. I don't want Lillian or Grace to have to referee. I'll get the ladies sorted with their tea and snacks. You take the guys their Irish coffees."

"What do you need me to do?" Jason asked.

"Stir." She handed him a spoon, winking. "Then we're making out until the tea is ready."

Two minutes later, Maggie held a steaming mug of coffee in each hand as her stomach flip-flopped. She took a deep breath before she walked through the front door of Becca's eco-inn onto the wrap-around porch. The cool air was fresh, a heady contrast to the warm mugs she held. Carefully, she leaned her shoulder against the door, closing it behind her with a soft click.

When she looked down the porch, she noticed Tanner Stone's tall form immediately. He was seated on one of the Muskoka chairs, his long legs stretched out in front of him. She soaked in the masculine sight of him.

If she ever let herself take a romantic leap, he would be it. Just the thought of getting tangled up with him brought a heated flush to her cheeks.

"Maggie!" Tucker, Becca's brother, spotted her.

Stone immediately sat up, tucking his long legs in, out of her way. She walked forward, smiling cautiously as she tried to ascertain if she had interrupted something touchy—Tanner Stone was the unclaimed, product-of-adultery. A half-sibling to the rest of the Tanners. His presence was a charged, mixed blessing for more than just her. "Becca thought you guys might appreciate something hot."

"Spiked coffee?" Tucker asked hopefully.

Maggie nodded, stepping past Stone to hand Tucker a mug.

"You're a godsend," Tucker said in thanks.

Maggie smiled at his exuberance. According to Becca, since Tucker and HRH Princess Grace became an item, his recovery from being shot at point-blank range had rebounded dramatically. Tucker was more and more like his old self again, not that Maggie would know firsthand. Maggie had only met half of the Tanner siblings at Meredith and Bruce Tanner's disastrous wedding earlier in the year. Meredith had been horrified to learn Bruce hadn't invited the rest.

Maggie held out the mug she had brought for Stone. "Here you go, Tanner."

His hands were out, accepting the mug she had brought him when she had called him by his first name. His whole body tensed, and for a second, she thought he would drop the mug.

"Just Stone," he reminded her as he adjusted his grip on the mug. His strong fingers briefly cupped over hers, and she forgot to breathe.

"Sorry, I knew that. I don't know why I said Tanner." She finally let go, feeling jealous of a mug.

"Thanks for the coffee." He looked up, his expressive eyes on her. "Did you draw the short straw?"

Her hands now free, she toyed with the small crystal pendant she wore. "I'm neutral—fringe, really, to everyone else." She might be Savannah's best friend, and Meredith was an auntie to Maggie in all the ways that mattered. Still, Maggie knew she was only passing through.

"Flying under the radar's not so bad."

Maggie crossed her arms lest she be tempted to run her fingers through his hair. She tilted her face up to the warm sun, eyes closed. "I like that, *flying under the radar*." She'd fly under the radar forever if it meant being included in the Tanner family Christmas festivities. She was having an incredible time, even with the super-charged family dynamics erupting and her unexpected crush.

Tucker scoffed. "Yeah, right, you're an honorary Tanner." Tucker lifted his mug. "Maggie, you're stuck with us."

Maggie's eyes widened. "Tucker … that means a lot. Thank you." More than he could know. But she darted a worried glance at Stone. He was a Tanner by blood, the late Bruce Tanner's unacknowledged biological son only recently connected with his Canadian half-siblings.

Stone held her gaze, and she felt a fissure pass between them.

Tucker, oblivious to the pinballing undercurrents, said, "You'll be on the family group texts in no time."

Again, Maggie's gaze found Stone's, and he lifted his mug in mock salute to her exalted status. "I need your phone number then."

Stone choked on his coffee.

Tucker slapped him on the back.

Stone cleared his throat with a final cough. In a deep voice, he said, "I'm not on any family group texts."

"He will be," Tucker promised.

Stone glared at him.

"I should go back in." Christ, she had practically begged the man for his phone number. Maggie didn't date, and she sure as hell didn't embarrass herself in front of others. "I need to go back in. There are very well-meaning moms and aunties in there trying to plan Lillian's baby shower." Lillian Kensington— badass war correspondent, former MI6 courier, and Colt Tanner's baby momma and wife—was no pushover, but the imminent arrival of the next generation was causing quite a bit of overly helpful pole positioning.

Tucker blanched. "Oh, good Lord. My mom and Meredith … like together, are planning?"

Stone was looking at her.

Maggie pressed a cool hand to her cheek. Was she still blushing? "Hmm, mmm. *All* the moms and aunties." Stone gave the slightest flinch at her words. Distracted, she pulled her gaze away from Stone's and looked at Tucker. "Don't worry, Lillian, Becca, Savannah, and Grace are holding their own." She inched closer to the front door as Tucker preened at the mention of his sweetheart, the Princess of Jordemorden.

"Thanks for the coffee," Stone said. He had recovered from the chink in his armor.

"Yup." She fled into the large ranch inn.

And ran straight into Gabe Tanner.

"Sorry!" Maggie righted herself, grabbing for Gabe's bent-over form. She clutched his shoulder and pulled. Her best friend's serious boyfriend had been reaching for his boots when she collided into him. "You okay?"

"I'm fine." Of course, he was. Gabe Tanner was solid as a fucking rock, literally and metaphorically.

"Savannah's looking for you—are you all right?" Concern immediately clouded his eyes when he finally looked at her.

"Me?" Maggie squeaked. "I'm great. Totally peachy. Why?"

Gabe's brow actually furrowed. "Because you just came in here like a bat out of hell."

Be cool. Do not blurt a damn thing about Tanner Stone's sexy voice, his sexy body—"Becca made fancy coffee, I just brought Stone and—"

Gabe's frown could have peeled paint. "Did Stone say something to upset you? Because if he did, I swear I'll take care of it."

Maggie felt her eyes widen. "Of course not. Tucker's out there, too. I brought them both coffee. Everything's fine." She hesitated. "Are you fine?"

Gabe's face went stony.

Maggie hoped she wasn't stepping in it. "Is there anything I can do to help? You and Stone—"

"There is no 'me and Stone.'"

Gabe's voice wasn't quite glacial, but it made Maggie reroute. "Right. My mistake. Excuse me, I'll go find Savannah." She ducked her head, wishing to make another escape.

"Maggie, wait—" Gabe stood stock still, everything about him held tense. Pain, as much as anger, radiated off him.

God, this family was hurting.

Maggie stared at the wall beyond Gabe's large shoulder. A framed mountain picture hung on the wall beyond the foyer. It was lovely in its stark beauty. Softly, she said, "It's okay, Gabe. It's none of my business."

"Stone is … a touchy subject." He looked almost bewildered before suddenly straightening, his stoicism back in place. "I'm sorry I was rude. It won't happen again."

"Do you miss him?" Maggie asked the question before she could talk herself out of it, now unwilling to make an easy escape.

Gabe frowned. "We never had the chance."

We. Maggie's heart tugged at the unintentional slip.

"Maybe someday you will."

It wasn't much as far as seeds went.

But that was the thing about seeds. You never knew when one would take.

CHAPTER THREE

Maggie was off limits.

Stone watched her go. She was a complication he wanted but sure as hell didn't need, and as soon as his brain arm wrestled his dick back for the blood supply, he'd convince himself to fuck off.

"She's a sweetheart."

Stone snapped his head around.

"I meant for you, dipshit," Tucker said. "You're totally rough around the edges, but like I said, you're growing on us, and she's clearly … curious about you. If that wasn't flirting, I don't know what is. And I heard her tell Grace your accent was dreamy."

Stone immediately squelched the flicker of hope that had sparked at Tucker's words. Maggie was Savannah's best friend, and Savannah and Gabe were solid. That meant Stone could never act on the attraction. Something sizzled just beneath the surface every time he saw Maggie.

Tucker pressed, "You could do a lot worse than Ms. Monroe."

"Gabe would shoot me." On this, Stone wouldn't blame him. Maggie deserved more than a bastard son.

Tucker frowned. "Why?"

"Because—" Stone blew out his retort. Tucker wouldn't understand—*couldn't* understand. Stone resettled in the porch chair. "Never mind. Besides, you're bananas over Grace."

"What does that have anything to do with it?"

"It's affecting your judgment." Stone had heard just how into each other Tucker and Grace were when he had made the unfortunate choice to go for an early morning horseback ride and heard their screaming adoration in the apartment above the barn.

Tucker beamed. "I am. Love will do that."

Stone tried not to roll his eyes.

"All I'm saying is being loved by a good woman ... it changes you."

"I'm good, thanks." Sex was real, love was a fairytale, and people didn't change. Besides, Maggie was too good for Stone. End of story.

Tucker snickered. "So was I, bro, until I wasn't."

Stone's body clenched.

Bro. Tucker tossed the word out like it was ordinary, like they were actually brothers.

Stone leaned heavily against the opposite armrest, putting distance between him and Tucker. If Tucker noticed, he didn't say anything. He just hooked his thumb toward the front door. "I'm telling you, that librarian would be good for you."

Stone did a double-take. *Librarian?* "Christ, I would have read a thousand books—"

"I know, right?" Tucker hooted. "She's completely oblivious, too."

Stone cupped the coffee mug she had brought him with both hands. "What's her story?" He would have guessed artist or beekeeper—something random and vibrant.

Not hot librarian.

Tucker's mouth turned down. "Kinda sad, really. I guess she and her twin brother were raised in separate boarding schools."

"What happened to their parents?"

Tucker shrugged. "No idea. She let that much slip last night and then clammed up. Kind of spooked her to share that much. You know what that means."

Stone did. In an interview, those were the fractures he always looked for to chase. "Where's her twin brother?" Just because Stone rarely spent holidays with family didn't mean everyone was as lonely as him.

"She never said. She just changed the subject and slipped out of the room."

Stone frowned. Most people were like shallow water. Stone was pretty sure Maggie was more like the Mariana Trench— deep and complicated as fuck to explore. Her inclusion in the festivities definitely made Stone's Christmas holidays more interesting. As a rule, though, he didn't do deep or complicated.

He was pretty sure Maggie Monroe was both.

The front door opened again, and Stone felt his heart rate bump.

It wasn't Maggie, her natural brightness banishing all the dark shadowed places of his soul.

It was Gabe.

The man's face equally fell when he saw Stone. "Oh ... hey."

Immediately, Tucker motioned to one of the empty Muskoka chairs. "Sit down, take a load off."

Gabe hesitated. Finally, he shoved his hands in his jeans pockets and walked past the first empty chair. He sat down on the other side of Tucker.

"Smooth," Tucker muttered. Stone gripped the mug tighter, fighting the urge to leave, while Gabe just stared out across the ranch yard. Silence hung awkwardly between everyone.

Drip, drip, drip. The melting snow that had sounded lyrical only moments before now scratched Stone's nerves. He stood. "I'll see you guys later."

Tucker looked apologetic. Gabe didn't look at him at all. The rejection would have stung if Stone wasn't so used to it. He had better things to do than stick around as his older half-brother ignored him.

Teague Alans was out there.

Stone was going to find him and wrap this case up once and for all. Then, once he knew they were safe, he could shove these newfound siblings as far away as possible.

CHAPTER FOUR

France

Sebastian Monroe waited to die. It was a peculiar thing, being tortured. In the dark moments of life, when he had grappled with the abyss of their turbulent childhood and felt the unconscionable pull of a promised oblivion, it was the hope for a noble death, something tragic and poetic, that had always stayed his hand. Not wanting to burden Maggie further had kept him alive.

Suicide wasn't noble or poetic.

Now, with his twin sister as settled as she would ever be, happy with her work and the new friends she met over Christmas—Hearthstone Ranch, she had called it, and he was happier than he realized possible with Phoebe, Sebastian *wanted* to live. But fate was a cruel bitch. Too late, he had realized Teague Alans was a lunatic, not the benevolent benefactor to his research that Sebastian had thought.

It was the second worst mistake of his life.

A jolt of electricity pumped through Sebastian's system, scattering his quasi-lucid thoughts.

They had discarded breaking the rest of his bones and moved on to electrocution. He could no longer keep track of what physically hurt, what had gone numb, and what body parts simply wouldn't work anymore. He supposed it was an evolutionary advantage, shutting off perceptions of physical pain. Sebastian pondered further—it didn't mean his body wasn't still being brutalized. The synapses in his mind had simply stopped reporting it. Sebastian was going to die at the hands of Teague Alans's crew. Even now, the two imbeciles were taking turns destroying his body.

Another jolt of electricity, stronger this time, pumped through his system, and in between spasms, his mind raged at their idiocy. His brain—chaotic though it was—was worth a thousand of them. Sebastian's research was a world-changer, the breakthrough humanity had been waiting for. While their contribution to the planet was non-existent, their existence utterly useless. Sebastian would tell them they were a waste of Earth's resources if he could figure out how to use his mouth.

Then everything went black, and Sebastian grasped for consciousness.

At least he thought he did until he realized he was floating. Looking down, Sebastian was suspended above his body. His rational mind knew it was impossible, yet here he was ... some sort of embodied consciousness floating above his physical body.

He lifted his hand, staring at the etheric translucence. The air was different like he was suspended in a prism instead of the atmosphere. Was he dead?

"Shit, I think he's dead," Imbecile number one said, still holding the wired cable.

Imbecile number two launched himself at his partner, pushing him violently. "You weren't supposed to kill him."

From the weird twilight of his untethered vantage above, Sebastian watched their shoving match deteriorate into a full-blown brawl. They slammed against the table and walls and finally, against the weird chair he was strapped into. His body was dumped unceremoniously onto the floor.

They stopped fighting, both breathing hard, and stared at his motionless body.

"Woah, he's like dead-dead."

"What should we do?" Imbecile number two asked.

"Let's wrap him up," Imbecile number one suggested.

"Good idea."

"What are we going to tell Teague?"

Imbecile number two shrugged. "Self-defense?"

"Works for me."

Sebastian winced from above as they manhandled his body, stuffing him in a sleep sack for god sakes. Grunting, they dragged his body down the hall before crossing a loading area. The sleeping bag caught on the edge of the metal door, and they heaved, once, twice, knocking his unresponsive body about with their clumsy efforts. Once the bag was free, they launched him into the back of a van. Sebastian viewed all of this with a curious detachment like watching someone else's movie. When he felt his consciousness slipping again, he welcomed the promised surrender.

So this was what dying felt like.

Maggie had tried to tell him once over the phone. They had been at separate boarding schools, an ocean separating them, and she had nearly drowned in gym class. He had gently chided her New Age sensibilities as she tried to explain her near-death experience. His science mind—and the abject terror of nearly losing her—simply would not compute.

At the time, he had dismissed his twin sister's experience as irrational.

Now he knew better.

He fought hard against death's hypnotic pull, refusing to die. The seductive oblivion Sebastian's body was begging for tempted his shockingly abused senses, and he willed his battered body to stay alive, to fight like he had when he was ten.

He couldn't leave his twin sister alone in the world, and he wouldn't leave his beloved Phoebe.

Sebastian fought to stay conscious, to let himself feel the pain and abuse that was even now shutting down his body. His desperate scream for life stuck in his tortured throat. He was trapped, a hair's breadth away from death, unable to move or feel.

Until he wasn't.

The van had hit a bump, and the jarring recoil shot through his body even as elation swelled within him.

He wasn't dead.

He couldn't be. He had *felt* that. Every battered inch of his body protested the rough ride, even as a euphoria spread through him.

He would survive.

Sebastian thanked every persistent teacher, every awkward friend, every act of kindness from a stranger, even the sense of responsibility and obligation he had felt that he couldn't finally end all his pain because that would mean leaving Maggie alone with their wretched family. Everyone had conspired to keep him from taking his own life. They hadn't been wrong to be kind to him. *Goddammit*, he was going to survive this. He would protect Phoebe and Maggie. And Teague Alans could burn in Hell.

Sebastian was rocked as the van swerved to the side, and he used the motion to burrow deeper into the sleep sack. They cut the engine. The bulky sleeping bag hid his shallow breaths, and he kept his body a deadweight as they pulled him out. Grunting, they heaved him over a guardrail.

And pushed him over the edge.

CHAPTER FIVE

F rance

Officer de Police Judiciarie Phoebe Freres hid shaking hands as she bagged the bloodied shirt in an evidence bag. Sebastian had been wearing that shirt when he had left their apartment yesterday morning. Alive.

She had known something was wrong. He liked to call or text, said it soothed him. But Phoebe hadn't heard from him since he had kissed her, smiling that sad smile he always had while assuring her again that everything was going to be okay. He was making sure of it.

It was the only time he had lied to her.

Nothing was going to be okay. His phone lay silent where he had left it in the copper bowl on the counter, and she was holding his bloody shirt, not him.

Her hand gripped the large plastic bag tight as she hugged the evidence bag to her chest. She hadn't screamed when the abandoned vehicle that had been called in was Sebastian's, nor when she had walked closer and saw the inside was covered in biological material. Now, she stared at the ground, her breathing unnatural, fighting the abyss she had seen scores of victim families topple into when their loved ones had been taken away from them violently and way too soon.

For years, she had bore witness to their pain and unconscionable loss, but she had never experienced the abyss. Until now. She hugged the evidence bag tighter and fought to take in a full breath.

"Freres?" Several OPJs were on scene, waiting for further direction. She barked out final orders. No one questioned her. If anyone noticed the redness of her eyes, they didn't say anything. She followed every protocol. Evidence was meticulously collected, and comprehensive notes were taken.

Her mobile rang. She nearly dropped it in her haste to answer, so hopeful that it would be Sebastian, that he was all right after all.

It was her colleague, Virunga. "I just started my shift. Need me to run anything in for you?"

Phoebe rubbed her forehead, pinching her thumb and fingers together over her tense flesh. "We're just about done here, and the drive will be a good wind down."

After a long pause, Virunga's deep voice vibrated over the phone. "There's nothing soothing about that commute."

Phoebe made a non-committal, desperate sound as silenced screams clawed up her throat.

Another heavy pause. "Let me know if you need anything." Virunga knew something was up.

"I will," she promised, her fingers finding the silver pendant at her throat Sebastian had given her for her birthday.

Virunga grudgingly signed off.

After the scene had been processed, she insisted on personally waiting for the flatbed truck that would transport the vehicle to the lab. One by one, OPJs and techs drove away, hustling to new crime scenes. New lives shattered.

Sebastian's vehicle was picked up.

Phoebe got back into her car, alone for the first time since she found the crime scene. Violent sobs wracked her body. She wrapped her arms around herself, rocking.

No one knew of her relationship with Sebastian. She had wanted to keep things quiet, see where they led. He was different, nothing like the Frenchmen she had dated. She had been afraid others would judge his eccentricities and laugh at her eclectic choice. Now she just wanted to see her beloved alive.

Phoebe swiped at her eyes and started her car back up. She pulled into traffic and, thirty-five minutes later, dropped the evidence bags at the lab.

The next several weeks were a nightmare.

Desperate to find Sebastian alive, she searched in vain, calling in every favor and following up on even the smallest shreds of evidence.

He wasn't found alive. He wasn't found at all.

They had finally identified the second crime scene, where Sebastian had been tortured, and the third, where the perpetrators had dumped his body. They had recovered the bloodied sleeping bag Sebastian had been wrapped in. The biological material—so much blood—had been confirmed to be Sebastian's.

His body was never recovered. Sebastian had been dumped in a ravine, a natural area with active wildlife, and it was assumed his body had been scattered by wildlife.

There was nothing of him to bury, nothing to hold onto. She had left his mobile in the copper bowl on the counter and his plaid shirt where he had left it over the back of their couch like he would be coming back. But he didn't, and she couldn't bear the thought of sleeping in their apartment without him. She had shut the door and hadn't gone back.

Swiping at her eyes, Phoebe dialed Maggie Monroe's number.

She had to tell Sebastian's twin sister he was dead.

CHAPTER SIX

Maggie Monroe had expected crime scene tape across the door; something—anything to declare something unconscionably heinous had happened. Again.

She stood with her wheeled carry-on in the hallway outside her twin brother's apartment in the Seventeenth Arrondissement of Paris and rubbed her red, jet-lagged eyes. Crying, instead of sleeping, on a transatlantic flight would do that. The hallway was well-lit and tiled, the walls freshly painted. It was obviously an old building and smelled like apartment buildings everywhere—the pungent mix of people, and their cooked food, coexisting.

This hadn't been the crime scene, and there was no tape, just a solid, old wooden door with a sleek, very contemporary-looking keypad. She pushed in another sequence, and the expensive-looking keypad shrilled in annoyance.

Another wrong code.

Think Maggie. Sebastian was complicated, a tortured genius. It made sense he would have an equally tortured, complicated security code, not something so simple as the birthdays and anniversaries she had been trying. Maybe she had the wrong apartment. She pulled out her phone and double-checked her map app before she confirmed the address the police had sent. She cross-referenced that with the address she had listed for Sebastian in her contacts app. She looked at the door again. The small, metal 3B hadn't magically changed. She was in the right spot.

Maggie swallowed the sob that had bubbled to the surface and punched in another variation of Sebastian's birthday with more force than necessary. She bit back an unexpected sting when her birthday digits didn't open the door, either. Maggie spun around and leaned against the door, slinking to the floor. She wrapped her arms around her legs and dropped her forehead to her knees, her phone clutched in her hand.

She missed her twin brother *now*. The police could grant her access to the apartment, but she would have to book a different appointment for that. Maggie wanted into her twin brother's apartment tonight. The rift in their family—an understatement if there ever was one—had wedged a distance between her and Sebastian that had only widened over the subsequent years. They had always had each other until their world, wobbly and tumultuous as it was, had been obliterated. In her lonelier moments, she had even contemplated reconciling with the rest of their family. They had made serious mistakes; legal, ethical, unconscionable mistakes. But Maggie desperately wanted to believe people could change. The police detectives and parade of therapists had strongly discouraged it—in their jobs, they saw too often what would happen. Lonely or not, she knew deep inside they were right.

Sebastian had been all she had left, and he had been murdered.

Maggie scrambled to her feet. She was getting into the damn apartment. She was a librarian, for fuck's sake. Her job was to help make knowledge accessible. Surely in her repertoire of know-how, she could figure out—suddenly, inspiration hit. Still holding her phone, she opened her browser app and searched the nerdiest thing she could think of as a door opened down the hall. A moment later, Maggie heard footfalls approaching. A young man was headed toward her.

Did he know Sebastian?

Did he know her brother was dead?

Would he question a strange Canadian woman breaking in?

Maggie sucked in a deep breath. She had never imagined she would be breaking into her dead twin brother's apartment the first time she finally saw Paris.

Be sad and scared and exhausted later. Open the fucking door now.

As pep talks went, it was ruthlessly awkward. But it worked. By the time he passed, Maggie gave the stranger a polite but aloof smile and murmured a *bonjour* as she pocketed her phone. She kept her gaze to herself and punched in zero-two-zero-seven-one-nine-zero-six.

The heavy-duty locks labored open to Hans Bethe's birthday.

Her brother—bless him—was such a nerd. Maggie hadn't known the Nobel laureate's digits, but that's what a data plan with roaming could get a determined person—unlimited access to obscure information while breaking into an apartment.

Thrilled at the small victory, she grabbed her wheeled carry-on's handle and let herself into the apartment, shutting the door quickly behind her. She noticed the deadbolts. All three of them. Frowning, she eyed their obvious robustness. Sebastian had never been overly cautious, and the neighborhood didn't look particularly dangerous. The police hadn't been forthcoming with the details of her brother's death nor returned any of her calls since scheduling their meeting.

Frowning, Maggie engaged each of the locks. The sound of metal sliding against metal scraped her already raw nerves. She rolled her carry-on into the small apartment before finally kicking off the wedge heels she had worn since dashing out of her Calgary walkup nearly twenty-four hours ago. Her feet ached, her head hurt, and she desperately needed a shower. Her long jersey cotton skirt, loose blouse, and scarf—all ocean colors, were as rumpled as she felt. She sniffed. Something didn't feel right. She sniffed a second time.

The apartment wasn't stale.

If Sebastian had been gone for months, the air would have felt *stale*. Her walkup did every time she went away for a girls' trip with Savannah and Meredith, and those were a week tops.

Flickers of light caught her attention. Across the room, a wide apartment window stood bare, revealing a glittering Eiffel Tower in the distance. Maggie crossed the space and stared at the icon through the window, the view exquisite. It was the Paris of post-cards, the Paris she had dreamed about her entire life.

Not the nightmare of the past twenty-four hours.

Suddenly, the dancing lights stopped. The iconic tower stood simply illuminated against the deep indigo sky. Why had she never come before … this? What had held her back? A shiver spread through her body, and Maggie rubbed her arms through her thin blouse. She should *feel* if her twin brother was dead. Instead, she felt … nothing. Her mind simply refused to wrap around the possibility that Sebastian was gone. She could only sense a terrifying blackness, not death, but not exactly life, either.

The night lights of Paris twinkled through the window as Maggie pulled out her phone with unsteady hands. She dialed her brother's number, an Alberta number she knew he still kept, desperate for it not to have been shut off.

It was ringing.

It clicked over to his voicemail after the fourth ring. She pressed the phone tighter against her ear, pressing his voice close. It clicked again, this time for her to leave a message. She scrubbed her face. "Sebastian … it's me. I miss you so much. If you get this, please, just—just stay safe. If you're still alive, I'll find you." Maggie hung up, feeling raw and stupid.

You're delusional.

The French police officer hadn't actually called her that, but that's what it had felt like when Maggie had insisted there must be some sort of mistake. Sebastian couldn't be gone.

Assassiner. Murdered.

The female officer had started kind and rather compassionate as she delivered the brutal words, but she had turned sharp at Maggie's dogged questions. Maggie wondered if all French police officers were as forceful as *Officer de Police Judiciarie* Phoebe Freres. The woman had nearly bit Maggie's head off at the suggestion that Sebastian might still be alive. Maggie hadn't meant it as a personal affront to the woman's professional integrity, but the woman had been so cross she obviously took it that way.

When would Maggie learn to just shut up and stay down? She constantly saw possibilities no one else dared to notice, connections others dismissed. She was sick of people brushing off her ideas.

Despair and fatigue threatened to overwhelm her.

Her phone vibrated, and she rushed to answer it. "Sebastian?"

There was a brief pause before a soft, "It's Meredith, darling."

The small flare of hope extinguished. "Meredith—" Maggie swallowed fresh tears. "Thanks for calling."

"How are you holding up?"

Maggie stared at the traffic on the rue below. Parallel ribbons of light, one row white, the other red. "Awful."

"It was never going to be easy." Meredith's melodious voice and deep concern smoothed over Maggie, a balm for all the sharp edges pain and hurt had created. Savannah's aunt was the only actual maternal figure Maggie had known as a kid.

The older woman asked gently, "Is there news?"

Maggie turned away from the window. "Just wishful thinking. He … he doesn't *feel* gone." She couldn't bring herself to say *dead*.

"Is there anything I can do?"

Maggie smiled, grateful Meredith hadn't questioned her lack of acceptance of Sebastian's murder. "I'll be all right." Maggie cleared her throat. "Really, thanks for checking in, though."

"Anytime, darling." Meredith paused. "Maybe you should stop at the cottage for a few days after you're back."

Maggie heard what the older woman wasn't saying.

Rest.

Regroup.

Take the time she needed.

Meredith would know. Last year her new husband, Bruce Tanner, had tried to murder her, his daughter Becca, and Becca's fiancé, Jason.

"Thanks for the offer. Maybe I will." As she said it, the idea blossomed, bright and full of possibilities, inside Maggie. Meredith's cottage was on Lake Muskoka in southern Ontario. Maggie had been going with Savannah since they were teenagers. The water, trees, and rocks of the southern edge of the Canadian Shield were a world away from the wild mountains and glacial rivers Maggie loved so much in the west. Though it was more built up and noisier, the eastern lake was a sanctuary in its own right. It had been on one of those visits, when her best friend had gone into town to run errands, that Maggie had confided to Meredith the truth about her past. It had felt good to share her story with an adult she trusted.

"Whatever you feel is best. Call anytime." Meredith signed off.

Maggie took a deep breath. She wasn't completely alone and needed to remember that. She slid her phone into her purse and looked around her twin brother's apartment. To her right was the living room, edged by a hallway. To her left a small contemporary kitchen. Nondescript except for a bowl of lemons decorating the dining area and a small copper dish with a cell phone resting inside it. In disbelief, she picked up one of the lemons. It was real. She held it to her nose. And fresh. Since when did her brother decorate with fresh lemons? Maggie picked up the cell phone, and her shoulders sagged. She had called a phone sitting right here. Of course, the battery was dead. She didn't know why she would have expected different. Maggie tucked it into her purse next to her own phone. If she was lucky, she could charge it and at least see the image on his home screen. It was probably something science-y, like an image of an atom or distant galaxy. Maybe she could figure out how to unlock it.

Two mugs sat on the counter next to the sink, and a couple of plates and cutlery were stacked in the sink. They must have been rinsed. No mold grew on them. Apparently, the police did not tidy up someone's apartment after a murder. She wasn't sure why she had thought anyone would.

Maggie returned the lemon to the bowl. She dropped her purse on the brown leather chair separating the living room from the kitchen and surveyed the space. Though obviously updated, the apartment was older than Canadian Confederation. Maggie let her fingertips trace one of the walls. They had the lived-in scars of age, though the soft peach paint covering them looked recent enough, if not a color her brother would have willingly chosen. The floors were a patterned tile. A few nicks could be seen, though they were well-aged and added character instead of detracting.

An ornate cuckoo clock hung on the wall, and a metal umbrella bin stood in the corner, holding a bouquet of three hockey sticks. Maggie blinked her suddenly damp eyes. The sticks would be signed by Canadian legends. She knew because she had gotten them for him. Sebastian hadn't completely dismissed his roots—or her—entirely.

She walked to the back of the chaise, her hands resting on a plaid throw draped on the back. The apartment seemed normal, ordinary even. No one would guess it belonged to someone who had been murdered.

Maggie looked down. Her hands weren't resting on a small throw blanket. It was a plaid shirt carelessly tossed across the chaise back, like Sebastian had discarded it before he left and would be back any minute, laughing and alive.

She bunched the soft material in her fists and brought the shirt up to her nose, inhaling. It still smelled like him, and

31

foolish hope flared. What if the police had gotten it wrong? What if her brother was still alive?

Fresh hurt squeezed her lungs, and her hand flew to her chest. Maggie rubbed her tight chest. She couldn't breathe. Dropping the shirt, she scrambled across the room to the wide window overlooking the rue. She ran her hands over the window frame, desperate to find the latch and fling open the window, to gulp fresh air as if she could breathe away the pain.

The window was nailed shut.

She darted to the second window, throwing open the privacy curtains, and realized it was a balcony door overlooking a courtyard below. Patrons from the restaurants, cafés, and bars below spilled into the quaint space. Fingers fumbling, Maggie unlocked the door and opened it, gulping in fresh air.

Rough laughter erupted below as party music cranked louder. Maggie recoiled, the boisterous crowd too much for her raw emotions even as her Spidey-sense flared.

Something wasn't right.

Nothing's right. Sebastian was murdered!

She closed the balcony door, scrambling to lock it, before darting a look across the room, confirming she had locked all three deadbolts. Maggie wrung her hands as she stood at the balcony door, box breathing and watching the courtyard below, willing herself to calm the fuck down. *Breathe, hold, exhale, hold.*

Sebastian would have chided her fanciful imagination and how she was always wound too tight, not like the balanced weight of their cuckoo clock. He was brilliant, socially awkward, and way too trusting. What if he had trusted the wrong person?

Maggie blinked, her gaze stopping at a man below. He stood beside a bistro table, holding a folded newspaper, and looked uncomfortably familiar. Before she could place him, a soft click sounded.

Maggie turned toward the front door.

A scratching sound followed.

Adrenaline exploded. Maggie looked around for a weapon

before launching herself toward the metal bin, grabbing one of the hockey sticks.

Two clicks sounded.

Tightening her grip on the hockey stick, she crept toward the door. Hockey, let alone slap shots, had never been her thing, but she understood the basic mechanics of a club in her hand.

At the last minute, she realized her folly.

There were two of them.

One at the door, the other was on the balcony.

CHAPTER SEVEN

S tone picked up the tiny espresso mug and took a dainty European sip. He could be surfing Pippi Beach right now, riding lonely waves, instead of watching some dead guy's apartment.

His phone vibrated. Only one family had this number. Frowning, he pulled it out and stared, dumb-founded. This time it was Lillian Kensington who had just texted him. Stone was now included in the Tanner family's group text, had been for several months, and it still floored him. He rubbed his jaw and stared at the image of his half-niece, Emma. Colt Tanner, in all his cowboy glory, was holding the little munchkin in his arms and looking beyond smitten.

A daughter.

Stone shuttered. Ties like that scared the shit out of him.

He scrolled through emojis to respond, but none quite communicated *cute, looks terrifying as fuck* without being a dick. Stone's thumb hovered over a smiley face, but he simply pocketed his phone. He and Lillian had run in a lot of overlapping circles when she worked as a war correspondent and MI6 courier, and it still shocked the shit out of him that she chose to settle down with his cowboy half-brother in the Canadian foothills. Not that Stone begrudged the couple. He just didn't understand what the hell they were thinking.

His phone vibrated again. His half-sister Becca had answered with appropriate cooing exclamations before inviting everyone to a summer barbecue at her eco-inn. Stone shoved his phone back into his pocket. He had to wrap up this case so he could untangle himself from the Tanners and all their extended family bliss.

Stone downed his espresso, setting the miniature mug on the small table with more force than required, startling a man and a woman holding hands. They detoured a wide circle around him, and he reminded himself he was supposed to be covert. Stone re-crossed his long legs around the pint-sized bistro table and pacified his face. He was rewarded when the next couple walking past in the swelling crowd simply nodded in his direction before leaning into each other and their conversation.

The quaint venue was filled with popular restaurant bars, cafés, and boutiques, all circling a shallow fountain pool with a sparkling central fountain, complete with a light show timed to the piped-in music. The space definitely had an attractive ambiance, and the building crowd proved it.

Suddenly, blaring music punctuated the night. One of the establishments had cranked up their volume as the party had spilled into the now-packed courtyard.

Stone didn't like it, and not just because he hated crowds. Something felt off.

His gaze tracked the scene. Merrymakers thronged around him. Stone strained to hear his earpiece as it buzzed to life, and he heard Agent Diaz's voice, *"A woman just entered the premises."*

Feral anticipation sparked. Stone had been chasing ghosts for a long time. Bruce Tanner's criminal associates had rigged international elections, falsified environmental records, had whistle-blowers assassinated, and found pressure points to turn good cops bad. They used intimidation, extortion, murder— anything to build their empire. Even set up their own blood.

Stone didn't like Gabe, but he sure as hell didn't want the guy murdered. Bruce had leaked stolen classified documents, leading to Gabe being ambushed while on a CSIS mission. Gabe had been shot in the head and nearly died. When Gabe had joined CSIS, Stone had left just enough breadcrumbs for his big brother to find him. He still wasn't sure why he had done that.

Banishing the troubled memories as sure as his older half-brother had banished his existence, Stone casually stood, shifting the folded newspaper to hide his sidearm better. Whoever the woman was in the apartment, she would lead them to Teague Alans, and Stone could finally walk away. It was time to cut and run. Last Christmas had been an aberration.

He glanced above and froze. It wasn't some woman in the window of the dead man's apartment. It was Maggie Monroe, the hot librarian from Christmas. Stone hesitated as impossible connections refused to fall into place. He didn't want to consider how she might be involved.

A shadow moved on the balcony above, on the other side of the glass door from where Maggie had stood only seconds before. In less than a heartbeat, the figure raised his arm and struck the balcony door. The glass shattered, albeit silently, unable to compete over the loud, disjointed music.

Stone sprinted through the crowd of partygoers, desperate to reach the apartment stairs before it was too late.

CHAPTER EIGHT

The balcony glass door shattered, and Maggie screamed. Deafening music sounded as a man in black tactical gear charged in.

She swung the hockey stick with all her might. The stick sent a jolt of recoil up her arms as it connected with the intruder's skull and neck.

The man dropped to all fours, dodging her second swing, and rolled into her like a steamroller. Her legs crumpled as he plowed through her, his face sinister. As she fell, Maggie dropped the stick and taloned her fingers. She aimed for his eyes.

He uttered a tortured scream, and she pressed harder, digging her fingers into his eye sockets.

A rough hand grabbed her hair and yanked hard. Distant memories flooded her, bringing a spooky calmness. She allowed herself to be pulled off the first intruder and, instead of fighting it, leaned into the momentum.

Caught off guard, the second intruder fell backward, releasing her. She nearly fell, too, but barely managed to keep her footing.

A moment later, an awkward snap sounded.

Maggie spun around in alarm.

Two more men—dressed in plain clothes—had entered the apartment. One sprinted past her. He disarmed the man with the bleeding eyes who had just aimed a gun at her. A sick thud sounded as he cracked the gun against the side of the man's head, dropping him.

She instinctively jerked away and saw his partner holding the second attacker's head at an odd angle. The man calmly let the body slump to the floor before reaching out, tapping the apartment door closed. He pulled out his phone and turned, giving her his shoulder as he spoke briefly into it, his voice privately hushed.

Maggie stood frozen in place.

Her mind raced after the violent altercation. The two men still standing had just saved her life, yet were completely ignoring her. Should she make a run for it?

The taller one snapped his fingers. "You, stay."

Maggie blanched at the clipped, barbaric speech. Her gaze landed on the first attacker, unmoving on his back where he had fallen. The second, also unmoving, was slumped at an odd angle. Both were decked out in tactical gear from head to toe.

They would look very dangerous if they weren't dead.

Maggie's stomach heaved, and she sprinted to the kitchen sink. Violently, her body retched over and over. A gentle hand touched her back. "Let it out. You'll feel better after."

His words were kind and unexpected, though she really didn't have a choice—her stomach and throat were screaming. It was her body's intuitive way of releasing the trauma. The gentle hand at her back made slow circles as her stomach turned inside out. A final shudder wracked through her. She rinsed her mouth, and he handed her a clean-looking tea towel that had been slung through a kitchen cabinet handle.

"Better?"

She accepted the towel, nodding.

"Maggie—"

Fear spiked even as something familiar tugged at her senses. She staggered back, away from him. "How do you know my name?"

"You're serious right now?" His voice was incredulous. Maggie took another step back, trying to place that accent as he snapped, "You seriously don't remember me?"

She gauged the distance between her and the front door. He took a step forward. "Don't even think about it. We need you to stay, *Maggie*."

She shivered.

Maggie. Only one person in the world said her name like that. She hadn't heard it in months. A provocative image from last Christmas ignited in her mind. Maggie had been invited to the Tanner family Christmas and this man had sat next to her at the boisterous Christmas dinner. She had savored the invite, and being included. She usually spent Christmas alone. It had been an explosive mess of chaos, international spies, monarchies, and unexpected healing. Even as an outsider, it had been the best Christmas of her life.

Relief flooded her. "Ohmygod, *Stone*? What are you doing here?" It was going to be okay. Stone was a Tanner—definitely someone you could count on in a crisis.

"I could ask you the same thing."

She recoiled. His voice held a challenge that hadn't been there when he had said her name so … intimately. "What's that supposed to mean?"

"Why are you here?"

"In Paris?"

"In this apartment," Stone clarified crisply.

She stared at him. Her mouth opened, but words wouldn't form. Why was he treating her like she had done something wrong, like she hadn't just been attacked?

His partner appeared at their side. "Time to go."

Still looking at her, Stone shrugged. "Fine, don't tell me. We'll take you in and get this whole mess sorted."

Maggie found her voice. "You're not taking me anywhere."
Maggie might have shared a Christmas cracker with the guy, but
the only place she was going was to the police.

"There's a leak in the *Préfecture de Police de Paris*. It's not safe
to take you there."

Of course, he would have to have a perfect French accent,
too.

"I have a meeting there tomorrow."

Stone and his partner exchanged a look.

"Yeah." It was her turn to snap. "Apparently, they schedule
one when they tell you someone was murdered."

Stone moved his body subtly. Was he trying to make her feel
cornered? His voice did not invite interpretation when he stated,
"I'll take you."

"Not a chance. You're looking at me like this," she motioned
to the two felled attackers, "is my fault. I don't even know you,
let alone trust you."

His eyebrows rose again.

She wanted to slap the look he was giving her off his face.
She crossed her arms instead. "Tonsil hockey does not constitute
knowing."

"I'm not familiar with the term." Stone's voice had gone
completely void of emotion.

His partner smirked, apparently having no trouble
translating.

Maggie and Stone had shared a steamy-as-fuck midnight kiss
on New Years. There had been a lot of champagne flowing, and
Stone was just so damn chiseled, foreign, and totally leaving. It
was the only reason she had considered briefly suspending her
moratorium on romantic entanglements. He had been, in a word,
perfect. She acutely remembered the charged kiss, every inch of
what he had felt like, the cadence of his voice.

But apparently not his face. Weird.

Now he was all attitude. "I'll drop you off at the Canadian
embassy and take you to the *Préfecture de Police* tomorrow. I need

you not dead. Savannah and Meredith would kill me, and my half-brothers would help if anything happened to you."

She wasn't imagining it. There was a definite frost to his voice.

Maggie had heard enough from Savannah to know Bruce Tanner had tried to murder his family and, before he had over-dosed, had several international spy agencies looking for him and his partners. Something about rigging elections to position their coal and oil interests. Stone was one of those spies—and Bruce Tanner's unclaimed bastard son.

"Why are you mad? I was the one attacked."

He dropped his head back and blew out a breath toward the ceiling. "Right. We'll get you to the embassy. You can get your boyfriend's things later."

"You think Sebastian was my boyfriend?"

Stone's partner stepped forward. "You're not his girlfriend? Who the hell are you?"

She looked between the two men. "No, I'm not Sebastian's girlfriend."

Something flashed in Stone's eyes. "Maggie, why in the hell are you here?"

Maggie hesitated, hoping she wasn't making a mistake.

"Sebastian's my twin brother."

CHAPTER NINE

"Sebastian, the guy working for an international criminal, is your brother?" Stone swore. He wasn't sure which sucked more, Maggie being Sebastian's sister or that she hadn't remembered him without prodding. It was hard not to take the overt dismissal personally.

"Twin brother," Maggie clarified.

Stone took in her rumbled clothing and wheeled bag. Color was returning to her cheeks, though she looked too pale. Yet, she still managed to be the brightest thing in the room. "You just fly in?"

She nodded before adding. "Just because he was murdered doesn't make him a criminal."

Sometimes Stone wished he could still live in a fairyland like civilians did. World-weary, he filled her in. "Your twin brother is working for Teague Alans to develop compact nuclear fusion bombs. That criminal enough?"

Her eyes widened. "I thought compact nuclear fusion wasn't possible?"

"*That's* what you took from that? Your brother is working for an evil fuck hell-bent on sending the planet into oblivion—"
Stone broke off and forced a calmness into his voice he didn't

feel. "Do you have any idea what weaponizing that will look like?"

Maggie blanched. "That can't be. Sebastian flunked out of school. He's a recluse. He couldn't possibly—" She stopped.

Stone snapped. "Open your eyes. Your brother is creating bombs that make nuclear fission seem like child's play. Pull apart an atom, and it makes a catastrophic boom. Bring atoms together —it's a goddamn world builder or destroyer."

She shook her head. "No, that can't be possible."

"He's playing with stardust to wipe out life when he could be saving it—" Stone broke off, scrubbing his hands over his face.

"Dramatic much?" She was eying him like he had grown a second head.

He hadn't figured her for a head-in-the-sand denialist. It pissed him off. "You don't have to be a granola-eating tree hugger to recognize the ticking clock. Climate disasters are piling up. It is no longer some nebulous, esoteric threat to human life. Climate change is taking lives *now*. It's costing trillions *now*. Dead people can't buy shit they don't need. Your brother could have chosen to help instead—"

"Twin brother," she corrected him for the second time.

Stone narrowed his eyes.

She had another brother.

"Twin brother, my mistake," he said smoothly.

"You're telling me Sebastian's research actually worked?"

He nodded.

She looked so stricken. Stone wanted to believe Maggie had no part in her twin's ambitions. That might just be his dick talking. Unlike her, he remembered every moment with her over the Christmas holidays and the smoking hot kiss on New Years.

Still, she had to know the truth. "Your brother is not helping anyone but himself and Teague Alans." Maggie's brother was a terrorist, and he said so.

Maggie whispered, "It doesn't make sense. How could Sebastian achieve what no one else has? He's a dropout. He'd need a lab. He'd need financing—oh. *Oh.*" Dark realizations clouded Maggie's expressive eyes.

"Yeah, *oh.*" Stone wished he could shove information into people faster.

"You think Teague Alans is financing my brother's research so they can weaponize it."

Stone spread his hands wide in a what-else-could-it-be gesture.

Her frown deepened, sinking her whole face into a look of absolute agony, and he almost felt sorry for her. Except he knew how easy it was to act affronted, to put on a show of distress. He did as much when the job required it. Better to just yank off the bandage. "Your brother's breakthrough could pivot the world's fossil fuel transition in a matter of months. He went the other way."

"It's that black or white? He's either helping people or obliterating the world?"

"From the intel, yeah, it's like that."

Agent Diaz lifted his wrist. His ginormous watch blinked red. "Time to move this reunion. The sweepers are two minutes away."

"We'll take you to the Canadian embassy. This yours?" Stone motioned to the wheeled carry-on still standing by the door.

"I'll get it." Maggie snapped, her frown replaced by anger. Stone tracked her movements as she retrieved her purse from the leather chair and slung it across her torso before grabbing a plaid flannel draped across the back of the couch. She had to step over one of the disposed attackers and jerked away as fast as she could before whispering, "Are they dead?"

"Does it matter?"

Her eyes widened.

"They were here to kill you," he reminded her. Stone wasn't a monster. He had simply learned what to replay in his mind and what shit he had to let go. He would have imploded years ago if he hadn't.

Maggie shoved the plaid into her oversized purse and strapped into her wedge heels before gripping the wheeled bag's handle and clutching her purse tight against her body. "Please take me to the embassy."

After a brief tug-of-war with her carry-on that he won—as much from the gendered manners his parents had drilled into him as any protocols concerning civilians—Maggie followed him down the apartment stairs. Agent Diaz covered their back.

Stone led them through a narrow throughway between two buildings where a dark, nondescript SUV with heavily tinted windows waited.

He opened the back door and placed Maggie in the back seat, motioning for her to scoot over. He slid in next to her.

Agent Diaz filed into the front passenger seat. A woman Stone had only ever met in passing was behind the wheel and drove off before the doors clicked shut.

The Paris night flowed around them.

Fucking Paris.

CHAPTER TEN

"*Sebastian ... it's me. I miss you so much. If you get this, please, just — just stay safe. If you're still alive, I'll find you.*" Sebastian's heart stuttered as he listened to the message on his voicemail. It had been months since he had heard his twin sister's voice. She sounded sad and scared, and fresh pain lanced through him. He had done that to her.

His body had recovered from near death, thanks to the old hippie couple and their patient son, the only doctor they would allow near them had been visiting when Sebastian had stumbled, mostly dead, into their remote yard in the French countryside. The couple lived off the grid, didn't trust institutions, and had found Sebastian's tortured state, further proof of their conspiracies. His duress had sparked their protective natures. Weeks of home-grown nurturing, and their son's astonishing medical skills, had worked miracles.

Weeks had turned into months. Sebastian needed a plan if he were to have any chance of getting his life back and stopping Teague Alans. He had unknowingly stumbled headfirst into breaking the law when he had allowed himself to be duped by the likes of the ruthless criminal. If he wanted to beat Teague at his own game, Sebastian would have to fight fire with fire. He didn't like it, nor would Phoebe when she found out, but it was the only way to get his life back and keep the people he loved safe while he did it.

He would find Teague Alans's pressure points and show no mercy.

CHAPTER ELEVEN

This was not tourist Paris.

Maggie gripped her purse against her body and tried to breathe slow and low through her nose. The Paris the guidebooks didn't show raced past her window as she simultaneously tried to make sense of what had just happened, as well as quell the overwhelming sense of panic.

Sebastian had a breakthrough in his research.

He hadn't told her.

She hadn't realized just how big the chasm between them had become.

Maggie folded her hands in her lap and dipped her head. She could be dead right now—would be dead right now if Stone and Agent Diaz hadn't shown up. She had spent a lifetime looking over her shoulder and had done everything she could to prepare herself for the family she was born into. Most of them were criminal, some simply narcissistic. All except Sebastian would fuck up her life again if given half the chance.

The irony wasn't lost on her.

Maggie had kept on the straight and narrow, trusted few, and took the grittiest self-defense classes she could find.

Nothing had prepared her for the violence she had just narrowly escaped.

She flinched as a moped pulled alongside her window before darting through traffic across the next intersection. Two cars honked as the moped sped away, seemingly unfazed.

She missed Alberta. Maggie had always considered it boring, a perfect match for her boring life. Sure, it had world-class scenery and record-setting sunshine. The overdosing addicts and the gun violence spilling across the border weren't exactly tame, but everything always seemed so … static. Even its history of boom and bust economies was glaringly predictable. Maggie wished she was home right now, eating her favorite takeout and scrolling through boring news stories on her phone. It wasn't exciting, but it was safe.

Maggie desperately wanted to be safe right now. And to sleep for a week. She was exhausted and clutched her purse as the Paris night flashed past her window. It looked terrifying after the attack.

They turned down a series of alleys, each more narrow than the last. The driver pulled the SUV into another tight corner and killed the engine. Maggie swallowed a protest. A ten-foot-high metal fence was less than a foot from her window. She'd have to crawl over Stone to get out of the vehicle.

"Let's go," Stone said.

Everyone opened their car doors. She darted a look at Stone, but he simply motioned for her to get out. Hesitating, Maggie did the same.

Her door opened easily.

The metal fencing had been a gate, and the small space they had pulled into was a receiving armory. Light standards illuminated the space with a harsh white light. She grabbed her carry-on and scrambled out of the vehicle.

Two uniformed soldier-looking types greeted them. One checked her passport. She glanced at Stone, but he and Agent Diaz were speaking to a third uniformed soldier—an officer, by the looks of it, that had just joined them. She was given back her passport and stood there, awkward and alone, as the trio spoke heatedly. The soldiers who had checked her passport stood several paces away from her.

Alone, Maggie shifted her weight from one foot to the other, clutching her carry-on handle with one hand and her purse to her body with the other.

Finally, Stone and the officer walked over to her.

"Maggie, this is Officer Jonas Saul. He'll answer any questions you have and get you sorted out."

The officer's lips tilted briefly in a polite smile.

Stone walked away.

"You're going?" Panic rose swiftly within her.

Stone stopped. "You wanted to go to the Canadian embassy." He pointed to the building. "This is it."

Maggie eyed the covert receiving area. Overwhelmed didn't begin to cover how she was feeling.

"This isn't the public entrance, but it's the Canadian embassy." Stone added, "You're safe now."

Maggie scrubbed her cheeks with both hands. Twenty-four hours had barely passed since she first found out her brother was murdered, took a twelve-hour trans-Atlantic flight, and was violently attacked. She wrapped her arms around herself to stop from shaking.

"Maggie, this is a secure location," Stone said gently. "I wouldn't have brought you here if I didn't trust you'd be safe."

Exhaustion and fear threatened to swamp her. Maggie spread her hands helplessly. "I don't know how to navigate your world."

"It's a Canadian embassy. It's your world."

"Will you come with me? I don't want to go in with someone I don't know."

He smiled at her. "I thought we didn't know each other like that?"

Maggie had known those words were going to bite her in the

ass. "As you pointed out, your tongue has been down my throat. We know each other enough."

Stone moved closer, and her heart began to hammer, anticipation momentarily hijacking fear.

"I don't recall revealing that private moment to the group."

"Yet you managed to communicate it just fine." She had wanted to sound contrary. Instead, her voice had taken on an embarrassing breathless quality.

"So you do remember."

Of course, she effing remembered.

Even now, her lips tingled, remembering how masterful his mouth had moved over hers. Maggie had avoided men like Stone—way too sexy for *her* own good—her entire adult life. Their brief, single make-out session had been her only slip, and fall she did.

Stone held out his hand.

This time, she handed him her carry-on.

He gripped the piece of luggage. "Come on, then. Let's get you inside."

Relief made her legs feel like jelly; she wasn't alone. Maggie was pretty sure at that moment that she would follow him anywhere. She was so damn scared, and he was so damn strong.

A door banged open, and a dark, fit man jogged down the grated stairs.

"Omran?" Agent Omran Forest stood in front of her. She turned to Stone, thrilled. "Are Thorsen and Charles here, too?" She looked around, hoping the rest of the covert Christmas dinner guests were lurking in the shadows, ready to thwart any bad guys.

"You remember them?" Stone asked. "How many of us did you make out with?"

Before she could rebuke his asinine remark, the British agent was upon them. "Ms. Monroe, what are you doing here?"

"Just Maggie—"

Stone interrupted, motioning toward the door. "We'll explain inside."

Omran glanced between her and Stone, his eyes giving away nothing. "Sure, mate."

Suddenly, an icy fear swept through Maggie, and she darted her gaze around the small area.

"Maggie, what's wrong?" Stone scanned the space, mimicking her search. "What is it?"

She couldn't move fast enough.

Maggie was frantic to get them out of the small, tight space. Something felt *very* wrong.

"Maggie?" This time it was Omran. He took a few steps toward her, concern etching his face.

Stone got to her first, and she pushed him away from her hard. "*No. Go, go, go!*"

"What the—"

"*Move,*" she shouted, pushing him away harder, desperate for him to get out, to get away. Something was *wrong*.

She heard a soft click and turned.

The SUV exploded.

CHAPTER TWELVE

Maggie was thrown to the ground. Instinctively, she curled in on herself, arms automatically protecting her head. Her ears rang, and it sounded like she was underwater. Thrown pieces of the SUV burned indiscriminately around them.

Suddenly, Stone was there. He wrapped her up in his arms, ushering her through fiery debris. She stumbled, and his arm cinched tighter around her, bolstering her. Smoke clogged her lungs and made her eyes sting as she clung to his large frame. She squeezed her eyes shut and held on.

Maggie heard men shouting, but her ears were still ringing, and she couldn't make out what they were saying. Stone pushed her ahead of him, and she opened her eyes. A side door yawned wide ahead, and she ran up the short flight of stairs. Ducking inside the door, she turned, expecting Stone to be behind her.

He wasn't.

Several armed men had swarmed in during the chaos. One of them had grabbed Stone.

Fury screamed through her. Maggie launched herself off the stairs, landing on the assailant's back. She snaked her arms around his face and yanked. Hard. All three of them tumbled to the ground. Maggie whipped her heel at the assailant's windpipe.

It was the opening Stone needed. A gun appeared in his hand, and Stone pointed it at their attacker, out of range of Maggie.

The man froze.

Maggie kicked him off of her and scrambled to stand. All of the assailants had been subdued and were now surrounded by armed embassy soldier types. In a coordinated hustle, the attackers were bound and forcibly escorted through an unmarked side door.

Maggie gave Stone a skeptical look. "You sure the Paris police station is more dangerous than this?"

Stone swore.

Omran was breathing hard with a fresh scrape on his forehead. He gave a quick look around. "Get inside."

"You guys were never just dropping me off, were you?"

Neither man confirmed nor denied.

Omran motioned with his hand. "Inside. I'll brief you both, and then hopefully, we can figure out *what the fuck* that was."

Stone picked up her carry-on before she could grab it but stopped.

"What is it?" she asked him, wringing her hands instead of reaching for one of his.

He pointed at a piece of metal embedded into the brick of the building.

"What's that?" Maggie asked.

Stone was looking at her, his face dead serious. "I would have been skewered if you hadn't pushed me out of the way."

The metal looked like a tie rod.

It would have eviscerated Stone.

Maggie felt her stomach lurch again. Her cheeks puffed, and she pressed her fist against her mouth, willing the nausea down.

Stone eyed the courtyard a final time. "Let's get you inside."

CHAPTER THIRTEEN

Teague Alans screamed, grabbing the assault rifle out of its case. His hands shook as he tried to assemble the weapon as the SUV burned in the clandestine courtyard below. His manicure was ruined with the barbaric task, and he swore violently, throwing the useless components on the floor. Christ, this was so beneath him. This was why he hired assholes to do his dirty work. Teague hadn't stomped his way to the top by getting his own hands dirty.

Perspiration beaded at his temple, and he darted a glance through the tinted windows at the spectacle below. His worthless crew were being bound and led inside an unmarked door. This was not the plan. The men he had hired were supposed to be professionals. They were supposed to be the best, and a woman had bested them.

A goddamn librarian.

Teague looked at the weapon's pieces he held in his hands. Bruce used to brag about killing prostitutes. He said there was no rush like taking the life of another, especially brutally. Teague had thought his old friend's little hobby rather base, grotesque in its absurdity. There was no money in it, and killing a prostitute certainly wasn't a demonstration of power. But Bruce had been on to something. It was time Teague got his hands dirty. It had been fun wiping out those two mercenaries.

He picked up the assault components on the floor, a new plan forming. Bruce Tanner had promised him a return on investment, a foolproof plan to secure billions. It had been the promise of the astronomical payout that had caught Teague's attention, but it had been the chance to play global puppet master that had cinched the deal. Bruce Tanner wanted money, respect, and power. Teague was smarter. He didn't give a fuck if people respected him. He wanted them to fear him and what his money and power could do to them. Sebastian Monroe's research was a global game changer, and Teague owned it.

He had been more careful than the rest of Bruce Tanner's consortium. He had been smarter, stronger. Teague had outlived the others. Fixing international elections, massaging environmental records, silencing whistle-blowers, intimidation, extortion—they had done what they had to, to secure profit and power.

Teague would get his due.

He would use Sebastian's sister and find what Sebastian had hidden from him. Then, he would find what Bruce had hidden for him. Bruce's final act of familial betrayal had been to leave Teague the land he had promised to his daughter Becca. Bruce might have been a weak son of a bitch—it hadn't been hard to turn the arrogant ass an addict, though he took longer to OD than Teague expected—but he had his moments. There was a reason Bruce left that land to Teague. Of course, it wasn't legal, but what did that matter? The lawyers would be tied up fighting that for years.

Teague would find what Bruce left him. Being hounded by a damn international task force led by none other than Bruce's bastard son would lead him straight to it.

CHAPTER FOURTEEN

Maggie hustled to follow Omran through the side door. She could feel Stone only inches behind her as they snaked left and down another corridor before entering an unmarked elevator.

The elevator doors closed, and she felt the subsequent lift. It seemed unnaturally normal after nearly being blown up. Violence did not stop the world from spinning.

Somehow it felt like it should. If the world stopped, people would notice. Violence would be noticed. Maggie looked at her hands. They were cut and bloodied, and she was standing in an elevator. She turned her head. Stone and Omran were speaking in hushed tones. Her ears were still ringing, but she hadn't lost her hearing. She was grasping at that bit of good fortune as the elevator stopped. The doors pinged open.

Omran stepped off the lift. She didn't want to leave without Stone.

"I'm coming." His voice was gentle.

Maggie nodded, unsure what words to say. Stone walked a half step behind her and a little to the side. Immediately to the right was another unmarked door. Omran unlocked it and opened it for them. He pointed to a second interior door. "There's a washroom in there you can get cleaned up in."

Stone hesitated.

"We have what we need. She can wash off," Omran said. "I'll be right back."

Omran disappeared through another door.

Maggie waited until the door had shut behind him. "You know him? I mean, more than just from Christmas dinner?"

Stone nodded.

"Do you know Lillian Kensington, too?" Thinking of the feminine powerhouse galvanized Maggie. Over the Christmas holiday, Maggie had sat enraptured listening to the elegant woman humbly answer questions about her extraordinary life and career.

"We were in overlapping circles only."

"And Omran?" Maggie wanted her eyes wide open with what was going on here.

"Omran and I met several months ago. We're working together."

Puzzle pieces snapped into place. "You were tracking Bruce Tanner."

"Bruce Tanner is dead."

The cold finality of his words made Maggie shiver. She looked down at the dried blood that had crusted on her arms and hands, and her face suddenly stung. She lifted her hand to her cheek and came away with fresh blood. "Is Paris always this ... aggressive?"

Stone opened the bathroom door, and a ghost of a smile played on his lips. "I'm the wrong person to ask."

He motioned Maggie into the bathroom.

She brushed past him. The contact was warm and all too brief. She felt cold to her very bones. "Why's that?"

"I hate Paris."

"Said no one ever—" Maggie broke off on a yelp.

She had nowhere to hide in the small room.

She was a disaster.

Her reflection in the wall-sized mirror revealed cuts and dried blood everywhere. Her hair was disheveled, and her blouse was torn. She had no idea where the ocean-shades scarf she had been wearing went, and her long cotton jersey skirt now sported an indecent gash.

Stone was less bloodied, but his frown more than made up for it.

He had stepped forward, alarmed at her exclamation. "Are you hurt?"

The bathroom door clicked shut behind him and their gazes met in the mirror, the small space suddenly intimate.

"Are you hurt?" Stone repeated.

Maggie shook her head, staunchly avoiding her reflection. She turned on the faucet and shoved her hands under the running water. Blood and dirt mixed with water, turning the rivulets in the sink shades of dirty pink. She scrubbed faster, desperate to wash away the last two hours. She swiped the back of her wet hand across her face, suddenly, a hairsbreadth from falling apart. She bit the inside of her cheek. Maggie could let herself fall apart later when she was alone.

Moving slowly, Stone retrieved soap from the dispenser. When he took her hands in his, Maggie's breath hitched. With a slow, steady touch, he washed her hands and her arms. Gently, he cleaned off the blood and grime.

She stood motionless, soaking up his kindness. For long minutes, she let his gentle ministrations of her hands and arms ease the aftershocks of violence.

Stone wetted a paper towel and motioned to her cheek. "This okay?"

She nodded.

Gently, he gripped her chin as he dabbed the blood off the angry cut on her cheek.

She watched him as he avoided her gaze.

"You shouldn't have jumped on that guy." His words were quiet, unexpected.

"I was trying to protect you." Seeing Stone attacked had unleashed something primal inside of her. She had reacted on instinct, putting into practice years of training she had hoped she would never need again.

"No, I mean, it was too dangerous. You shouldn't be taking those risks. Not for me."

"Why not you?" Maggie leaned toward him. "You saved my life."

Stone avoided her gaze. Instead, he glanced around the small space. He found a first aid kit in the cabinet above the paper towel dispenser and set the oversized pack on the counter, unzipping it.

"Stone, why not you?" Maggie pressed.

He rummaged through the first aid kit. "As I said, if anything happened to you, Savannah would kill me, and my half-siblings would help. Gabe would happily take a shot at me."

Maggie had noticed tension over the Christmas events but had chalked that up to the months of chaos and ruthless violence the family had endured. "Why do you say that?"

He shrugged. "I'm the half-sibling bastard."

"Is being a bastard still a thing?"

Finally, he looked up. "Of course it is."

"Sounds like bullshit to me."

"It's not bullshit. It's how it is."

"If you say so." Maggie selected a tube of antibiotic cream. Stone took it from her hands. Softer than she imagined possible, he doctored her cuts and scrapes. Bruises were starting to appear. She would look like hell in the morning.

Maggie watched him as he worked. He was so close she could feel the heat of him. She watched his biceps stretch the short sleeves of his V-neck T-shirt. "I doubt your siblings think that."

"Half siblings." He corrected before glancing at her. "Gabe hates me."

"Gabe hates not realizing you were an agent."

Stone's hand hesitated, the only indication he gave that he had heard her.

Maggie continued. "Gabe's a good guy. A bit overzealous when it comes to responsibility, but a good guy. He doesn't hate you. You surprised him. I don't think that usually happens, and according to Savannah, it's been catastrophic the few times it has. Cut him some slack." She knew Gabe had paid off his student loans by becoming a CSIS agent. After a nearly-lethal ambush in the field, he had left CSIS and went back to being an archaeologist a few years before he met Savannah. It hadn't sat well with Gabe that the intel he could find hadn't identified his half-brother as a foreign operative. If Stone had been from an unfriendly nation, it would have been more easily explained. He was from another commonwealth nation and had purposely stayed several steps ahead of his older half-brother.

Stone made a noncommittal sound.

Maggie pressed. "Becca would wrestle lions for you."

"Don't be ridiculous."

"Whether you like it or not, the Tanner siblings—your siblings—and their significant others have adopted you into their fold."

He parroted her words back. "If you say so."

"I know so," Maggie insisted. "Becca, Colt, Tucker, Jason, Lillian, and Grace all would." It was plain to her that the Tanner siblings had accepted him. Stone must have some serious blinders on to miss his siblings' loyalty.

"You didn't mention Gabe and Savannah."

Maggie placed her hand on his arm, staying his administrations.

He looked at her, his eyes bleak. "What?"

Maggie's heart squeezed at his obvious pain. "Give them time."

"It's not like we can be one big happy family."

"Why not? When Colt brought Lillian around, there were way more fireworks than you've managed to spark, and now Gabe and Savannah are going to be the godparents."

Stone stilled.

"People *can* change," Maggie insisted. "They love you. You're part of something really special."

What she wouldn't do to belong to a found family of loyal, kind people like that.

"Bruce was our biological father, and look what he did."

"Bruce is a dead monster. He doesn't count," Maggie snapped. "He deserved to die alone in a pile of his own excrement, slowly choking on his awfulness and dumb ass choices." She was breathing hard as fresh anger flared.

Stone whistled. "Wow, that sounds personal."

Maggie swiped at her eyes. "Meredith was like an auntie to me, and that piece of shit tried to murder her. There's also the rest of your family—whom I adore, by the way—that he tried to murder, too. And he never claimed you. Fuck him." She wondered if this anger would ever go away. When she met Bruce Tanner, she hadn't liked him on the spot. She had been loathe for Meredith to marry the guy but hadn't had anything concrete. She had no rational reason to dissuade Meredith from getting mixed up with the likes of him, just a *feeling* that the guy was off.

Stone cleared his throat. "He can't hurt anyone anymore."

Maggie looked up. "Isn't that why you're here? Because even dead, that jackass is still causing global problems?"

The edge of Stone's jaw ticked. Something was just below the surface. He was thinking of telling her something. She just wasn't sure what. Maggie waited, but Stone simply administered a topical cream to one of the bruises on her arms.

A few moments later, he said, "*Maggie?*"

"Yeah?" She loved when he said her name like that.

"Don't jump on terrorists for me."

"No promises."

"*Maggie.*"

She smiled to herself again. "Is that arnica?"

Without checking the tube, he said, "Smells like it."

He moved on to her other elbow, where a goose egg was swelling. "I thought you were a librarian."

"I am a librarian."

"Where'd you learn to fight like that? You're positively combustible."

Maggie dropped her gaze to the floor. "Here and there."

Stone didn't quite stop applying cream, but she noticed his hesitation. "I meant that as a compliment. Fire is a good thing."

She fought the urge to scoff. Not in her world, it wasn't. Being bold as a kid had put a target on her back. Apparently, she was *tough enough* to take it. He was eying her too closely, though, so she shrugged. "If you say so."

He smiled at her choice of phrase. "A lot of people wouldn't have fought back, let alone with such ferocity, or land as many hits. You're a natural."

Maggie did scoff this time. Fighting skills should be an aberration, not a natural tendency.

"I meant it as a compliment."

She blew out a breath. "I know you did. I just don't like fighting."

He glanced at her, gently rubbing arnica cream. "You're good at it."

"I wish I didn't need to be," she said softly.

He turned his head swiftly at her comment when a knock sounded.

Fear shot through her.

Maggie hadn't noticed there was a second door.

CHAPTER FIFTEEN

S tone had seen trained agents lose their shit after considerably less than Maggie had dealt with. Even now, battered and bloodied, her gaze was scared but steady as she looked at Stone for direction. She was holding up incredibly well—adrenaline toured people through a lot of touchy emotions. He was pretty sure it was just a matter of time before she snapped.

Stone held up a forefinger to his lips before returning the knock.

A staccato drummed back as Maggie watched him with that unnerving focus.

Satisfied they were safe, he opened the door. Agent Forest stood on the other side.

"Just checking." Stone had been reasonably sure Omran had knocked, but he hadn't been prepared to bet Maggie's life on it.

Omran nodded, his face serious. "You should be."

The door opened into a room with a small conference table and chairs. Three of the walls were painted a light green. The fourth was floor-to-ceiling glass. A small office bullpen was beyond.

Stone and Maggie joined Omran in the small conference room.

Omran held a large file and sported a butterfly bandage on his forehead. "We're on a ticking clock. That infiltration was—" He made a frustrated sound. "Let's just say Ottawa is not happy."

"Really, how can you tell?" Stone asked, deadpan.

"Hilarious, mate." Omran used a droll tone.

"I can't believe you're slamming my country of origin," Maggie muttered without heat.

"I'm exercising whimsy," Stone countered. Was this where she finally lost her shit?

"Why, because the alternative is to fall apart?" Her tone was too light for the darkness in her eyes. She was holding up, but she was hurting.

"Something like that." His own dark sense of humor was how he didn't leap into the deep end after every day at work. Stone moved closer to her, wanting to offer shelter to the storm she was in. Omran gave him a warning look before he pointed to the handful of chairs ringing the small conference table. "Have a seat."

Stone waited until Maggie was seated before he took the chair next to her. Omran sat across from them.

"Ottawa's not mad at us?" Stone asked.

The Brit shook his head, opening the file folder he had brought in. "We kept a Canadian civilian from getting dead twice. Including at the embassy. We're good." Omran looked up. "Sorry, love, that came out wrong."

She gave him a tight smile. "It's okay."

Omran's smile didn't quite reach his eyes as he nodded and flipped through the folder.

Maggie started to fidget, finally blurting, "He's not dead."

"Sebastian?" Stone asked.

"Yes. My twin brother isn't dead. I would feel it."

Omran folded his hands over the folder. "Maggie, these things are hard—"

"No." She shook her head. "We've not always seen eye-to-eye, and we could drive each other nuts, but I'd feel it if he were —" She had pressed her hand to her chest. "It doesn't *feel* like he's gone."

Stone jumped out of his seat. "We can finish this in the morning. You've got to be exhausted." She'd been through enough. They could face whatever Omran had to tell them after Maggie got some rest.

Omran stared at him. It was the Brit's *what the hell* look. Stone stared right back.

Maggie shot her hand out, staying his arm, and Stone froze. Her touch unhinged him.

"I shouldn't have said that out loud. I'm fine." Maggie gently tugged on his hand. "Please, we need to finish this now. When I drop, it's going to be hard."

Stone relented and did as she bid, albeit grudgingly, and sat down.

Maggie hadn't let go of his hand. Under the table, their fingers remained intertwined. The look Omran was giving him said he knew and didn't approve. "Stone's right. I can brief him now, but you don't have to hear this."

Maggie squirmed in her seat, gripping Stone's fingers tighter, and he translated, "You can't un-know or un-see something."

She shook her head. "Do you have any idea the novels I read? You guys have no idea how graphic and worse-case scenario my imagination is. It's entirely possible what I'm imagining is worse than reality."

"Are you sure?" Omran said, but something in his voice sounded almost … triumphant.

Maggie promised she was.

"Stop us at any time." Omran opened the large file he had brought in and picked up his pen. "How did you know the SUV was going to explode?"

Maggie dropped Stone's hand. "Is this an interrogation?"

Stone wondered the same thing.

"Of course not," Omran said smoothly before repeating, "How did you know the SUV was going to explode? Did you see something, hear something?"

Maggie scrunched up her face and closed her eyes. "The whole thing just suddenly felt *wrong*."

"What do you mean, wrong? Like protocol was off—"

Maggie glared at him. "How the fuck would I know your super spy protocol?"

Omran gave a placating smile. "I'm just going through my list. So, you felt something was off?"

Maggie's shoulders fell. In a gentler voice, she said, "Yes. I don't know how to explain it besides something just felt … *off*. Then I got really scared and yelled at you guys to get out of there." She looked at Stone. "Sorry I pushed you so hard. I had to get you out of danger."

She had. Maggie had taken the brunt of the blast and saved his life. "You did. I would have been skewered."

Her eyes rounded, and he found her hand under the table. "My sense of humor sucks."

She squeezed his hand back.

Omran managed not to roll his eyes and instead pressed on. "Who exactly contacted you that your brother was murdered?"

Maggie's head snapped up.

Stone tried to catch the other agent's gaze, but the Brit pressed on, "If there is any chance your brother is still alive, we need to find him. Who contacted you?" Omran paused for effect. In a soft tone, he added, "It might help us find your brother."

The bloke was good. And it most certainly was an interrogation, a skilled one. Omran's tone was reasonable, yet with enough structure to give firmness without crowding. He had disarmed Maggie's suspicion. Even now, she was leaning forward in her seat, and without hesitation, she said, "I assumed they were the Paris police. That's where Sebastian lived. They rattled off their credentials, but it was in French, and it all just ran together."

"Could it have been an *Officer de Police Judiciarie*?" Omran asked, rolling the pen between his hands.

She shrugged. "I don't know. Paris police. When I picked up the call, it didn't dawn on me to record it for replay." She paused. "The woman said her name was Phoebe Freres. That I understood."

Stone shifted. "The evidence and reports were first tampered with before disappearing entirely. There's an insider at the *Préfecture de Police de Paris*. What was the officer like on the phone?"

Maggie considered his question. "Nice, sympathetic at first. When I kept badgering her with questions and asking if it was possible they had made a mistake, she got mad."

"We have reason to believe Sebastian Monroe was working for Teague Alans to develop compact nuclear fusion. We tracked them here. The *Préfecture de Police de Paris* had opened an investigation into Sebastian's murder. No body was ever recovered, and the evidence and reports have gone missing."

Omran was giving him *the look*. What Stone was sharing was definitely in the gray area.

Maggie was looking a little green. "Sebastian's a recluse. He flunked out of school. What evidence do you have that my brother is working for Teague Alans—wait, isn't he the one who messed with a bunch of elections with your dad?"

Stone let go of her hand and rubbed his palms on the sides of his pants. "Don't call him that, ever. He's not my dad." Stone needed this fucking case closed.

The tension in the room crackled.

Maggie eyed him. "Noted. Didn't mean to hit a nerve."

Omran just sat looking at him, waiting for Stone to pull his head out of his ass.

Stone sat up straight, crossing his arms. "Teague Alans and Bruce Tanner were criminal business partners. That's why we're here. We know your brother was mixed up with some very dangerous people. Do you have reason to believe he was coerced into working with Teague Alans?" There. No one could argue that Stone wasn't in complete control again.

"No, I had no idea Sebastian knew him."

"So, no idea if he was a willing partner or a victim?"

Maggie shook her head. "No, but I can't believe my twin brother would willingly sign up to hurt anyone."

"People aren't always what we imagine." Stone didn't know he had it in him to watch his biological father overdose when he had a kit in hand to save him, but there you go.

"Tell me about it," Maggie muttered, her voice wobbly.

Stone had an uncomfortable feeling that she was talking about him. He uncrossed his arms and cleared his throat. "Did you recognize either of the men who attacked you in Sebastian's apartment?"

Maggie shook her head again.

Omran checked his phone. "The guys who attacked Maggie in Sebastian's apartment are low-level mercenaries. Likely a dead end."

"What about the woman?"

In unison, Stone and Omran asked, "What woman?"

Maggie stared at them.

"What woman?" Stone repeated.

She glanced between the two of them. Slowly, she said, "That apartment was dotted with feminine touches. You thought I was his girlfriend. I just assumed—" She stopped, letting the thought hang. "Never mind, you guys are the experts."

"Your brother didn't like … feminine touches?" Omran asked neutrally.

"Seriously?" Maggie looked ready to throttle the Brit. "Was I *not* supposed to mention the weird shit I noticed? Because I assumed that would be what you secret agent types would call a *clue.*"

There was the adrenaline crash. Stone leaned forward, making a hushing sound. "Easy, Maggie."

She turned on him like a cornered animal. "Back off. You're pissed I called your biological dad your dad, yet I can't have an informed opinion on how my twin brother would or would not decorate his house? Fuck you."

It felt like the floor dropped out from underneath him.

But she was right. "We're trying to get to the bottom of this. You're not in trouble—"

"I know that," she snapped. "I didn't do anything wrong."

The charged tension in the small room was claustrophobic.

Maggie exhaled and rubbed the dark circles under her eyes. "This has been a really shitty twenty-four hours. I'm … sorry."

Stone felt like an ass. Without trying, the woman was dragging out decades of his unresolved, suppressed anger. He didn't like it, but instead of floundering, Stone should have noticed how wrung out she was. He should be the one apologizing.

He offered up information instead. "We had one shaky piece of intel that suggested a girlfriend, but we haven't been able to substantiate it."

Some of the tension drained from her. "I can tell you my twin brother is not the type to have bowls of lemons lying about or ornate soap dispensers by the sink. A woman—or someone inclined to softer touches, spends a lot of time in that apartment." Maggie hesitated. "But how would my brother get a girlfriend?"

Stone and Omran looked at each other.

Stone ventured, "Uh … the normal way?"

"No, I mean, my brother is a recluse. At the risk of sounding like an ass, my brother's kind of weird, in a boy genius sort of way, I mean. He's never had a girlfriend, not one that has been around long enough to decorate, anyway."

"We'll check Sebastian's apartment," Stone added. "If you're correct, we could find something to lead us to the woman."

"We'll go tomorrow," Omran said.

"Excellent," Maggie said, looking relieved.

Stone sat up. "He meant me and him. You're not coming. It's

too dangerous." Maggie had almost gotten dead the first time she went to that apartment. There wasn't a chance Stone would be the one to risk her life for intel. Not to mention he hadn't been exaggerating. His half-brother might not give a shit about him, but Gabe was protective as fuck of Savannah, and Maggie were best friends.

"Right, of course."

Stone frowned. She had agreed way too readily.

"*Maggie?*"

"What? I said okay."

Omran looked between the two of them before asking, "When was the last time you spoke with your brother?"

"Twin brother." Maggie crossed her arms. "How is that relevant?"

Stone looked at Omran. Red flags were pinging all over the place.

Stone asked, "What aren't you telling us?"

"Nothing."

"*Maggie?*"

"Don't even. Being attacked and nearly being blown up wasn't enough. Now I'm getting shit for how often I talk to my brother?" She swiped at her now damp eyes. "I was minding my own business on another continent when I got a call from the Paris police, and some Inspector Freres says my twin brother was murdered—" She pressed her palms against her eyes. "I've told you all this. Shouldn't you guys be, I don't know, chasing bad guys?"

A buzzing sound could be heard.

Omran looked around. "What's that?"

Maggie reached for her purse. "Relax, it's not another bomb. It's my ringtone."

"Who knows you're in France?" Stone demanded. Smooth.

"Do you *not* interrogate everyone like this?" Maggie had been damn near putty in his hands in the bathroom. Now she was getting pricklier by the second. "As a matter of fact, yes."

Omran was giving Stone a considering look. Damn. Stone's infatuation with Maggie was a liability. It certainly wouldn't help him close this case any sooner, but if he wasn't careful, it could jeopardize it.

Omran turned to Maggie, clarifying, "You and Savannah are best friends, and Meredith is Savannah's aunt, which makes you like an adopted niece to Meredith?"

Maggie had noticed Stone and Omran's unspoken subtext. "That's right. Savannah and Meredith are the only ones who know I'm in France."

She checked her phone and made a strangled sound. Her face went white.

"Maggie?" Stone asked, alarmed. "What is it?"

She held up the phone.

"This is Sebastian's number." Maggie dug in her purse a moment before holding up a second cell phone. "But this is his phone."

CHAPTER SIXTEEN

Maggie's heart was hammering. "Should I answer it?" Her twin brother was assumed murdered, she had just been attacked twice, she was exhausted, jet lagged, and her blood sugar sucked. She was not ready to deal with whatever terrorist bullshit the asshole on the phone was about, so she handed her phone to Stone. "I can't."

He accepted it and punched the speaker and record buttons. "What?"

A menacing distorted voice crackled, "We have your brother."

Maggie grabbed the phone back. "What kind of sick joke is this?" she demanded, even as hope flared.

"We have your brother. Bring the—"

"Put him on," Maggie demanded. *"Put him on."*

Several moments later, a voice sounded. "It's me, Sebastian."

Maggie gripped the phone tighter. "Sebastian, we're going to figure this out, all right. Do what they say. We'll figure this out." She swiped at the tears streaming down her face. "I miss you, Sunbeam."

"Me, too." There was a brief burst of static before the distorted voice returned. "Meet me at—"

Maggie screamed, *"Do not fuck with me."*

Omran reached to take the phone, but she jumped to her feet out of reach before screaming into the phone, "You don't have my brother, you creepy fuck. You're a piece of shit scraped off—"

The phone went dead.

Stone and Omran were gaping at her.

Maggie's heart was hammering as she paced. "Don't look at me like that."

Stone asked, "Why did you do that?"

Maggie exhaled. "Because he was lying."

"How could you possibly know that?" Omran asked, his voice thick with anger.

She froze. It couldn't have been Sebastian. The voice hadn't answered her correctly.

A sick feeling rolled through her. What if she had been wrong? What if her outburst cost her twin brother his life?

"Maggie, I'm going to ask you something, and I need you to tell me the truth. Why do you have Sebastian's phone?"

"I didn't do anything wrong," she repeated, nervous at Stone's tone.

Silence met her declaration, and she rushed to fill the space. "He's my twin brother. I took his phone when I saw it sitting in that copper dish he has on his counter. I just wanted to see another picture of him. His screen image, something. It needs to be charged. I don't know what's on it." Her hands shook as she groped in her purse. Her hand collided with soft flannel.

"Maggie, we don't—" Stone broke off when she tugged her twin brother's plaid flannel out of her purse. She pushed her suddenly cold arms into the sleeves, gently turning her nose into the collar. Self-conscious, she wrapped her arms around herself.

The left breast pocket crinkled.

Slowly, Maggie reached her hand into the pocket. Her fingers touched a slip of paper. It was a folded piece of paper with two rows of numbers on it. A stylized cartoon duck with a kilt on grinned from the corner. She ran her thumb over the printed duck, thinking. The top number she recognized. *Zero-two-zero-seven-one-nine-zero-six.*

Without hesitation, she held the paper out to Stone.

He accepted it, frowning. "Weird duck. Do you know what any of it means?"

"The top number opens Seb's front door. No idea what the second row is."

Stone passed the slip of paper to Omran.

Omran took a photo of it and started typing into his phone.

Stone was looking at her. "Maggie, why did you say the voice was lying? You sounded … sure of yourself."

Omran stopped typing and looked at her, too.

She swallowed. "Because Sebastian and I have a security code, so we would always know if the other was actually in trouble. Whoever that was, he didn't answer it correctly."

Carefully, Stone asked, "Why would you and your twin brother need a safety net like that?"

Maggie swallowed, wrapping her arms around her tighter. "Because this is not the first time a kidnapper has called."

CHAPTER SEVENTEEN

Teague Alans slammed the phone down. Maggie Monroe was going to be a problem.

He didn't like problems, nor women who didn't know their place. She had the audacity to scream at him ... *at him*. Her asinine display of anger had been most unappealing. *He* was the wronged party here. Her brother had taken his money. Sebastian Monroe was the reason Teague was in this predicament. It was all his fault.

"What do you want us to do, boss?" The new mercenary stood to the side. Three men stood behind him, waiting, alert. They were a hundred times better than the jackasses who had fucked up a simple case of torture and lost the goddamn body or the assholes who had gotten caught at the embassy.

They cost almost a hundred times as much, too.

Teague wanted what he had bought and paid for. He owned Sebastian Monroe, and that included his fusion research, goddammit. Since he couldn't take it out of Sebastian, he would take his pound of flesh from the man's sister. The four men had found her in a matter of hours. It was all where one knew to look.

"What are they going to do next?" Teague demanded to know.

The mercenary in charge shrugged. "Dump her in a safe house and wait for further instructions. This is an international incident. They have to wait for the appropriate coordination. It shouldn't take long."

"I presume you know where these safe houses are?"

The mercenary's face was impassive. "That's what you pay us for."

"Good. Find out which one and report back."

"Just report?" The mercenary confirmed.

Teague's smile was cruel. "Yes. I want the pleasure of breaking Sebastian Monroe's harpy sister. Not before I get what's mine from her."

First, he had another problem to take care of.

CHAPTER EIGHTEEN

S tone was not surprised very often. Maggie's admission positively chilled him. Not to mention Teague Alans's brash kidnapping ploy. "I'm calling it. This interview is over. Maggie, you look like you're going to topple over. When was the last time you ate anything?"

Maggie shrugged, her eyes had an eerie blankness to them, and it was like her energy had caved in on itself.

Omran sprang to motion. "Sorry, love. Let's get you sorted. Give me a moment." Omran made an eating motion, and Stone nodded. Omran hurried out of the room.

Maggie still had her arms wrapped around herself and looked like she had checked out.

"He doesn't trust me." Her voice was flat, lifeless. It made Stone uneasy.

"Omran?"

Maggie nodded. "He was interrogating me, wasn't he?"

Stone paused before nodding.

Her mouth turned down in a frown. "That sucked, but I get it."

"You do?"

"I'm not a secret agent, but I'm not an idiot."

Stone wasn't sure what to say. She was tough as nails, way tougher than him, but admitting she was the most resilient person he had ever met might come out sounding trite.

"Where'd he go?"

"Food. It won't be much, but it'll help." Stone glanced at the door, willing Omran to hustle faster.

"Thank Christ, I'm starving." Maggie pressed the heels of her hands against her eyes. "This has been, without a doubt, a shit ass day, and I've had some doozies."

Stone shot her a look but refused to pry. People were entitled to keep some secrets.

It was like she read his mind when she answered, "It's okay. I'll tell you. Just not now. I feel like I've been gone nine rounds with a truck." She tipped her head back and closed her eyes. "Teague Alans knows I exist. He knew it was me who answered Sebastian's phone."

Stone had been hoping she hadn't caught that. That latest development worried the shit out of him.

Omran appeared, and Stone jumped up. The Brit set a large, pre-packaged sandwich and bottle of juice in front of Maggie. "It's not fancy, but it'll fill the gap."

"Thanks," Maggie mumbled, reaching for the juice first.

Omran motioned for Stone to follow him.

"I'll be right back. You okay?" Stone asked her.

Maggie had already uncapped the juice and taken a long swig. "Go. I'll be fine here."

The door shut with a click behind them, and Stone and Omran walked several paces away from the glass wall. Maggie was tucking into her sandwich.

In a hushed voice, Omran said, "She might be part of this."

"I know."

"How did she know the SUV was going to explode?"

"I said, *I know.*"

"You have to stay objective, man, stay neutral," Omran pressed.

"No shit."

Omran made what sounded suspiciously like a growl. "You like her. Don't deny it."

"Wasn't going to."

"That's it? You gotta give me more than that."

Stone rocked back on his heels. "That's all I got. I know what I'm doing."

"Do you?"

Stone and Omran had been working closely for the last several months. Stone knew the guy was doing his job, and he had a point. He even liked the guy a lot. Omran was solid. Still, he didn't need a fucking lecture. "You done?"

"Unless you fuck up."

"I won't."

Omran gave him a long look. "Think it was Teague Alans?"

"Behind our SUV exploding, probably."

"Think we got a leak?"

Stone exhaled. "Fuck, I hope not."

Both men stood, absorbing possibilities. Omran spoke first. "When do you want to head back to Sebastian's apartment?"

Stone checked his watch. It would be daylight in an hour. He wasn't leaving Maggie until she had a proper sleep, got rehydrated, refueled, and was coherent. "Dusk? That should give me enough time to get her to the appointment with the police."

Omran agreed. "You taking her to your place?"

Stone nodded. It was the safest place he could think of.

Omran let out a long breath. "Good. If she's innocent, I don't want her ground up in all of this. Lillian would never forgive me."

"Were you two ever ..." Stone let the half-question hang. Agent Forest had been assigned as state security for Lillian's high-ranking grandmother. He was one of the few agents Lillian still trusted after her trumped-up treason charges were dismissed.

Omran shook his head. "Nah, she's the closest thing I have to a sister, though."

Stone nodded like he understood what that would feel like. "And if Maggie's not innocent?"

Omran's dark eyes clouded. "You know what these guys are like. Don't you dare let her pull you under." The Brit clapped him on the shoulder. "I actually like working with you, bro."

Stone returned the weary smile, suddenly aware Omran was precariously close to being as much a brother-type to Stone as his half-siblings were.

As they walked back to the conference room, Stone digested that latest revelation. "I actually like working with you, too."

Omran laughed. "Easy there. I didn't ask you to move in."

Stone grinned, remembering Omran was bi. "Now that just hurts."

The two were smiling as they returned to the small conference room. The empty juice bottle and half a sandwich were on the table.

Maggie wasn't there.

CHAPTER NINETEEN

Maggie had devoured half the sandwich and juice before her stomach protested. She stood in from of the mirror, clutching the edge of the sink, taking steadying breaths. A fresh wave of nausea hit her as she washed her hands.

Loud banging thundered on the other side of the door. *"Maggie."*

More violent pounding.

Her heartbeat spiked, and all traces of nausea evaporated. She snapped off the taps and yelled through the door, "Stone?"

The pounding stopped. She heard a slump against the door.

She flung open the washroom door, fearing the worst and ready for battle.

Off balance at the sudden open door, Stone almost toppled into her. At the same time, his gaze raced over her person. "You're okay?"

Relief flooded her. Instinctively, she grabbed his forearms. "I'm okay, my stomach was just queasy again. What's wrong?"

"When you weren't in the room, I—"

Maggie pulled him in for a tight hug, her mouth at his ear as she repeated, "I'm okay. I'm safe."

She felt his strong arms wrap around her and hold on.

Holy shit, he had been *really* scared for her.

"It's okay, Stone. I'm okay." Her arms around him were just as tight. "I ate too fast and didn't feel well, that's all."

Stone straightened, pulling away. "You scared the shit out of me."

"I'm sorry." Now that there was no danger, her stomach resumed its unsettled roll, and she placed her hands on her belly as her eyelids fluttered closed. She needed sleep badly. Maggie had been up for nearly thirty-six hours, unable to sleep during the twelve hours she had been in the air or the seven hours she had been in three different airports, let alone the last couple of hours. She was ready to drop.

"She all right?" She heard Omran ask.

Maggie swayed, and her eyelids opened in a rush. She gripped the wall. "I'm fine. I just need sleep. I wasn't kidding. I'm going to drop."

Stone wrapped an arm around her shoulders. He led her out of the bathroom, snagging the handle of her carry-on. "Come on. I'm going to take you somewhere safe to sleep. We can sort everything out later."

She leaned into him, eyes closed, utterly exhausted.

Maggie heard Stone and Omran speak briefly, but she was too drained to register what they were saying.

Soon, she was tucked in the front passenger seat of an SUV. Stone came around the vehicle and got behind the wheel.

"Where are we going?" Maggie's eyes were still closed.

"Someplace safe," Stone replied.

She forced her eyelids open and whispered, "Am I in trouble?"

Silence met her question for so long that she didn't think he would answer.

"I hope not." His voice was serious, quiet.

The lights of Paris flashed by, and Maggie pressed her hand against her stomach. She couldn't believe this was happening again.

CHAPTER TWENTY

"The woman cop doesn't know a damn thing." The younger of the two mercenaries Teague Alans had paid to rough up Sebastian Monroe spoke. They were standing near the door of the plush hotel suite.

Teague Alans glanced from the well-stocked sideboard. He finished pouring three drinks. "That's not what I heard."

The mercenaries glanced at each other nervously. The younger one spoke again, "We kept everything quiet, just like you said."

"You lost the goddamn body. There shouldn't even have been a body. I said torture, not murder." Teague wanted to spit on the miserable excuse in front of him or slit their throats. When he hired professionals, he expected results. The larger one widened his stance, setting his shoulders back. "We kept your name out of it. I told you, we *are* professionals."

The first one straightened, trying to mimic his partner. "She's just a stupid cop. She didn't get a peep out of us—" The larger one cut him with a quick, icy look, and the younger man shut up.

Teague weighed his options. He knew how to manipulate, defraud, embezzle, and creatively blackmail with blinding clarity. Killing was a new toy to him. The large man in front of him had dead eyes and a body hardened by violence. Teague would never last in a physical fight with the likes of him, which is why he had come prepared. He turned his back to his visitors, discreetly slipping two tablets into their respective drinks. The younger one was different, weaker. Perhaps Teague would try physical violence with that one, see if Bruce's hysterical obsessions held any merit.

He picked up one of the drugged tumblers and his before circling the two men. "I told you to get Sebastian Monroe to talk, and instead, you killed him." He leaned over the shoulder of the larger man. "That wasn't very professional."

The assassin stared straight ahead. "The target was more fragile than we thought."

The younger one darted his partner a look, his eyes panicked.

Teague paused. "Oh, I see. *He* killed Sebastian."

The larger one remained stock still. Teague smiled, handing him the drink. "I knew it couldn't be you."

The man accepted the tumbler, easing his stance a fraction.

Teague tipped his glass in salute before downing the expensive whiskey. His paid assassin did the same while the younger partner looked on, frowning at being excluded.

Teague waited a beat, anticipation building. The large assassin's eyes rounded, and his gaze shot to Teague's. It was filled with pure loathing. Too late, the man understood what was happening. Suddenly he grabbed at his throat, rasping. The young apprentice ran to the assassin, but it was too late. The large man was convulsing on the floor. "What did you do?"

Wisps of anticipation shot through Teague as he picked up the ceremonial dirk he had brought just for such an occasion. He caressed the decorated metal, careful to stay clear of the blade's wicked edge. It had been a gift from Bruce. How fitting. "I paid for a service. You didn't follow my instructions."

"But he didn't mess up, I—" The young man broke off, realizing his mistake. He stood slowly, wary eyes on Teague. In a smooth rush, the young man suddenly charged Teague.

The blow knocked him to the ground, and the dirk flew out of Teague's hand. The young assassin started pummeling him. Teague was taking the beating of his life when a garbled sound came from the large assassin on the floor. The young mercenary halted, hope filling his expressive eyes. He shoved Teague aside and scrambled to his comrade.

It was the show of weakness Teague needed.

Teague grabbed the dirk from the floor. Before the rookie mercenary knew what he was about to do, Teague plunged it deep into the older assassin's chest.

The young man launched himself over the dead man's body. It was just the reckless move Teague had hoped for. He yanked the dirk out and flipped his wrist. The young assassin impaled himself. He gave a grunt of surprise, gripping Teague's hand, still holding the embedded dirk.

Teague twisted his wrist.

Surprise turned to hatred as the young man stared back at him. Blood dripped from his mouth as it poured out of his mutilated stomach. Teague saw the exact moment the life blinked out of the young man.

A fevered rush raced through him.

Bruce Tanner had been right.

Murder felt good.

CHAPTER TWENTY-ONE

S ebastian stood motionless in the shadows of the suite's second bedroom, his hand unflinching as he videoed the brutal exchange. He tried to feel something other than cold indifference at the carnage in the suite in front of him. He had always been a quick study and felt nothing beyond getting and securing the proof of Teague Alans's treachery.

Phoebe would be so disappointed in him.

The few times she had spoken of her job, how it had desensitized her to normal human reactions. How she had stopped experiencing physical and emotional reactions to revolting scenes and brutalities. To do her job well, she had learned to compartmentalize the horrific details of crime scenes, the evidence collected, and the depravity investigations uncovered. She had found comfort and purpose in Sebastian's naïveté.

He wasn't naïve. His and Maggie's childhood had blown that shit wide open.

Still, the innocence Phoebe saw in him was proof he wasn't irrevocably broken, wasn't undeserving of her love. The shit he and his twin sister had endured at the hands of the adults meant to raise and protect them hadn't forever sullied his soul.

Tonight Sebastian realized he was wrong. There was no innocence left in him. He was just as broken as the two dead guys who had brutalized him all those weeks ago and the lunatic who had just murdered them. Sebastian's steady hand and unflinching gaze, as he recorded the odious deed, proved it. Even now, Teague Alans was standing over the dead bodies with an unholy glint in his eyes, and Sebastian kept recording.

The terrorist first booted the large man like he was kicking tires. When he was met with zero resistance, he kicked harder, laughing. Suddenly, he spun to the younger body. The blood had long since stopped pumping out of the stomach wound and looked to be congealing. Teague dropped to his knees and grabbed the hilt of the dirk. He pulled it from the motionless body and, with a howl, plunged it back. He giggled as blood dribbled down his wrist. Teague pulled the knife out before drawing it back down. Sebastian kept filming as Teague stabbed the corpse again and again before repeating the desecration on the larger man.

Sebastian's stomach lurched. Teague Alans was one sick son of a bitch.

He felt bile rise up the back of his throat when the lunatic started playing with the congealing blood, and he slapped his hand to cover his mouth.

Teague Alans suddenly sat up. "Is someone there?" He scrambled to stand. His meticulous suit was covered in the blood of dead men. He dropped the dirk. It made a dull sound as it landed on the soiled rug. He tugged at the lapels of his suit. "I didn't think so."

Sebastian felt the hairs on the back of his neck rise. A moment later, he heard the suite door open. "What the hell did you do?"

Teague gave the newcomer a dismissive glare. "I need this place cleaned up."

"Jesus, Alans, you don't clean that much blood. You burn it."

"Fine. Give me twenty minutes, then torch the place."

The door clicked shut.

Teague took out his phone, snapping several selfies with the corpses, before retreating to the bathroom. Sebastian heard the shower turn on. He waited until he heard the uneven spray of Teague in the shower before he hit sync to upload the video to the cloud.

The file was huge, but Sebastian didn't dare move before confirming it had been saved.

Several minutes passed.

The suite's door opened quickly. "Your twenty minutes is up."

Steam billowed out when Teague opened the bathroom door. He wore a ridiculous outfit better suited to a snotty North American golf course than Paris.

The man frowned at Teague but got to work. The sharp sting of accelerant hit Sebastian's nostrils as the man started dousing the space. Sebastian's gaze flew to the phone in his hand. The file had finally finished syncing. Thank Christ.

"I had the sprinklers disarmed. I need you to sound the alarm after the fire takes. You'll get paid after."

"Where the hell are you going?"

Teague rounded on the guy. "I don't pay you to ask questions." He pulled out a lighter, igniting it before tossing it between the dead bodies. A whooshing sound filled Sebastian's ears.

"*Jesus!*" The newcomer launched himself and Teague out of the suite as a fireball lit up.

Flames erupted as high as the ceiling in the main suite.

Sebastian's exit was blocked.

CHAPTER TWENTY-TWO

Stone parked in the single underground garage, closing the garage door behind them. Maggie had fallen asleep. She sat in the passenger seat, unmoving and with her neck at an uncomfortable-looking angle. Stone checked his watch. All the security icons looked as they should.

Not wanting to startle her, he softly said, "Maggie, we're here."

She turned in her sleep, reaching for him.

"I'm going to unclip your seatbelt," he said.

No verbal response, just her hands curling in his shirt as she resettled, still deep in sleep.

Out cold, and still she reached for him.

He wished they could have met someplace far away, just the two of them, without anyone else's bullshit influencing their lives. Just a boy and a girl free to be smitten with each other if they so desired. And dammit, he desired.

Squashing down useless feelings, Stone continued giving Maggie the play-by-play as he carried her into the townhouse and tucked her into the only bed. He retrieved her carry-on and purse and placed them in the room so she would see them when she woke up. He started to close the bedroom door, ready to leave her in peace, but she stirred and called his name.

"It's okay," he whispered. "I'll just be in the other room. You're safe."

"Please don't leave," she murmured, sounding still asleep.

"I won't." It was a vow.

She smiled then, murmuring something unintelligible, her eyelids fluttering closed again.

That was nine hours ago. Several hours ago, Maggie had cried out, and Stone had rushed to her. She had been crying in her sleep. It had gutted him to leave her alone, but he hadn't wanted to wake her. He figured she needed sleep more than comfort.

He'd have to wake her up soon so they would make the appointment with the police.

Omran called. Stone answered it on the first ring. "What do you got?"

"I found something."

Fear squeezed Stone's stomach as he waited.

"In the apartment?" Stone hadn't wanted to leave Maggie alone when Omran went back to Sebastian's apartment.

"No, that was clean." Keyboard clicks could be heard. "They changed their last name. Sebastian's past has been scrubbed, but Maggie's hasn't. I'm sending it to you now."

Stone already had his laptop open on the kitchen table and clicked on the file Omran had sent.

The newspaper article was old, back when newspapers were still printed.

Twin ten-year-old terrorized in parents' ransom scheme.

Stone braced himself and read on. The article showed a pixie-faced Maggie and a serious-to-the-point-of-sad Sebastian. The differences were stark. Their parents and far-older sibling had orchestrated Sebastian's abduction in an attempt to extort ransom money out of Maggie and Sebastian's estranged—though wealthy—grandparents.

It had worked. Until Maggie found out. In a dramatic confrontation, Sebastian had been rescued, their parents and older brother had gone to prison, and Maggie and Sebastian's newfound grandparents passed on raising their parentless grandchildren.

Maggie and Sebastian had been assigned a court guardian and been dumped in separate boarding schools. Their grandparents had been prepared to open their checkbook—if not their home—to the devastated twin ten-year-olds.

Stone felt eyes behind him and turned.

Maggie stood in the kitchen doorway. Her eyes were clearer than they had been yesterday, and her skin had most of the color back.

Relief nearly undid him. He cleared his throat. "Uh, are you hungry? I can make you something."

Her sleepy expression darkened, and she pointed to his laptop screen. "Where did you get that?"

Stone swung the laptop to face her better. "It's part of our intel on your brother."

"And me." Her voice held accusation.

He nodded. What could he say? It was the truth.

"You guys didn't even know I was part of this until I showed up at Sebastian's apartment."

Stone nodded again.

The color drained from her face. "Oh my god, I led you guys right to my brother."

"No. The Paris police called you." *Shit.* The Paris police had called her.

Maggie frowned. "How would they know if you guys didn't?"

"That's a good question."

Maggie pulled out one of the dining chairs and dropped into it more than sat down. She exhaled a long breath. "What if the woman I think exists in Sebastian's life works for the Paris police?"

SARAH KADES

Connections started popping through Stone's head. "Tell me exactly what you mean?"

Maggie drummed her hands on the top of the table. "You work for ASIS, and Omran is British intel, right?"

Stone nodded.

"So how could a metro police department have better intel than you guys?"

"It would be unusual," Stone admitted.

"Unless a Paris police officer had a specific connection, insider information."

Stone hadn't thought of that and told her as much.

Maggie added, "How else would they have known to call me, and that I was Sebastian's next of kin?" The color drained from her face. "Oh my god. What if she called our parents and older brother?" Her voice had pitched higher.

"When was the last time you spoke with them?"

Maggie pulled her legs up on the chair and wrapped her arms around her knees. "Fifteen years ago." She pointed to his laptop. "I'm sure it's all there. My dad and oldest brother are out of prison, but my mom broke parole and went back in."

Stone tensed. "Could they be behind this, setting up your brother?"

Maggie frowned. "Maybe. I doubt it. They're cruel but not terribly bright. That's how I caught on to what they were doing in the first place when I was ten." She hesitated before swearing. "They are charismatic. And isn't prison just a business mixer for criminals?"

"What are you saying?"

"Does Teague Alans have known associates in Alberta prisons?"

"Yes."

"So he could have gotten to my family." Maggie dropped her legs to the floor and leaned forward. "What if they have something to do with this?"

"It's possible. Teague Alans isn't above putting pressure points on family members—"

"He wouldn't have had to. He would have just had to offer them money." Her words held the bitterness of betrayal. She scrubbed her hands over her face. "Sebastian and I changed our names so they couldn't find us when they got out. Problem is, you did. You found us. They could, too."

Stone hated to ask. "Could Sebastian have reached out to them? Scheme together?"

Maggie shook her head. "No way. Sebastian is a lot of things —he's got that eccentric, weird scientist thing going on. But he's not motivated by money or power. He's kind. And he knows what it feels like to be abused. He would never willingly hurt another, let alone team up with them." Her voice shook. "He had been terrified I had been taken, too, that he couldn't save me. He didn't know it wasn't real, that it was all just to extort money."

Stone wanted to comfort this woman but wasn't sure how to do that without being an ass. He still wasn't convinced of Sebastian's innocence. "That's why you and your brother have the code."

She nodded.

"Why'd you change your name to Monroe? Is it a family name?"

"Hardly." Maggie smiled. "Cora Monroe from James Fenimore Cooper's *Last of the Mohicans*."

Stone wracked his brain. "The movie?"

"No, the book. *Last of the Mohicans, A Narrative of 1757*." Her eyes went wide. "Damn. Cora dies in the book." She looked at him, her eyes still rounded. "Why didn't I pick a heroine that lived a long, happy life? One that died peacefully in her sleep only after an epically awesome life? Instead, I picked—"

"She's fine in the movie," he interrupted gruffly.

Maggie stared at him. "You're trying to make me feel better."

Stone remained silent.

She gave him a considering look. "Thank you. It's nice to have someone to talk to about this."

He frowned. "What about Savannah?"

Maggie looked at the tabletop. "Savannah doesn't know about any of this."

Red flags started popping. "I thought she was your best friend?"

Maggie looked up sharply. "That doesn't mean I have to confess the darkest shit of my childhood to her."

"No, it doesn't." Stone would never break Maggie's trust, but if Savannah or Gabe ever found out Stone knew and hadn't told them—and shit like this had a way of coming out, it would be yet another thing for Gabe to hold over Stone's head. Another reason he couldn't be trusted.

Maggie cradled the sides of her head in her hands, elbows propped on the table. "I'm sorry, I shouldn't have snapped. It's a sensitive topic for me."

"I won't tell," Stone promised. "I was just … surprised, that's all."

Maggie blew out a breath. "Savannah is my best friend, and she's had her share of crap. I just don't know if she'd get this, ya know? I don't want her to get weird about it." Maggie shrugged. "I buried that part of my life a long time ago."

Stone understood that better than most.

Maggie gave him a pointed look. "I don't talk to people about it."

"Like usually?"

"Like ever."

"You're talking to me." She had been clear. Whatever they were, it wasn't close.

"Don't worry, it freaks the fuck out of me, too." She hesitated. "Do you think my parents could be mixed up in this?"

"I honestly don't know."

Maggie swore. "If my brother is alive, we need to find him. I wasn't strong enough to fight back when we were kids, but *no one* is going to use him again, not if I can help it." Her back was ramrod straight, and her eyes were dark with conviction.

At that moment, Stone was pretty sure he'd walk through fire for her.

He would have to—dead or alive, Sebastian had unfinished business with Teague Alans, who wouldn't stop until he got what he wanted. Just like his crew had done to Sebastian, Teague Alans would press Maggie as hard as it took until he got what he wanted.

Or broke her trying.

CHAPTER TWENTY-THREE

The force of the fireball had knocked Sebastian on his back. He scrambled up, rushing to close the side bedroom door. Smoke streamed under it. The suite beyond was an inferno. Sebastian grabbed towels from the bedroom's en suite, stuffing them across the bottom of the door. It wasn't perfect, but it would buy him some time.

The hotel bedroom had filled with an alarming amount of choking smoke. Sebastian ran back to the en suite, shoving a hand towel under the tap. Sopping wet, he wrapped it around his head, covering his nose and mouth.

Think. How was he going to get out of here?

The bathroom was tiled. He would need a sledgehammer to knock his way out. He darted back into the bedroom. The room was on the seventh floor. There was a single, secured oval pane of glass. He pressed his forehead against the glass. Below was a pool deck, three, maybe four floors down. Colorful awnings matched the pool deck umbrellas.

An eerie crackling sound split the air before a crash reverberated through the floor. Sebastian instinctively ducked. By the sounds of it, the ceiling was crashing down in the main suite. It would only be a matter of time before this room was engulfed, too, and this ceiling came crashing down on him.

He grabbed one of the decorative bedside lamps. It was a hefty crystal. Sebastian yanked the cord free and stopped. The lamp had hidden a folded sheaf of papers. He pocketed the stash before yanking the shade off the lamp. He raised it, intending to slam it against the window pane, but ran back into the bathroom, such as he could in choking smoke. Wrapping a towel around his hand, he picked up the lamp base and heaved it against the glass.

Nothing.

He hammered at different spots on the glass, needing a weakness.

On his fifth attack, a fracture appeared. He battered the lamp base against the glass again and again. The fracture became a spiderweb of cracks. Heaving with all his strength, he struck the oval pane again with so much force that he nearly fell out the window as it shattered, raining glass below.

A half second later, he realized his mistake. The door to the bedroom blasted open as a fireball scorched in. The force launched him out of the gaping hole.

Sebastian windmilled his arms, grasping for purchase.

There was nothing but air.

He was in a free fall.

CHAPTER TWENTY-FOUR

Maggie sat at Stone's kitchen table in his Paris apartment, still reeling that it had felt so *right* to share the deepest shadows of herself with him. She was good at plastering a convincing smile on her face, but she lived her life in constant fear. It was one of the reasons she had chosen to be a librarian—she could have adventures and travel the world, all within the safe confines of books.

Last night she had woken up at some point, frozen in terror and with no idea where she was. She had strained to hear something that would orient her when she had heard Stone's low voice speaking quietly on the phone. The whole mess came flooding back, and she burst into silent tears.

But she hadn't been silent. Stone had come to check on her, whispering her name and asking if she was all right. Maggie had feigned sleep. She hated feeling weak, especially when he was so strong. After a long hesitation, Stone finally retreated.

He was in front of her now. If Maggie leaned forward, she would bump into him. That's how close their chairs were.

It made her feel needy. She didn't like it. Instead, she sat up straighter. "What am I going to do if my parents are back? They are ticking time bombs."

"We'll figure it out." Stone moved his hand, then stopped before flexing it. Did he want to reach for hers? Why did he stop himself?

Maybe it was *need*—not neediness, she was feeling.

Maggie kept her hands completely accessible, just in case, and joked, "I could have used a secret agent like you in my life when I was growing up."

"I'm in your life now." He was looking at her with such intensity. She realized it would have frightened her even a few days ago. Now she knew better; Stone was fierce strength and protective instincts, with an intelligence as sharp as his sense of humor. The only thing she had to fear was how hard she'd fall for him if she let herself. Maggie smiled at him then. Getting to know him was the only good thing to come out of this latest shitstorm.

Stone reached for her hand.

His watch beeped.

He swore softly.

"What's that for?"

Stone turned off the alarm. "Time to wake you up to make it to the appointment with Inspector Freres."

Maggie darted her gaze toward the window. The afternoon sun filtered through closed blinds. "I slept all day!" She swung her gaze back to him. "You didn't go to my brother's apartment."

"I didn't want you to wake up alone."

Could the man get any hotter?

Maggie looked down, unable to meet his eyes. What she was feeling for him was way more complicated than simple safety. His gentle acceptance of her past was like a bright light, and the shadows she had feared her entire life lost some of their bulk. It didn't hurt he was also hot as fuck and lit up everything feminine in her body. "Thank you. I ... thanks."

Stone closed the lid on his laptop and stood. "No problem."

SARAH KADES

They were suddenly on a new footing. An intimacy had sprung between them. He seemed as disoriented as she.

Maggie tucked a wayward strand of hair behind an ear. "What did Omran find?"

Stone took a step away from the table, putting distance between them. "Nothing besides what you already noticed—decorative touches, clean sheets, nothing growing in the fridge. It was a quick look, mind you."

"I'll find something." Maggie forgot to temper the conviction in her voice.

"I believe you."

She sprang up from her chair. "You do?" By now, Maggie should be used to her ideas being dismissed. If she was lucky, people circled back. It was a time-consuming cycle as others caught up to the patterns and connections she always seemed to notice before others did. It was why she had lost her shit at the embassy when Omran and Stone had doubted her.

"Of course I do. We know Sebastian on paper. You *know* know him, I mean, the guy's your twin brother. I just don't want you to be in harm's way. That's why I resisted—the only reason I resisted," Stone clarified.

"I can help. I know I can. We can go after the appointment." Even she heard the earnestness in her voice.

He hesitated, and her stomach dropped. Stone was going to tell her no.

"Maggie, you're enough."

She swallowed. "What did you say?"

"I said, you're enough." His soft admission caressed all the neglected, scared parts of her soul. Emotions she had blocked for years threatened to overwhelm her. Maggie couldn't have spoken if she wanted to; she had no idea what to say.

She hugged him instead.

Stone had just reached into the darkest, scariest part of her and yanked out a festering thorn she had never been able to articulate. Some kids never get over striving to please unappeasable parents. Apparently, Maggie was no exception.

He held her close as her whole body shook.

A final ripple shuddered through her, and he pressed his lips against her hair. "When this is all over, whatever happens … I wanted you to hear that. You need to know that."

She nodded, her head still burrowed in the crook of his neck.

He thought she was enough.

Maggie squeezed him tighter.

Stone brushed a kiss across her hair. "You don't have to put yourself in danger. If anyone could find something in that apartment, it would be you, but you don't have to."

She leaned back to look at him. "You'll be there. I'll be safe."

"*Maggie.*"

She wiped at her eyes. She didn't want to discuss how scary and dangerous all this shit was or fall apart again, even if his big strong arms were the place to do it. Maggie leaned to the side, looking around his massive shoulders. "Do you have any food?"

He gave her a long look before turning. "Sure. Any preferences?" She liked the feel of her hand in his as he led her deeper into his kitchen. "Peanut butter and a spoon. I'm not picky."

"We can do better than that." Stone released her hand and opened the pint-size fridge under one of the counters. Squatting, he pulled out items, stacking them on his cradled left arm. He stood, closing the miniature fridge door, before placing a container of grapes, a chunk of gouda, salami, and a small bottle of spiced mustard on the counter. He reached for a baguette. "This is fresh. If you like, we can go proper grocery shopping later."

Stone pulled out a small cutting board and knife and started slicing the salami and cheese. She liked watching the play of his shoulder and back muscles under his shirt.

Maggie ripped off a piece of baguette, making a mini sandwich. She took a bite and groaned. It was as delicious as he looked. "How can you possibly hate a city that produces this?" She held up the mini sandwich in her hand. "Seriously, try this."

Stone leaned forward like it was the most natural thing in the world, eating from her proffered hand.

His lip briefly slid across one of her fingers, and the butterflies in her belly noticed.

Maggie swallowed as he slowly chewed the delectable snack. He cleared his throat.

Her voice felt all throaty when she asked, "Was it good?"

Stone shook out his pant leg. "I might have to revisit my views on this city."

Maggie smiled as she reached for the knife and sliced off another piece of gouda. "Thanks for going with me to the appointment. I hate that people respond differently to men and women—"

"No way. That's a thing?"

She snapped her head up.

Stone mock ducked. "Woah, I was totally kidding. Remind me not to tease you when you're wielding a knife."

Maggie quickly set the knife down. "Guess I'm still on a hair trigger."

Unfazed, Stone picked up the piece of cheese she just cut. "Seriously, where did you learn to fight like that? You were ready to throttle me."

Maggie carefully picked up the knife and sliced a piece of salami. "Self-defense classes."

His eyebrows rose. "From where, a SEAL team? I've never seen a civilian move like that."

"Former U.S. Army Rangers," she said a bit defensively. "They came recommended."

"By whom?"

For years, well-meaning therapists had recited trite self-help mantras. Her last therapist had suggested she take high-level self-defense classes.

Those had helped more.

"Eat this." She shoved the piece of salami at him.

He dodged her ministrations. "I didn't mean any weird gender shit. You just surprised me."

Flashes from her childhood taunted her, daring her to believe him.

"You know I don't think women are somehow less than men. You know that, right? I would never—"

She did know that and told him so.

Stone pressed, "Because if I fucked up, I'm sorry—"

Maggie held up her hand. "I've lived with misogyny. Trust me, you're not it."

"See, I hear you." Stone pointed to the knife she was holding up. "But could we maybe talk without you having a knife in your hand?"

Horrified, Maggie set the knife down. Stone picked it up and cut a huge piece of cheese. "Who was the misogynist?"

He had moved to stand next to her at the counter. He didn't crowd her, nor would they have to make eye contact. It was subtle, his body positioning. Maggie noticed and appreciated it.

"My dad."

He nodded like he had already guessed.

Embarrassed, she asked, "You know the whole story?"

He brought his thumb to his forehead, scratching it. "Omran found newspaper articles and the court transcripts."

Shame flooded Maggie. She had only been a child, yet she felt the deep shame of being part of a family so intrinsically … broken.

Stone handed her the ginormous piece of cheese. "We use gender bias in investigations."

She accepted the gift. "You harness bias?"

"All the time." He grabbed a handful of grapes and started popping them in his mouth. "People see what they want or expect to see. Works like a charm."

"What did you see when you met me?"

"The Mariana Trench."

He didn't pause or hesitate. Just fired out the brief, cryptic answer like he had it locked and loaded.

Maggie stared at him. "I don't know what that means."

Stone blew out a breath. "Deep and complicated as fuck to explore."

Something wild blossomed inside her.

Unsure what to say, Maggie reached for a grape. "Thanks for letting me tag along to Sebastian's apartment."

"You would go on your own if I didn't."

She could *feel* the guilty expression on her face.

Stone laughed. "Relax, I would, too." He paused, his eyes suddenly dead serious. "I know you can hold your own, but when we go, if I say duck, jump, whatever—do it, okay? Question me later, grill me. I don't care. But at the moment, I *need* to know I can trust you."

"You can trust me," Maggie promised.

He rubbed his forehead. "I really hope I don't regret this."

"You won't." She held up the baguette. "Still hungry?"

It was the wrong thing to say, standing a nibble away from Stone in his Paris kitchen. His eyes sparked with heat. "Yes, I am."

Maggie shoved the baguette at him. "I'll be ready in three minutes."

"Maggie—"

She fled the kitchen before she grabbed his face and shoved her tongue down his throat. She was halfway down the hall when Stone's words stopped her. *"Maggie, I'm sorry.* I shouldn't have said that." He rounded the corner, stopping several paces from her. His hands flexed at his sides. "I shouldn't have said that."

Maggie's heart was racing. "You simply remarked on the food ... sustenance is important," she finished lamely.

"You know I wasn't talking about the food. That's why you ran. It won't happen again—*can't* happen again."

"Why not?" Understanding dawned. "Oh, *oh.*"

His expression shifted.

Maggie was quick to fill in the blanks. "I get it. You don't know if I'm one of the good guys or not, and you have a job to do. You're right. Of course, nothing can happen between us."

"That's not—"

Maggie gave him a sad smile. "It's okay, I understand. I'll just go get ready." She half-turned. "Please still be here when I get back. I'll hurry, I promise."

Stone's face was granite, but his eyes were a storm of emotions. "I'll be here."

Maggie ran down the hall before he changed his mind.

CHAPTER TWENTY-FIVE

S tone had fucked up. Bad. He should have reassured her and told her he trusted her explicitly.

He didn't.

He would have been lying—Stone didn't trust anyone.

Maggie stood silent as they waited at the counter of the *Préfecture de Police de Paris*. On the drive, she had dutifully answered his questions in brief, monosyllabic responses. She had even managed to navigate them around a grid-locked detour without betraying a single emotion.

It pissed him off. This contained version didn't suit.

Maggie had a flashpoint she had kept well leashed in Canada, but here in France, she had sparked with fire and depth. Omran had a right to be concerned—there was no way Stone could stay objective where Maggie Monroe was concerned.

Her dynamic self captivated him.

And she was giving him the silent treatment.

Because he had damn near nibbled her as she fed him, then hadn't been able to correct her that he knew she wasn't caught up in this whole mess. Stone really was a bastard.

An officer walked up to the counter. He wasn't smiling. To Maggie, he said, "*Bonjour Madame. L'officier Frères n'est pas là.*" A murmur rose from beyond the front desk. Several officers sitting at desks looked their way.

Maggie looked at Stone. "My French sucks."

"Officer Freres isn't here," Stone translated.

Maggie frowned. "Tell him I have an appointment with her." Stone did as she asked.

The officer shook his head. *"La officer de police judiciaire n'est pas là."*

Maggie drew in a deep breath before pulling out her phone. Stone glanced at the raised heads. Several officers were watching them.

Maggie had pulled up an email on her phone and showed it to the officer. "I have an appointment."

The man shook his head, repeating, *"Elle n'est pas là."* Several more heads turned to watch. The mention of Officer Freres was causing a stir.

Maggie shoved her phone back in her purse and mumbled, "Merci." She turned away from the officer at the front desk, arms tightly crossed, and whispered to Stone, "I have to get out of here."

Stone rushed to catch up. Maggie was stalking toward the door, her skirt fluttering around her shins. "You're right. Paris sucks."

His heart squeezed. Stone wanted to be the one to add joy to her life, not take it away with his ornery stereotypes. There were a hundred places he wanted to show her, beautiful places of Paris, that would be positively exquisite with her. Maybe someday, when they weren't chasing murderers, and he knew she had nothing to do with any of this, and if she ever didn't think him an ass. "Don't say that."

"You've been telling me this the whole time we've been here. I should have believed you."

"Not the whole time," he said quietly.

She slowed her steps. Her voice had a huskiness to it when she whispered, "No. Not the whole time." She pushed through the doors and walked into the bright sunlight. She waited until the doors closed behind them. "That was weird, right? You saw how they reacted to us mentioning Officer Freres. It's not just in my head?"

"It was weird," Stone agreed. "I overheard a couple of officers talking. It sounded like she took an unplanned leave."

Maggie's gaze shot up. "What if Teague Alans got to her? She was investigating Sebastian's disappearance. What if she's hurt or kidnapped or—" She broke off. "Sorry, my head races ahead sometimes."

"You care." Stone grumbled as he held open the SUV door for her. Just being near her was unlocking decades of accumulated ice he hadn't even known he had barricaded around his heart. He was softening in her presence.

It was unnerving.

"You okay?" Maggie was looking at him, concern etching her face.

"Of course."

"I'm sorry I had to get out of there." A shutter rocked her body. "Everything suddenly felt overwhelming, and it didn't feel like they were going to have the answers we're looking for, anyway."

"Stop apologizing."

Her gaze snapped to his.

"You've got great instincts. If more people listened to themselves like you do, I would be out of a job."

Maggie was staring at him. Finally, she offered a soft "Thank you."

"You're welcome." Stone closed the door harder than necessary and walked around to the driver's side. He would stare, too. God, who talked like that?

Thirty-five minutes later, they stood outside Sebastian's apartment door.

"You know the code?" Stone asked.

Maggie nodded, punching it in. *Zero-two-zero-seven-one-nine-zero-six.* He committed it to memory and opened the door.

The location had been secured by the sweeper crew, but he confirmed it. The balcony glass door was in one piece, and the apartment was set to rights. No bodies or blood littered the floor. The bathroom and single bedroom were empty, too.

Maggie stayed close while he swept for bugs. He found none and told her so. She immediately started exploring the small space.

Arms crossed, he took in the apartment, trying to see the space with fresh eyes. The print on the bowl of lemons matched the print on the matching throw pillows. Even the hockey sticks in the corner were in a decorative bin. He sniffed. Was that lavender? Stone had a few apartments around the world. If any of them had matching décor, it wasn't on purpose. Even his apartment back home in Brooms Head was functional at best.

"Where did you find your brother's phone?"

Absently, Maggie half-turned. "The copper bowl on the island counter."

Stone glanced over. The copper bowl sat empty and rested on top of a sailing magazine. He recognized the popular periodical and picked it up. It was last month's issue, and the name and address matched Sebastian's. He flipped through it, stopping at a notated page.

"Did you know your brother sailed?"

She stiffened. "No. Not really. I mean, Sebastian took a week's summer school class at the reservoir when we were kids, but that hardly counts, does it? It's no Bondi Beach or where ever Australians sail."

Stone held up the magazine. "He won a local regatta last year. There's a picture in the year-in-review write-up." Stone's intel had said as much. It didn't explain why the recent magazine was sitting on a dead man's counter.

Maggie raced to stand next to him. He handed her the magazine.

The picture showed a crew of men celebrating. Sebastian was on the end, tanned and smiling at the camera with his arm slung around an equally striking woman. Stone watched her. She had taken great pains to paint her twin as an uninspired, socially awkward scientist. The man in the photo looked like he was on top of the world.

"He looks so happy." Her voice was low, a mix of sadness and surprise. Maggie shook her head. "He had a whole other life here that he never shared with me." Her shoulders drooped. "I thought I'd find something, thought I knew him. I don't know anything about Sebastian, not anymore."

Stone frowned. People didn't change *that* much. "Where would you have looked before?"

Maggie surveyed the room, her gaze landing on the cuckoo clock hanging on the wall. "In there."

Stone closed the distance between them. "Up you go then."

Maggie stared at his proffered hand. She grasped it before stepping onto the plush armchair. Balancing on the uneven surface, she let go of his hand to put a steadying hand on the wall. With her other hand, she gently slid her fingers inside the cuckoo clock's front doors.

Maggie gasped, turning toward him with wide eyes. "There's something in here."

He smiled at her enthusiasm.

She pulled out her hand, ducking to eye the inside of the clock. She slid her fingers back in, rotating her wrist slightly. "Got it."

Gently, she pulled out her fingers, holding something.

It was a small packet made from folded printed paper. A kilt-wearing cartoon duck grinned from the corner at them. Gently, Maggie unfolded the small package.

A set of keys lay inside.

Maggie turned them over in her hand before handing them to Stone.

It was a floating keychain. "These are boat keys."

Her enthusiasm waned. "First, a woman I didn't know about,

now a boat. I don't know Sebastian at all. It's like I'm losing him all over again."

She looked devastated.

"How did you know to check the cuckoo clock?"

Her face fell further, and Stone hurried to hold up his hands. "It's okay. Forget I asked."

Maggie sat on the chair and clasped her hands together in her lap. "When we were kids, Sebastian and I learned we had to hide things to keep them safe. Our treasures were small, of course. A pretty hair elastic a friend gave me for my birthday. Sebastian hid a lighter he had found. Once, we got a deck of cards from a piñata at school."

Stone felt his anger rise. "Safe from who?"

"Our older brother. Our parents. They'd wreck stuff in front of us, show us they had the power." Maggie paused. "I hated that feeling of helplessness."

Stone's heart squeezed at the image of Maggie and Sebastian as children, hiding their small treasures to protect them from tormenting family members. Feeling helpless to stop them also explained why Maggie trained so hard physically.

She pointed. "The floaty keychain thingy has a logo on it."

Stone looked at the keys in his palm. A water nymph inked on the miniature float was giving him a side-eye and reminded him of Maggie. In stylized letters, the word *Venus* was wrapped around the nymph. *Port Carling, Ontario*, was printed below it.

Stone looked up. "Isn't Port Carling in Muskoka?"

Her eyes rounded. "Are you serious?" She grabbed the keychain. Stone heard what she hadn't said. Why hadn't Sebastian told her when he was in Canada? Or that he was there often enough to keep a boat there?

Maggie handed him back the keychain. "Port Carling is in Muskoka. Meredith has a cottage there. She asks Savannah and I to join her there every year."

"Do you?"

"I try to make it. We always have fun, but it's too crowded

for me, and I don't really fit in."

Stone couldn't imagine Maggie not fitting in somewhere. "I don't understand."

"You will," Maggie promised. "They'll like you. You're Australian."

"They don't like Canadians?" Stone was seriously lost now.

"They don't like Albertans," Maggie corrected. "That part of Canada sees Albertans as redneck assholes hell-bent on blindly destroying the planet."

Stone stared at her. "Becca's eco-inn is off the grid, and Tucker's police service did not weed that tree-hugging hippie out. The only Albertans I know are either lefties or central."

"Yes, well, those Albertans don't make the news. We also have a lot of American influence—both historical and contemporary." She shrugged. "We rub Eastern Canada the wrong way."

"Why would American influence matter?" American influence was all over the globe.

Maggie smiled. "A prof explained it to me as loyalist ambitions versus post-revolution colonial expansion."

"Ahh, generational feuds—that's another reason my job exists."

"Damn. You're right. Canada's no different than other countries. Memories are long ... sort of. We know we're not supposed to like others. We just forget why."

"You could be talking about Australia."

"Or most places," she reasoned.

"Touché." He hesitated. "How do Albertans see Eastern Canada?"

She gave a deep belly laugh. "Stuffy, over-consuming whiners desperate to steal our natural resource money while demonizing us for pulling it out of the ground in the first place."

"So, completely neutral then?"

She laughed again. "Point taken. I guess all sides could use a reality check, myself included."

He held up his hands. "You said it, not me."

Stone didn't want to break this fragile truce but felt compelled to mention, "That keychain could have come from anywhere."

"I know. But it's the only lead we have." She stopped. "Unless you're not telling me something? Where's Omran?"

Checking a dead body.

Not that Stone was going to tell Maggie a John Doe had been dropped off at the morgue. Instead, Stone hedged. "It would be an unbelievably long shot Sebastian has a boat docked at the Venus marina."

"A long shot is all I've got. Besides that creepy guy on the phone." Maggie shook off a shiver. "And whatever lead Omran is tracking down that you won't tell me."

If Sebastian were alive, it was *possible*. The police hadn't found his body, and Stone and Omran hadn't done any better. Maggie had been attacked and nearly blown up. If it were Teague Alans, he'd let his trail go cold. There was no new intel or chatter, just the same questions.

And a crackling, building tension between Maggie and Stone.

Stone pocketed the boat key. "Let's keep looking." Maggie continued searching the living room area, and Stone returned to the kitchen, checking cabinets. "Let me know if you find a mail key."

Finding nothing obvious in the kitchen cabinets, Stone eyed the dirty dishes and cutlery stacked next to the sink.

They had multiplied.

Stone called out to her, "Do you remember how many dirty mugs were here yesterday?"

Maggie popped her head up from searching under the couch on hands and knees. "Two mugs, two bowls, and two small plates. It's one of the reasons I suspected a woman. Why?"

"There's four of everything now." Stone touched the electric kettle.

It was still hot.

"Someone's here." He drew his gun. "Stay down."

CHAPTER TWENTY-SIX

Maggie made herself as small as possible and tried to breathe. She had positioned herself behind the side table next to the balcony door. She was tucked low but able to move quickly if necessary.

Stone, gun drawn, had disappeared down the hall.

She reminded herself he knew what he was doing, that he would remain safe, that she was safe. She just had to keep her wits about her. Even if Stone didn't entirely believe her, he would never have let her come if he thought there was a viable chance of danger.

The wild horses that had replaced her circulatory system were having none of it.

She wondered if she should check on Stone when a movement snagged in her peripheral vision. Maggie turned, looking toward the balcony, and a scream threatened to explode from her.

The privacy curtains had been pulled closed but silhouetted against the courtyard lights, a form crouched low on the other side of the glass.

Maggie launched herself away from the balcony door. She sprinted down the hall, hissing Stone's name.

He appeared in front of her instantly, gun still in his hand. "What's happened?"

"Someone is crouched on the balcony." Her heart was hammering so fast.

"Get behind me." Stone's voice was icy, and she instantly complied, filing close behind him as he stalked into the living room. "Get behind the island counter."

Maggie shot across the apartment to the kitchen, terrified the entire way gunshots would pepper them. She snaked her hand across the island and grabbed a chopping knife before she tucked behind the counter. It wouldn't stop a bullet, but it could help if the intruder got in.

She scurried low along the length of the island, peeking from the other side with a clear shot of the balcony door.

Stone pressed close to the wall. In a flash, he yanked the privacy curtain open.

Maggie held her breath, bracing herself.

Nothing happened.

No one was there.

Stone opened the balcony door and searched the small space. No intruder attacked or materialized.

Maggie stood, returned the knife to the butcher block, and wiped her sweaty, shaking hands on her skirt. "I swear someone was there."

Stone holstered his sidearm. "I'm getting you the hell out of here."

She swallowed. "I'm scared as fuck right now, but isn't now the best time to check the bedroom? There might be another clue, and whoever was hiding on the balcony is gone now. This might be the safest chance we get."

Stone swore. "You're going to be the death of me."

Maggie stopped on her way to the bedroom. "Don't say that. That's not funny."

He winced. "Jesus, my timing sucks. I didn't mean—" He broke off, looking truly horrified.

She rubbed her arms. "I worry about you, too."

Stone gave her a considering look. "I didn't say—but I do, worry about you."

"I know." She hesitated, wanting to tell him more but knowing now wasn't the time. "Let's just check the rest and get out of here."

Maggie led the way to the bedroom. He did a sweep of the space first before nodding to her. She went in. The curtains were pulled tight, though thin enough to allow light to filter through, softly illuminating the space.

A double bed was centered against the wall, with two night-stands flanking it. The duvet cover was a striped pattern, and there were matching throw pillows artfully arranged on it.

Slowly, Maggie turned around. Stone stood in the doorway watching her.

"Everything about this room is tidy. The whole apartment—save for the dishes in the sink—is tidy."

Stone shrugged. "So?"

"My brother's a domestic disaster." She picked up a decorative throw pillow. "At least he used to be."

Stone stepped forward. "I haven't noticed any computers, no technology."

Maggie surveyed the room. "*That* would have made sense to find. A makeshift office. Disarray. Old food in the fridge. Dirty clothes." She waved her hand. "Not this. This is creepy clean."

"Do you know if he has another place?"

Maggie couldn't imagine paying rent or a mortgage on an apartment she didn't use. She just managed to afford the one she had in a non-stabby-stabby part of town. "Why would he need two apartments?"

"A decoy, maybe?" Stone shrugged. "If I were neck deep in shit—my own making or otherwise, I'd have a few exit strategies."

"How did you guys know to watch this apartment in the first place? Did you check ownership or something?"

"After Sebastian got on our radar, intel tracked him here."

"Is his name on the deed or lease?"

Stone had already pulled out his phone.

"I'll check the closet." Maggie flung open the door. A wide, single rod spanned the length of the long, narrow space. A massive amount of blouses, jackets, and pressed trousers—all of a feminine cut, were crammed onto the rod. Maggie shuffled deeper into the closet. A considerably smaller section held masculine items farther down. Her hand wrapped around the sleeve of a tweed jacket. Sebastian had worn it to his master's thesis defense. He had dropped out before finishing his doctorate.

She blew out a breath.

Two low dressers were lined beneath the rod. She recognized her brother's ancient Calgary Flames T-shirt on top of the stack of folded shirts. There were also jeans, pajamas, socks, and ... ew —her brother's boxer briefs were in tidy rows, taking up the first dresser. The second held drawers of lacy lingerie, yoga pants, T-shirts, and folded sweatshirts.

Maggie found nothing untoward, even when she crouched low, guiltily checking if anything had been stashed in the recesses.

She pushed the drawers closed.

Her brother had a girlfriend serious enough for them to be living together.

He hadn't told her.

Maggie had felt the distance building between them and missed the closeness they had once shared. They had been insep- arable before the kidnapping, before they had been sent to boarding schools on different continents. The months had turned into years apart. She had been kidding herself that they had stayed close.

Maggie turned, uncoiling herself from her crouch. Scarves, a backpack, and two handbags hung from an oversized hook at the far end of the narrow closet.

A knob poked through the accessories.

"Stone," she said slowly while cautiously walking toward it. "I found a door."

Maggie had barely stopped talking before Stone careened into the closet. "*I'll check, I'll check.*" His voice was frantic and rushed.

He stopped inches away from her, and the narrow closet was suddenly very intimate.

Maggie swallowed. "Men's and women's clothes on the rod and drawers."

Stone's gaze followed where she was pointing before landing back on her. "Your brother's?"

She nodded.

He gently gripped her upper arms, maneuvering past her in the tight space. "I'll just make sure it's safe."

His broad back blocked her view as he unholstered his gun. "It's not locked."

Maggie hoped that was a good thing.

She crept forward as he opened the door and swept inside. Maggie held her breath.

"Clear … of a sort."

Maggie rushed in, stopping dead in her tracks.

It was a wreck. The space was nearly the size of the bedroom, with rows of over-packed shelves ringing the walls. Boxes were stacked everywhere, with binders, volumes, and printouts on every flat surface. Several desks were arranged in the center of the room with computers, monitors, black plugged-in boxes, and a maze of electrical cords. Some of the monitors were on, lines of data streaming down the screen. A single office chair faced perpendicular to its desk as if whoever had been sitting in there had rushed out, not bothering to tuck it back in.

It wasn't the untidiness of the space that was Maggie's undoing. It was the scent. Tears burned the backs of her eyes, and she made a twirling motion with her index finger. "The room, the mess, the *smell*. It's Sebastian."

Maggie wrapped her arms around herself. It was the second time in as many days that she had smelled her brother. How long did the scent of someone linger?

"You okay?" Stone had stepped closer.

She nodded. "It just took me by surprise. Hasn't a scent ever triggered a memory?"

Stone's face changed then.

"I'll just have a look around." Maggie unfolded her arms and stepped away, such as she could in the cluttered space, and left Stone to whatever memories had risen.

She stepped over a stack of books on the floor, stopping at one of the bookshelves. The chaos totally looked like it would be her twin brother's office.

"Bondo." Stone's voice was low, barely enough to register.

Maggie heard him and turned. "Like the car stuff?"

He nodded.

Maggie had smelled the bonding agent only a couple of times. Its scent was indeed distinctive. "Are you a grease monkey, Stone?"

"I'm not half the mechanic my dad is." He shrugged. "Fast cars are fun."

Maggie gave a half smile. "That's why Sebastian likes electric cars. Zero-to-crazy fast in an instant."

The shared moment held an unexpected closeness.

Stone cleared his throat. "This more like what you were expecting?"

Maggie swept her gaze around the chaos. "Absolutely."

"Good." Stone started rifling through the mess and snapping photos. He pulled something out of his pocket and fixed it between two crammed bookshelves. He punched something into his phone, waiting a moment. Satisfied, he turned to her. "Time to go."

Maggie spread her arms wide. "There are a million things to go through in here."

"I know. That's why we'll let the nuclear physicists on salary deal with it."

Maggie frowned.

"I don't want to fuck something up or miss anything, and I'm not a rocket scientist."

"Energy particles," Maggie corrected.

"Whatever. We'll let the scientists, science."

She led the way out of the room. "I've never heard science used as a verb."

Stone snickered, and she half turned. "What?"

"Just something Tucker said." Stone's phone pinged. When he looked up, Maggie's stomach clenched. "Dear god, what now?"

Stone's face had gone to granite.

"The name on the rental agreement paperwork for this place is Phoebe Freres."

CHAPTER TWENTY-SEVEN

S ebastian's fingers gripped the balcony's edge as his feet groped for purchase on the thick tangle of vines that flanked the side of the balcony. He had been catapulted from Teague Alans's burning hotel suite into thin air, plummeting to certain death in a mix of awe and terror.

Death had not been ready for him.

Sebastian had bounced off not one but three awnings before being dumped unceremoniously into the pool. The deep end. That was what had nearly done him in. The shock of not being dead had nearly drowned him.

He had come to his sensing and fought hard, kicking and crawling to reach the side of the pool. Sebastian had dragged himself out of the water, stunned but relatively unscathed, and fled before Teague Alans or his new crew realized what had happened.

He had been terrified he would be found, shot in the back, or worse.

Now he dangled precariously from the edge of the balcony, nearly getting caught breaking *out* of his and Phoebe's apartment.

Being dead was shockingly dangerous.

Sebastian scurried down the vine ladder and, with more determination than grace, landed on the balcony below.

He tucked under the bistro table nestled in the corner of the space among the vines, pulling potted plants around him and grabbing a fistful of shredded vine leaves to sprinkle on his head. Thank *Christ* he wore a mottled green shirt. He heard the door above open and froze, holding his breath. It would not do for the Australian to find him.

Swift steps paced on the balcony above him. Each time they paused, Sebastian squeezed his eyes shut like he could will himself not to be discovered.

The steps above retreated, and the click of the balcony door closing above felt like a benediction.

Sebastian waited. He had learned patience.

A click sounded, and Sebastian froze, still under the table.

The door to the balcony he was hiding on opened. An older woman walked out, smoking a cigarette and speaking into her phone. Sebastian tried not to wince as she recounted, in graphic detail, her date last night to whoever was on the other end. She laughed, ground out her cigarette, and went back inside, oblivious to the full-grown man hiding under leaves and her bistro table.

Sebastian took a full breath.

He had to move.

CHAPTER TWENTY-EIGHT

Stone negotiated Paris traffic while Maggie sat quietly in the seat next to him, using her phone to look up images of Phoebe Freres. He was starting to understand her nuances and that whip-smart brain of hers.

He pulled into a visitor spot at the *Préfecture de Police de Paris* and turned off the engine. "Are you sure you want to go back in there?"

"I want answers and to wring Phoebe Freres's fucking neck. Not once on the phone did she mention she knew my brother, let alone that she was living with the guy. I get a call from her that Sebastian's been murdered, and then she disappears when I come running. Did she kill him?" Maggie held up her phone. "Is this woman capable of murder?"

Stone didn't begrudge Maggie her outburst. The optics were not good. Still, he felt compelled to ask. "What if she has a legitimate reason for not being in today? What if she really was dating your twin brother?"

Maggie pulled her gaze away from her phone. "Are you a closet romantic?"

"*No.*" Even to his ears, he answered that way too quickly.

"I guess it's possible," Maggie said slowly. "Where has she

been, though? I mean, I was nearly killed in her apartment. Her balcony door was shattered. She would have noticed something."

Stone made a noncommittal noise. "The cleaner crews are good at what they do. If she was at work, it is entirely possible they could have gone in."

"Haven't you guys been watching the place? That's why you were there when I showed up."

God, the woman's mind was quick. "That only flagged when the *Préfecture de Police de Paris* declared Sebastian's death a homicide—if he is dead," Stone quickly clarified. He reached for the door handle. "Let's go get some answers."

Maggie put her hand on his arm. "Stone, *look*."

She was staring out the windshield. A woman was arguing with a man on the sidewalk.

"Let me see your phone again."

Maggie handed it to him, asking, "I'm not crazy. That looks like Phoebe Freres, right?"

"You're not crazy." Neither was he. The woman arguing with the man on the sidewalk looked like Officer Phoebe Freres. The man grabbed her arm, and Stone reached for the door handle.

"She's got it," Maggie whispered, stilling him with her hand on his arm.

Indeed, whatever Officer Freres had said had spooked the man. He hurried off and looked behind him several times. Officer Freres stood defiant, watching him go. Only when the man turned a corner down the street did her shoulders droop. She got in a vehicle parked in the staff lot on the other side of a chained area.

"We're following her, right?"

"Oh yeah." Stone started the SUV and pulled into traffic a few cars behind the Freres. He negotiated traffic, sometimes ahead of her, sometimes behind, keeping her in sight.

She drove back to the Seventeenth Arrondissement, several blocks from the apartment, and stopped on a tree-covered lane.

On the next street over, Stone parallel parked, leaving an expanse of canopied green space and a pond between them. The wind scuttled across the water, breaking the surface with a dancing latticework of trembling water. The trees had leafed out, though it was that in-between space where they hadn't quite finished unfurling and expanded to the potential only summer could tease out.

"Am I staying or going?" Maggie asked, assessing the location.

Stone smiled to himself. The area had at least a dozen spaces a shooter could hide in. Maggie was a natural. "Do all librarians have such situational awareness?"

She side-eyed him. "How did you know I was a librarian."

"Tucker told me."

"You guys were talking about me?"

He pointed. "Let's see where she goes."

"Smooth."

"I thought so," he retorted.

They watched and waited.

The officer stepped over the low fencing and crossed to a bench next to the pond. After several minutes, no one had approached. Phoebe Freres simply sat, arms wrapped around herself, staring at the wind-scuttled water.

Stone turned to Maggie in the passenger seat next to him. Sunlight angled across her profile. The effect made her seemingly glow. "What does your gut feel?" Maggie's instincts were better than most.

It also highlighted her childhood—she was not used to being safe.

She turned, surprised, before briefly closing her eyes. "It's safe. And I don't think she hurt Sebastian."

"Why do you say that?"

"Because I don't want to strangle her anymore."

His gut said the same thing. Stone held out his fist, and Maggie fist-bumped him.

"Let's go," he said, opening his door.

They walked around to the front of the vehicle, and Stone held out his crooked elbow to her. "We'll look less—" he broke off, searching for the right word.

Maggie snaked her arm through his. "Predatory?"

"I was going for inconspicuous, but sure, aggressive works." They started to walk around the path, circling the pond.

Suddenly, Maggie frowned. "Damn." She scanned the park as they walked. "I think I have more fire in me than I realized."

Picking up her thread, he asked, "You see aggressive as a bad thing?"

"Sometimes."

"I like your fire."

She turned to look at him. "It scares the shit out of me. My parents were always angry. I don't want to turn into them."

"Anger and fire aren't the same thing." It's all he had time to say. They were approaching Phoebe Freres.

"What's the plan?" Maggie whispered, gaze glued to the solitary woman sitting on the bench. Maggie's arm tucked through his tensed the closer they got to the officer.

He ducked his head as if he were nuzzling her neck and whispered, "Take my lead."

"Sure thing, mate. I'm a whiz-bang at improv."

Surprised, Stone whispered, "Really?"

"No," she hissed before shushing him. He hid his smile.

As they approached, Phoebe barely glanced their way, just gave a polite smile in their general direction.

Stone angled them closer, and Maggie was right there in lockstep with him. When they were nearly at the bench, the officer realized their proximity and jumped up. Stone crossed in front of her and sat down close. Without missing a beat, Maggie did the same, pressing in just as tight.

"Easy there, Phoebe. We just want to talk." The woman wasn't paying Stone any attention. She was staring at Maggie. "Maggie, is that you?"

Stone stared. *Not in a million years.*

Maggie's mouth dropped open. "You know who I am?"

The officer patted her hair self-consciously before running her hands along the tops of her trousered legs. "You're really here."

"Yeah, we had an appointment." Stone winced at Maggie's tone.

The woman was unfazed. "Sebastian told me so much about you—and you're really here."

"So you did know my brother."

The woman's lips trembled then, and she held up her left hand. A small solitaire adorned her ring finger.

Maggie reached for the woman's hand. "You two were engaged?"

The woman nodded, tears streaming down her face.

"So he's really gone?"

The officer stopped and looked at Stone. "Who are you?"

Before he could answer, Maggie did. "I trust him. He's solid. Tell me about Sebastian."

Something unfurled inside Stone; Maggie sounded like she meant it.

Phoebe rubbed her eyes. "I have been scouring every lead for weeks. I haven't found him."

Maggie had angled her body toward her would-be sister-in-law. "Why did you miss our appointment today?"

The woman frowned. "You canceled it."

"No, I didn't."

Phoebe looked closer at Stone. "I've seen you before. You've been following Sebastian." She swore. "I knew this was bad. You're with JSC, aren't you."

"I've been told I look the part," Stone said neutrally.

Without skipping a beat, Phoebe added, "Only in the third act."

Puzzle pieces rearranged in Stone's mind. Phoebe Freres wasn't just an *Officer de Police Judiciarie*, she was part of the larger international task force that Stone and Omran had been working on for months.

"It's how I met Sebastian," she explained.

"Will someone tell me what just happened?" Maggie asked.

"Freres and I are colleagues of a sort," Stone said.

Maggie blinked. "Of course you are. Could this get any weirder?"

Stone asked Phoebe, "So, you know the kind of people Sebastian was working with? Why I'm here?"

"I know the kind of people who targeted him," she corrected. "Sebastian refused to share his findings with them when he realized what they wanted it for, and th-they killed him." Phoebe's voice shook, and her eyes were bleak.

Maggie darted him a look but said nothing.

Stone hated saying what he had to. "They did a good job of making Sebastian look dirty. The offer must have been substantial."

Phoebe sat up straighter. "Sebastian was a kind, decent man. He had too much respect for science, for moving the world forward, to ever be tempted by something so base as money or power. Besides, with his work, the global power dynamics will shift."

Maggie adjusted herself on the seat. "What do you mean?"

"The stranglehold of those who currently hold the money and power is dissolving. This planet is about to get a serious overhaul. Finding where he stashed his work will accelerate so many changes."

Maggie looked thoughtful. "Did he work out of an office, or did he have a home office?"

Inspector Freres waved a hand. "He liked to call the collection of chaos at our place a studio, but sure, it could be called a home office. When he realized Teague Alans was a nutcase, he said it was too dangerous for me to know more. He moved everything specifically related to his most recent work to an unknown location. He'd be gone for weeks at a time." Her lip trembled. "He wanted to keep me safe."

Stone kept his voice noncommittal. "When did Teague Alans enter the picture?"

Inspector Freres swore graphically. "After Sebastian published his latest findings in an academic journal—I can't remember the name—Teague Alans contacted him, promising extraordinary funding, how Seb would be part of saving the world. It was all bullshit. Teague Alans is a terrorist."

"And you're on the clock."

Phoebe brought her hand to the ring she wore. "It's how we met. Sebastian didn't know it was a setup." She was quiet for a moment. "Falling for him was *real*."

Maggie's hand flew to her chest. He guessed it could come across as a romantic way to meet if you believed in love. Which he didn't. He was not a closet romantic, nor delusional. He was not someone who believed in something so airy fairy as love. "Do you know where Teague Alans is?"

"No." Phoebe's voice was bitter. "We picked up the two of his crew that murdered Seb but haven't been able to find Alans."

"Any leads from his crew?"

"There was a hotel fire in the Second Arrondissement a couple of hours ago. Two bodies were recovered. I'm waiting for confirmation, but preliminary evidence suggests it was them."

Maggie stared. "Seriously? Who'd sign up for that shit?"

Stone and Phoebe exchanged a glance. Regardless of country, most in law enforcement stopped asking that question.

"So we're looking for Sebastian's lab and Teague Alans," Stone summarized.

Maggie sat straighter. "And Sebastian. He's alive. I can feel it."

Phoebe placed her hand on Maggie's, her eyes bright with tears. "I know this is hard, and it doesn't feel like he's gone. Some-times I swear I can still feel him, too, even smell his cologne and

burned coffee. But I was at the crime scenes. All three of them."
She swallowed. "Maggie, there were lethal amounts of blood at
the crime scenes. I refused to believe it for weeks, but I have to
accept it. He's gone. Everything points to him being dead."

"He's not," Maggie insisted. "You feel it. I feel it. He's not
gone. I'm going to find him."

"We," Stone said.

Maggie looked past Phoebe to Stone. "You believe me?"

"If he's alive, we'll find him. Together. You're not alone."

"What about Teague Alans?" Maggie asked, cutting through
the bullshit. She saw him more clearly than anyone else on the
planet. Even his mom.

Stone looked out across the pond, coming to a decision.
"Omran and the rest of the task force can follow that trail."

Maggie launched herself across Phoebe into Stone's arms. He
caught her close, savoring the bright energy that was hers alone.
He probably was holding on too long, too tight, but Maggie felt
so right in his arms.

Phoebe had pressed herself against the bench back, averting
her gaze, giving them space. She neither complained nor interrupted the spontaneous moment flung across her.

Maggie was the first to pull back, and Stone instantly missed
her spontaneous embrace.

She gave an apologetic look to Phoebe. "I'm sorry, Officer
Freres," she ducked her head, "sometimes I'm a bit much. I'm
sorry if that was inappropriate."

"Please, call me Phoebe, and you're not too much. Never
apologize for giving yourself permission to feel." The woman's
intelligent gaze danced between Stone and Maggie before her
smile turned sad. "No one knew about Sebastian and me. He's
… different. Besides the investigation, I thought I would be
protecting him, not introducing him to my colleagues. Now I
would do anything to see him again. Shout out to the world how
I feel about him." Shadows crossed her eyes. "I don't know if he
ever knew."

"He knew," Maggie said, certain. "He's a genius, you're lovely, he knew." She paused. "So, did you two ever sail?"

Phoebe looked startled by Maggie's question. "Yes, as a matter of fact. Though, I hardly know how that's relevant?"

Maggie sat back a little, looking down. "He used to when we were kids. I just wondered."

Stone watched the interchange with interest.

Phoebe was quick to answer. "He took me to Canada, though I would hardly call it proper sailing. It was on a lake, albeit a big one. Kind of."

Maggie's gaze snapped up. "Lake Muskoka?"

"That sounds right."

Pride filled Stone. Maggie shared the truth, let herself be vulnerable, and built trust with the officer in seconds. She had gotten her answers in mere moments. He had seen seasoned agents take months to achieve similar results.

"Venus Marina, right?"

A small smile lit Officer Freres's face. "I was expecting something more … Canadian sounding. You call it *north woods*, right?"

Maggie laughed. The sound was as uplifting as sunlight. "You mean like moose or beaver?"

"I don't know, certainly not *Venus*." Phoebe laughed then, too. It was brief and ended when her face crumbled. Her voice was a whisper when she said, "He doesn't *feel* gone."

Maggie grasped Phoebe's hand. "If he's alive, we'll find him."

Stone eyed the two women. Were they simply delusional, or did they feel something he couldn't? His mom felt things others weren't able to. Doris could help everyone in town—friends, strangers, and all were helped by his mom's inexplicable *knowings*. She could tune into the intricate details of their lives, help them understand the greater picture playing out, and make decisions based on that beautiful, expanded awareness.

Yet she hadn't been able to see the truth of Bruce Tanner.

Stone's biological father had been a predator.

She had seen one truth. Doris knew Bruce wouldn't leave his wife and their kid on the way for Doris or their child together. That's why his mom had named him Tanner Stone, giving him his father's last name as a first name.

Stone hated it.

The women had stopped talking and were staring at him. Maggie asked, "Are you all right?"

"Of course," Stone bluffed.

He wasn't.

His mom had willingly had an affair with a married man—a murderous asshole.

"Stone—"

"I said I'm fine." The now-familiar anger simmered just below the surface. God, why was he *feeling* so much? He had gone his entire adult life being emotionally … controlled. His previous girlfriends had all said variations of the same thing: *Do you even have emotions?*

No, he didn't.

Until last Christmas.

When he met Maggie.

CHAPTER TWENTY-NINE

"We're going to Muskoka, right?" Maggie asked. She was sitting in the passenger seat as he drove them back to his Paris apartment. "It's a couple of hours north of Toronto. We could be there by tomorrow night." She waited a beat. When he didn't answer, she asked, "Stone?"

She sat still, yet he could feel her vibrating in the passenger seat next to him. He had never been able to feel someone's presence so keenly. It was unsettling.

Stone turned on his left blinker, changing lanes. Finally, he answered her. "I'm thinking."

"Think faster."

He smiled, delighted to be sparring with the fiery, unleashed Maggie again.

She frowned. "I shouldn't have said that. I'm sorry."

Stone reached across the SUV's console, taking her hand. He drove one-handed, holding her hand in his.

Maggie held his hand back.

Several blocks passed before Stone lifted their entwined hands and pressed a gentle kiss on the back of her hand. He kept his eyes on the road but felt her exhale.

They were almost at his apartment when she asked, "Were you serious about helping me find Sebastian?"

He pulled into his apartment's underground car park and shut off the engine. Neither made a move to open their door. The interior of the SUV felt like a cocoon in the dim underground light. "Yes."

She slid her hand out of his. "That's not fair to you. As much as I'd appreciate your help, I can't ask you to stop tracking Teague Alans to help me find Sebastian. It's not right."

"You didn't ask. I offered."

"Same difference."

"Not really."

Her gaze was heavy on his profile. "Why?"

Stone traced the steering wheel with his index finger, not looking at her. "I've been chasing a ghost."

"Your dad?"

Stone dropped his head against the headrest. "I never should have been assigned to the task force."

"Why were you."

He laughed. It sounded hollow in his ears. "My boss calls me too clever for my own good."

She reached across the console, closing her hand over his. He held it like a lifeline.

"It brought you to your siblings—*half-siblings*," she corrected herself. "That's a good thing, right?"

Unwelcome feelings rose at her reasonable assumption.

"I don't know," he answered honestly.

"Is it Gabe?"

Stone turned his head sharply. There it was. Maggie's uncanny knack for drilling straight to where he didn't want, but apparently needed, to go. "Gabe knew about me, knew I existed, and … *nothing*. Not a damn thing. I grew up not knowing I had four siblings because he couldn't be bothered to mention I existed."

"He was a child," Maggie reminded him, her voice gentle.

"And then he grew up." Maybe it wasn't fair, but Stone felt as abandoned by Gabe as he had by Bruce.

Maggie sat back. "*Ohmygod.*"

She was looking at him with unnerving concern. "What?"

"You're going to walk away."

How could she possibly know that? Stone hadn't told anyone —hell, he had just decided. Carefully, he said, "I promised Tucker I'd take care of Teague Alans, and I'll make damn sure the task force does that. I promised you I'd help find your brother—"

"Twin brother," Maggie corrected.

"Why do you always caveat that?"

Maggie rubbed her hands over her thighs. "It's complicated."

"What family isn't?"

She gave him a side-eye. "Is that why you're going to walk away?"

"How can you possibly know that?"

"I don't *know*," she said defensively.

"Fine, let's just drop it. What's so complicated about your brother, I mean, besides the obvious?"

Maggie sucked in a breath, and suddenly Stone wasn't sure he wanted to know. "Maggie—"

"Sebastian and I have an older brother, Lawrence," she blurted. "He's ... awful. That's why I always correct people that Sebastian is my *twin* brother."

Stone remembered the disturbing newspaper articles Omran had shown him. "Is Lawrence still in jail?"

Maggie snapped her head around, her gaze one of angry betrayal.

"Omran found articles about your family," Stone explained. He didn't mention the police or court reports. Lawrence's record was shorter than most. What he lacked in volume, he made up for in cold cruelty.

She looked down. Her whole body seemed to curl in on itself. "I don't know if he's still in jail."

Protective instincts flared. "Is he a threat to you, Maggie?"

"I don't know." Her voice was quiet but laced with unequivocal fear.

"What about your parents? Are they a problem?" Stone's mind immediately started lining up protective measures, how he would keep Maggie safe.

She put her hand on his arm. "I'm fine. At least, I think so."

Stone froze.

Had she just read his mind?

Maggie didn't notice. She brought her hand back to rest in her lap, caught up in her own memories. "I never knew if Lawrence was truly awful or simply a kid trying to survive. Seb and I had each other, and we got out when we were ten. Lawrence was eight years older than us." She swallowed. "It couldn't have been easy for him, growing up in that house."

Her compassion and grace shouldn't have surprised him. "Could your parents be behind this at all?"

"They'd set Seb up. They did it before. I just don't know how they would get on Teague Alans's radar. They're garden variety local criminals and really inept ones at that. I figured out their plan, and I was a kid."

"Your mind is incredible. Even as a kid, I suspect you ran circles around most people."

She stared at him, before her face lit into a slow, wide smile.

"What? It's the truth," Stone said as his cell vibrated a specific pattern.

He pulled it out, and his whole body tensed.

New orders had come in.

"What is it?" Maggie asked. "The color just drained from your face."

He cradled the phone's screen out of her view. "Just my boss. She's a bit of a terror—always grumpy and all that."

Maggie didn't look convinced.

Stone pocketed his phone. "Yes, we're going to check your brother's boat. We're booked on an overnight flight."

"How? We've been talking the whole time."

"Omran," Stone said.

Maggie's brow furrowed. "How did he know?"

Stone opened the SUV door. "Come on, let's pack. I need to check in with Omran before we leave."

Maggie raised an eyebrow.

She didn't know it, but knowing who booked the flights back to Canada was the least of her worries. The task force had reopened the Sebastian Monroe murder investigation. Maggie was the sole beneficiary to Sebastian's estate—including the patents he had taken out regarding his compact nuclear fusion work. She had also received a one hundred thousand dollar deposit from an offshore account with expected ties to Teague Alans.

Maggie had just been officially named a person of interest by the task force.

CHAPTER THIRTY

Maggie fluttered her eyelids open, unsure what had woken her. An airplane window was a body-width from her face—Stone's muscled torso width, to be precise. They were in one of the last rows with only two seats per side. He was sitting in the window seat, and she was curled into his shoulder at an impossible angle. The last several days came crashing back, and she stiffened, fighting the urge to sit bolt upright—Maggie wanted to wake him up about as much as she wanted a hole in her head.

She shouldn't be leaning on him.

Their crackling sexual tension had been usurped last night by an uneasy distrustful tension. It had started when Stone's boss had texted. Maggie hadn't the foggiest idea how to navigate a man's moods—she made it a life habit not to date—but the distance between them had grown exponentially wider, and she had no idea why.

Frowning, she looked out the window. Sometime during the flight, he had lifted the window shade back up. She straightened as covertly as she could, extracting herself from his warm body, before peering out the window. Inky blackness was punctuated by the night lights of towns and cities thirty-five thousand feet below. Scattered across the darkness were lights from farmyards or acreages, their lonely lights a sharp contrast to the collective glow from towns.

The plane banked, and Maggie saw the edge of dawn—a beguiling orange tracing the horizon interrupted the indigo night.

She tensed, holding in the sigh that had bubbled to her lips. Sometimes nature's beauty felt like it grabbed her whole body and shook her into feeling more than she wanted to.

Being outside dared her to feel alive and not scared.

The plane adjusted course, finding its highway in the sky, and the eastern dawn disappeared behind them again.

Maggie turned her head, studying Stone's sleeping profile. He was beautiful in the way a Greek statue was. Chiseled features and strong muscles corded his tall frame, stretched out, such as he could, in the minuscule plane seats. Closer, long lashes fringed his closed lids.

Maggie straightened, facing forward. She knew better. Don't lean on people. They only let you down.

Savannah never did, nor did Meredith.

Maggie felt an immediate softness. Those two women were the exception to the rule and Maggie's whole world. She didn't know what she had done in a past life to deserve such kind, incredible women, but their trio, despite their age differences— Meredith was old enough to be their mother—kept Maggie putting one foot in front of the other.

She glanced at Stone.

Boys came and went, *especially* ones that looked like Stone did. Whatever bug had flown up his ass last night could stay there. She'd find Sebastian's boat and, if she were lucky, *him*, alive. If not, she would keep looking until she found him or irrefutable proof that he was dead—either was tomorrow's problem.

She fished in her purse stowed under the seat and pulled on a pair of dark sunglasses, hiding fresh tears.

"Morning."

Maggie jumped. She adjusted her sunglasses and hoped she schooled her face. "I'm going to try and get more sleep."

She sat tense, waiting for Stone to drop the other shoe.

"You can lean on me again."

She lowered her sunglasses, her eyebrows lifting. "You sure about that?"

"What's that supposed to mean?" He had shifted, pressing against the window. It was a small move, but Maggie noticed. He was as far away from her as the small plane seats would allow.

She placed her sunglasses back on and closed her eyes. She faced the seat in front of her, her back ramrod straight. Maggie had never wished for a first-class seat more than she did at that moment.

"Maggie, what's going on?"

"You tell me." She hadn't moved when she asked it, save to open her eyes behind her dark sunglasses.

She felt more than saw him open his mouth to speak but then close it.

"Thought so," she muttered.

"What do you want me to say?" Stone asked.

"Whatever your boss said about me that put a bug up your ass." She scowled to hide the hurt. "I know it was bad. What I don't get is why you believed it."

Stone stared at her before scrambling to pull out his phone. He started taking it apart.

Perplexed, Maggie shoved her sunglasses to the top of her head. "What in the world are you doing?"

Stone was analyzing the pieces of his phone. Suddenly, he looked up, surprised. "There's no bug."

"There was supposed to be?" Fear exploded within her. Who was after them now? She craned her head around, assessing the people huddled in the cramped seats around them. Everyone was asleep except a teenage boy watching a movie on his phone.

Across the aisle, a mom was quietly nursing the infant in her arms. She gave Maggie a small smile when their gazes met, and Maggie quickly looked away, fearful her attention would somehow put the woman and child in danger. In a low hiss, she asked, "Who is after us?"

He didn't say anything.

"*Stone?*" Desperate, Maggie clung to her faith in him and his ability to navigate them safely through whatever curveball Teague Alans was throwing at them.

The look on his face shredded her. "*Oh.* You thought *I* bugged your phone." She sat back in her seat. When the fuck would she learn? Don't. Count. On. Anyone. The hurt was sharper than she remembered. She hadn't let anyone besides Savannah and Meredith close enough to hurt her in a long time.

He leaned toward her. "What was I supposed to think?"

"Jesus, Stone, a bug—really?" Maggie cradled her head in her hands. "Fuck you."

"How else could you have possibly known what my boss said?"

Maggie spun her head around and glared at him. "I have no idea what your boss said. What I do know is that before the text, you looked at me like you gave a fuck what happened to me. Since you're completely disgusted with me. Pick a lane, asshole."

Stone opened his mouth to say something but snapped it shut.

"I don't know if I'm coming or going with you. You're about as far away as you can get."

He had the grace to look embarrassed. "I'm sitting right next to you."

"You might as well be on the fucking moon." Maggie hugged her arms around herself. "It's not okay to pretend to care about someone. That's not fair."

"Maggie—"

"What did your boss say, Stone?"

His frown was as ferocious as hers.

He didn't answer her question.

"I'm going back to sleep." Maggie curved her shoulder away from him, angling herself toward the aisle, wishing he still cared.

She managed a fitful sleep, jolting awake only when the pilot announced they were preparing to land.

"I do care." Stone whispered the admission as she checked to make sure her seat was in its upright position.

Maggie blinked. *Trans-Atlantic flight, Sebastian is still missing, and Stone thinks I'm in league with Teague Alans.* She couldn't just wake up. This nightmare was real.

"How many times have I said I need to keep you safe?" Stone pressed.

Exhausted, Maggie scrubbed sleep from her face. "I don't want to fight. And I get it. You've said it like a million times. You don't want Gabe to get more grumpy with you." Christ, she needed a proper night's sleep.

Stone jerked in his seat. "What did he tell you?"

Fuck.

"Gabe didn't tell me anything. You did. You said you needed me, not dead, so you wouldn't have to hear about it from him. And something about your very existence bothering him—I'm paraphrasing the last part, but that's how you see it, right?"

Stone stared at her for several moments. "So Gabe or Savannah didn't say anything?"

His voice came out like gravel.

Maggie's heart begged her mind to scoop up the pieces of hope he so desperately wanted to put back together. Carefully, she hedged, "Savannah explained who you were, but you told me the rest, besides what I picked up at Christmas."

Stone's brow furrowed.

"You guys aren't exactly a subtle bunch. I read between the lines."

"And what, exactly, did you think you saw?"

Maggie recoiled at the sharpness of his tone. Whatever underbelly she had glimpsed was behind solid angst armor now.

The distance stung.

It was an effective reminder, though, of the lesson she should have learned in childhood. You can't make someone like you. You can be kind, you can hear them, you can do everything right, and still someone close, someone you desperately want to like you because love is just too much to ask—will dismiss you.

Maggie shoved her sunglasses in her purse, stowing it back under the seat as the plane started its final descent. "Nothing, Stone, my mistake."

CHAPTER THIRTY-ONE

S tone really was a bastard. He couldn't remember ever damaging someone's trust in him so swiftly. She saw him too clearly.

Maggie waited quietly for the passengers ahead of them to deplane. Stone stared straight ahead. He wanted to reach out and tell her everything.

That might put her in more danger.

Maggie turned her head away from him, and he followed her gaze. The woman across the aisle, a mom traveling with an infant, was having a hell of a time holding the squirming baby and collecting their things.

"Need help?" Maggie asked.

The woman hesitated only a moment before passing the tiny bundle across the aisle and into Maggie's arms. "She's a wiggle worm," the woman warned. "And strong."

Maggie's face lit up. "She's perfect." Maggie gently held the small human, making silly faces and cooing noises. The baby girl gurgled with delight.

Stone sat dead still. He had never considered having kids. Those dreams were better left to others. Family people.

The little girl wore a blue onesie with a stylized sun across her belly. She bounced up and down on Maggie's legs as Maggie held her.

Stone couldn't help it. He waved at the wee thing. Immediately, the little one started wailing. Maggie shot Stone a withering look, before shifting the baby in her arms to face forward. The baby resumed its happy gurgling, kicking her little feet.

Stone felt unreasonably judged by the bundle of contempt and mouthed *sorry* to the mother.

The woman laughed. "She's like the weather. Just wait a minute."

Sure enough, the little one looked directly at him and reached out her little hand.

Stone froze. "What's she doing?"

The mom smiled. "She wants to grab your hand."

"She was just screaming at me."

The woman shrugged. "Now she wants to hold your hand. She doesn't keep score."

Tentatively, Stone lifted his hand, curling his index finger out. The baby latched onto him with surprising strength. He bobbed his hand. "Wow. She's strong."

"Tell me about it."

Suddenly, the baby did a nosedive toward him.

"Woah." Maggie adjusted her hold on the infant. The kid was frantically clawing for Stone.

The mom looked up from packing. "She wants you to hold her. It's okay. I'll be done in a sec."

Stone cautiously held his hands out. "I can hold her."

Maggie's eyes rounded. "Seriously?"

Defensively, he said, "I can help." He wanted to. It wouldn't make up for the stupid fracture he had caused between them, but he wasn't completely useless as a decent human being.

Maggie passed the little one to him. He positioned her, holding the baby in the crook of his elbow, facing her mom and Maggie. The little girl was warmer than he expected and smelled like happy. She leaned, curling completely into his chest. This time reaching for Maggie's finger.

"Your husband is a natural," the woman said, fitting a baby carrier on. "Do you two have kids?"

"Oh, we're not … a thing." Maggie made it sound like something distasteful.

He deserved that.

What he hadn't expected was how crappy it made him feel.

The woman's face fell. "I'm so sorry. I shouldn't have assumed—"

I'm telling you, that librarian would be good for you.

His half-brother's words whispered through him as the woman apologized again.

Tucker knew it. The random stranger across the aisle knew it. Hell, even the baby knew it as she bridged the distance between Maggie and Stone.

They forgot to factor in Stone's proclivity to being a bastard.

"It's okay," Maggie assured her, smiling at the woman. "It'll be fun to tease him about it the rest of the trip."

The woman gave a relieved smile, and Stone marveled again at Maggie's easy camaraderie with strangers. He handed back the little one. As the mom adjusted the kicking infant into the front-facing baby carrier, Maggie gently tapped the baby's nose and, in a cooing voice, said, "You just made my whole week … yes, you did." Maggie made another silly face. "Yes, you did."

The baby kicked her feet out and gave a shriek of delight.

Stone wanted to be the one who made her whole week.

The passengers in the row ahead of them started to file out. Finally, it was their turn to exit the plane, and he asked the mom, "Need any help?"

"I've got it."

She did.

Stone stared. With the baby in the front carrier, the woman slung the single, large backpack onto her back. The woman's shoulders must be bionic. She waved at them. "Thanks again."

Maggie smiled, waving back.

The baby kicked happy feet.

The woman glanced at Stone before giving Maggie a wide smile.

"What was that about?"

"Nothing." Maggie answered too quickly.

He followed Maggie out of the seat and reached past her to retrieve her wheeled carry-on from the overhead compartment.

"Thanks," she mumbled.

He stepped to the side, and she cautiously filed ahead of him and down the narrow aisle, their truce awkward again.

Stone carried only a backpack. He slung it on his back and tried not to notice the way Maggie moved in front of him.

She greeted the flight attendants and pilots waiting for them to deplane.

Everyone smiled at her.

His muttered *thanks* and got a cooler reception. He wanted to say to Maggie, *See? I'm a bastard. Even the flight crew knows it.*

As they walked through the airport, Maggie drew attention. It was more than the swish of her soft skirt and bright scarf. *Everyone* smiled at her. It was weirding him out. In his experience, no one would ever accuse Toronto of being a laid-back city, nor its people eager to exchange pleasantries with strangers. Yet Maggie's simple presence was turning up smiles.

They walked through the arrivals gate, and he angled toward the car rentals, antsy to get out of the airport. He looked over to see that Maggie was okay with the pace.

She wasn't next to him.

He stopped and spun around, his stomach tightening.

A man in a suit nearly collided with him and barked his annoyance.

Stone ignored him, scanning the crowd of travelers for a splash of color as fear and adrenaline spiked. Forget Gabe. Stone would never forgive himself if anything happened to Maggie under his watch.

The man was still standing there and called him an ugly name.

Stone shot him a lethal look. The man's face went white, and he stumbled in his haste to get away from Stone, even crossing himself.

A hand grabbed his forearm.

Maggie.

"Jesus, boys are dumb," she muttered.

His heart actually stuttered as relief swept through him. Maggie was safe. Then her words sunk in. "What?"

"I can't leave you for a second." She sounded quite put out. "You nearly gave that guy a heart attack."

Stone turned and cradled her cheeks in his hands. Her eyes widened. Giving in, he lowered his mouth, then stopped, giving her a chance to turn away. She didn't. The kiss was firm and lasted longer than it should have. Finally, he dropped his forehead to hers, still cradling her face in his hands. "Please don't disappear like that."

She had wrapped her hands around his forearms, her forehead pressed against his. "Don't give me a reason to." They held each other for long moments. Stone drew in a haggard breath. "Fair."

"I know that, do you?"

He pulled back enough to slide his hands down and hold hers. He gave them a gentle squeeze. "Do you have anything to do with Teague Alans?"

She straightened, tugging her hands out of his. "*That's* what your boss said?"

"Maggie, please, just tell me the truth."

He held his breath.

"Does wanting to kill the guy with my bare hands count?"

"I'm being serious."

"So am I." She was shaking with fury. "The guy had my twin brother tortured and left for dead. Why the fuck would I have anything to do with him?"

A family of four, struggling with two carts stacked high with oversized luggage, stared at them before hurrying away.

Maggie grabbed Stone, pulling him over to stand by the wall. She leaned toward him, her voice a low hiss. "I have *nothing* to do with Teague Alans."

"One hundred thousand dollars was deposited into your bank account yesterday."

Maggie gasped. She drew back, shaking her head violently. "Not possible."

"It was traced to an account we suspect is Teague Alans's."

Maggie's hands shot up, fingers wide, palms facing her shoulders. "And I'm telling you that's not possible. The only person I know with that kind of money is Meredith, your stepmom ... well, kind of. Anyway, there is zero reason for her to give me that kind of cash, and even if she did, she'd give me a heads-up. For the millionth time, I don't know Teague Alans. The first time I heard of the guy was at Christmas when you secret agent types were talking. The second time was two days ago, in connection with my twin brother's disappearance. I don't know the jackass and don't want to. I just want to find my brother alive." Her breathing was ragged, and she shook with fear, anger, or both.

Stone angled his body, sheltering her from the next line of arrivals eager to leave the airport. "Do you have any idea why he would target you? You are a librarian, right? Not a nuclear fusion scientist?" Or international weapons dealer?

Her frown was ferocious. "Yes, I'm a fucking librarian. No, I'm not a rocket scientist. The only thing I know about fusion is what was covered in high school science classes. And before you ask, I'm not an arms dealer, or terrorist, or whatever the hell else your boss thinks I am. I went to Paris to find my twin brother." She pressed her hands together, her thumbs hooked under her chin and forefingers pressed against her nose. Her shoulders shook.

Stone was silent but angled his body more to hide her from

curious passersby. Behind her hands, tears streamed down her face. He had made her cry again. *Bastard*. In his line of work, he didn't think about what victims were beyond what was required to get the job done. He certainly didn't contemplate their families outside of job context. Those were slippery slopes that only ended in an abyss damn hard to claw out of. So, it was unfamiliar territory hoping like hell Sebastian Monroe was alive. Stone rubbed his forehead with his thumb, still blocking her from prying eyes. "Where were you going?"

Maggie had gripped the handle of her wheeled carry-on, rocking it back and forth in a tight fidget. "The parking lot."

Stone hooked his thumb. "The car rentals are back there."

"I'm not renting a car."

Fear for her safety and general annoyance at this whole damn case made him testy. "Why the hell not? Is there a magical bus in the parking lot that will take us to Muskoka, whatever the hell that is?"

Maggie glared at him, stepping forward. "Yeah, except it's a magical car fairy named Meredith. She had a car left for me in short-term parking. Your boss didn't leave you a car? Huh." Maggie spun around him, heading toward the exit.

Stone's long legs ate up the distance between them. "When were you going to tell me?" He easily kept pace with her brisk walk.

"I wasn't. I was going to walk out that door like a sane person. Whatever game you and your boss are playing, I want no part of it."

There was no hesitation in her voice. She'd do it. She'd go looking for her brother alone.

"I'm not looking alone. I'll call Grace and ask if I can borrow one of her secret service types. She has a goddamn roster of them."

Stone forgot about Princess Grace. Maggie and the philanthropic royal had gotten along famously over the Christmas holiday in Alberta. The Princess of Jordemorden had a well-trained army at her disposal and some of the most elite special ops in the world.

Then a more troubling thought occurred, and he stopped. "I didn't say anything about you looking for your brother alone … out loud."

Maggie hadn't stopped moving, and Stone chased after her.

Goddammit.

She'd read his mind.

Again.

CHAPTER THIRTY-TWO

"*M*aggie, *wait up*." Maggie felt as much as heard Stone following her. He had questions she didn't want to answer. It was a coincidence, nothing to get weird about. She couldn't read minds. Usually.

She gripped her purse close to her body and wheeled her carry-on behind her. Her legs felt like lead, and her head was fuzzy as much from emotional exhaustion as physical.

In a heartbeat, Stone was at her shoulder and keeping pace. "I can't believe I'm asking this—tell me you're not psychic."

She stared straight ahead, moving as fast as her legs and the blasted wheeled carry-on would allow. "I'm not psychic."

"See, I hear you, but that's the second time you've done that."

Maggie caught herself from snorting. It was a hell of a lot more than two, not that she was counting. Her unusual sense of *knowing* seemed tied to strong emotions, and Tanner Stone set off avalanches of emotions within her. Like when she knew when he was thinking about kissing her—which was a lot—and when he changed his mind—almost as much—making her disappointment more visceral. Each time she had felt this electric charge of *knowing*, a blitzy, heady sense of anticipation … and then a devastating void. It sucked, which was why she hadn't walked away when she had the chance. She had *felt* Stone's frantic panic as he searched for her. Like he cared about her more than whatever his stupid boss wanted him to get out of her.

Stone pressed close as a large group of rugby players passed them. Two passed a ball between them. Their merriment and obvious candor were lovely to witness. One dropped the ball, and it rolled into Maggie's foot. He trotted over. "Sorry about that."

Maggie smiled at the gorgeous player before bending to pick up the ball.

Stone beat her to it and fired the ball back at the player, making it unnecessary for the man to come any closer.

The player gave a conciliatory wave before winking at Maggie. He caught up to his teammates as Stone glowered next to her.

"Was that necessary?"

"What?" Stone's frown was fierce as he stared after the team disappearing around a corner.

"The guy dropped the ball. You didn't have to hammer him with it."

"He didn't drop the ball. His aim was spot on."

Maggie swept her lashes down. It was as close to flirting as she got. "Was it? I didn't notice."

Stone gave a grunt in reply. A second group of players came up, and Stone maneuvered to put himself between her and the players.

She smiled to herself.

"About you being psychic—"

Maggie grabbed his arm. "Can we continue this in the car?" She did not want to have this conversation in the middle of a large international airport.

"Uh, yeah … that means you won't try to ditch me again?"

"Unless there is any more of that bullshit about me being a

nefarious fucking terrorist in bed with Teague Alans. Then, I will disappear. I've been coming here every summer for fifteen years. I know how to hide." She wasn't sure once sneaking a hard cider when she was underage exactly counted as being adept at laying low, but Stone didn't need to know that. "Hustle up. We have a two-hour drive ahead of us."

"Lead the way." He followed her toward the exit, hiking his backpack higher on his shoulders. "*Nefarious*, really?"

Maggie dropped her head back, giving a long-suffering sigh. "Hashtag-read-a-fucking-book."

Stone burst out laughing. The sound angled straight to her lady parts. He draped his arm across her shoulders. "I love when you get all nerd snarky. I'm keeping you."

She eyed him. "Until your boss says you can't? Not fair, bro." She removed his arm from her shoulder. Her lady bits would just have to keep carrying on without him.

The look he was giving her reminded her of a bewildered puppy dog.

"Forget I said anything." She fished in her purse, pulling out her sunglasses. "We have our truce. Let's just find the car."

Stone eyed her as they walked out of the exit toward the parking lot. She knew he was trying to figure her out—felt it. His boss might have poisoned their time together, and he sure didn't trust her, but he didn't underestimate or dismiss her. It was a welcome change. What little time she had with him was a precious gift. She felt more alive with him, even … fiery.

Maggie stopped abruptly.

Stone looked at her, expectant. "This it?"

"What?" She stared at him. Shit, to keep herself safe, she had kept herself *contained*. She had insulated herself from life. Hell, she had even dismissed the books she had read about being psychic because it all felt way too dangerous. Better to fit in and go with the status quo, even if it felt like she was dying inside. Equally unsettling, people underestimated her because she never let them see her?

Except Stone saw her.

"You okay?" His voice was filled with concern. "I'm more than happy to drive. It's been a hell of a few days."

"Ain't that the fucking truth." Internally, she was freaking the fuck out. She didn't do fire or passion.

Stone was looking at her oddly. "You swear more when you're excited."

Her head shot up. "I'm not excited." Was her voice breathless?

"Riled?" Stone supplied.

"Doesn't everyone?" Unwilling to make a bigger fool out of herself, Maggie feigned checking the directions on her phone.

She had missed a call.

"No, everyone doesn't," Stone answered.

Maggie tried to swallow the fear that was bubbling up her throat. "What? Oh right. They're missing out," she retorted, pocketing her phone.

Stone put his hand gently on her arm, staying her. "Are you okay?"

Maggie refrained from grabbing Stone's hand. "The car's this way."

Years ago, her mom had broken parole and was back in jail.

The call was from the jail her mom was incarcerated in.

CHAPTER THIRTY-THREE

The black Land Rover was backed into a stall in the short-term parking, just as Maggie said it would be. She walked around to the rear passenger wheel and ducked, snaking her hand into the wheel well. A couple of moments later, she popped up, holding a magnetic key box.

"Meredith's sure full of surprises." Stone approved.

Maggie smiled, walking around the vehicle to the driver's side. "Not really, not if you know her. Check the back seat. I bet there's a care package."

Stone did as she said. An oversized rectangle-shaped basket, deep enough to hold an upright bottle of wine, sat in the back seat, brimming with fresh and packaged snacks ... and, indeed, two bottles of wine. A flat of assorted beverages sat on the floor of the back seat, also.

"Is she for real?" It had been years since anyone packed him a care package. His mom used to until he screwed that up.

Maggie climbed into the driver's seat. "She is. Kindest, most nurturing woman I know." Maggie paused. "Actually, she and Becca are tied."

Stone closed the back passenger door and let himself into the front passenger seat, remembering. Becca, the youngest of the

Tanner siblings, had reached out to Stone as soon as she had found out he existed and invited him into their family, welcoming him without hesitation. Stone would never forget that kindness, though it had taken him several months to respond to her messages. "No argument there. You going to tell me what just came in on your phone?"

"I am not."

It was worth a shot. Stone reached for his seatbelt but hesitated. "Do you want me to drive?" Maggie had gotten scraps of broken sleep in the last handful of days. The toll was there, in the dark smudges under her eyes and the parlor of her skin, not to mention whatever notification had come in on her phone that had spooked her.

"We're both short on sleep," she reminded him, starting the SUV and adjusting the mirrors. Her routine attention to detail continued to impress him.

"I might be more used to it." How sleep deprived could a librarian be?

She laughed, clicking on her seatbelt. "You're underestimating the power of a good book."

Stone stared. Maybe he was more tired than he thought. He didn't think he had asked the question out loud. "You've totally lost me."

Maggie put the vehicle in drive. "Put your seatbelt on. This week has sucked, what just came in on my phone was another shit bomb I have to deal with, but I'll let you know if I need to switch or take a break."

All right then.

Stone dutifully clicked his seatbelt and circled back. "You stay up multiple nights reading books?"

Maggie pulled out of the stall and headed toward the exit. "Don't you?"

"No."

"You're reading the wrong books."

Stone raised his eyebrows. He read maybe two books a year.

How many did she read?

Maggie pulled smoothly into traffic, and changed lanes, before merging onto Hwy 427 North.

"It's not all the time."

Stone blinked, trying to pick up the crumbs of the conversation. "Are we still talking about books?"

She glanced at him. "No."

"What are we talking about?"

"You asked if I'm psychic. I'm not."

"You've read my mind. Isn't that the definition of being psychic?"

Maggie kept her eyes on the traffic. "The definition is a moving scale." She shrugged. "Who knows which one people are talking about when they accuse you of being one."

Stone felt himself coil. "Do you get accused often?"

She shot him a quick look. "I've learned to keep my mouth shut." She paused. "Except with you, apparently."

A warm feeling spread through his chest. "So what would you call it? You did read my mind."

She shrugged. "I don't call it anything. I just … sometimes sense or know things. It's not on purpose. It just happens."

"Can you turn it off?"

"I don't know how to turn it on, let alone off. It just … happens."

Intrigued despite himself, Stone asked, "What's it like?"

Maggie was quiet for several moments. "Sometimes I get a feeling strong enough that it sways what I choose to do. Other times I just know something." She hesitated. "Like when I answered a question you didn't ask."

"Have you always been able to?"

She shook her head, hand slung over the wheel as the traffic thinned out. "Not until I was ten. At least, that's when I first noticed it."

It was a tender age to find herself saddled with such an

uncommon gift, especially given what she and her twin brother had survived.

"Right? I've always seen it more like a curse." Her eyes widened. "Shit, I did it again, didn't I?"

Stone chuckled. "You *do* swear when you're riled."

She gave him a dirty look. "I'm not riled. Cussing is simply choosing words that come with their own exclamation mark." She glanced at him. "Okay, maybe I'm a *little* riled. You called me psychic."

And basically, a liar.

She hadn't said or thought it.

His guilt had.

Stone was ashamed of how quickly he had jumped to believe his boss when everything within him screamed that Maggie was innocent.

"What do you think you are picking up on? Energy?"

She shot him a look. "That's an astute conclusion. I'm not a closet witch if that's what you're asking."

Stone had listened enough to his mom's musings to know some people could sense things, though the mind-reading part was new to him.

Maggie smiled, eyes on the road. "I thought witches were women."

Stone threw up his hands. "There goes my retirement plans."

She snickered. He enjoyed this, the comfortable banter between them when he wasn't blowing it.

"So, energy … it's just hanging around everyone, and some people can pick up on it and translate it?"

"Yeah, kind of. I think anyway, though mine isn't consistent or controllable." Her voice had dipped, and she cleared her throat. "From what I've read, everyone is constantly broadcasting energy. Some people can tune in and understand that signal, so to speak."

Stone frowned. "Isn't that invasive?"

"Heck yeah. That's where karma gets thrown into the mix

and needing to ask permission. Others postulate that you can only pick up what another willingly shares. From what I've read, there is no consensus on what does or does not happen when you read energy."

He stiffened. "You read books on this stuff?"

"Sometimes. I like reading books on random topics." Maggie was watching the road, relaxed. She gave no indication that she had read any of his mom's books.

"Sounds like you read a lot," he said cautiously.

"I *love* books." Her interest was palpable. "Books make knowledge accessible. That can be a game changer for people. People miss opportunities not because they don't have the smarts or the drive. They don't realize what's available. Dreaming big is relative. Books help. There's also fiction that introduces whole new worlds and perspectives, all through the innocuous novel." She ended with a soft sigh.

"Is that why you're a librarian?" Stone had never met someone who liked books as much as his mom.

Maggie paused. "I never really thought about it, but yes, I guess so. I find comfort in knowledge, in understanding things, and in exploring this incredible planet. And I like helping people. Libraries keep evolving how we help the community, so yes, it's a good fit."

"Maybe you should write a book."

She laughed. It was a full-bellied sound. "Oh my god, I thought you were serious there for a second."

"I was." Maggie was intelligent and articulate, with integrity and compassion. He suspected she would bring incredible insight if she ever undertook a book project.

She shot him an incredulous look. "*Other* people write."

Stone stared out the windshield. "I'd read your books. I imagine you're better at it than you realize."

She made a weird sound before clearing her throat. "Thanks."

"No problem." Stone kept his gaze out the window. Subdivisions dominated the landscape, punctuated by the odd farm holdout.

Maggie was quiet for a few moments. "I don't think my experience would translate."

Stone smiled to himself, happy she was contemplating it. "Tell me more about your process. How do you read energy?"

Maggie brightened, back on safer ground. "This sense of knowing kicks in. Sometimes it's mundane stuff, like finding a parking spot or knowing something random. Once, I was out for breakfast, and I asked the server her preference before ordering one of the multiple breakfast sausage options. As soon as I asked, I got this flash that she was a vegetarian and had never tried the different meat options. A half second later she said as much, but how would I know that? Stuff like that happens all the time." Maggie frowned. "Or it's more serious, like the feeling that came over me when those guys attacked. I would have appreciated a bigger heads-up on that one."

Stone traced the window frame with his finger. "Or the bomb exploding."

"Or the bomb exploding." Her voice broke. "I know how implausible it sounds, but I didn't have anything to do with that bomb besides *feeling* that something was very wrong and that you were in serious danger."

Stone made it a habit of compartmentalizing certain aspects of his job and promptly pushing them to the recesses of his mind. Nearly dying qualified. It happened less often than people expected in his line of work, but it happened. Stone didn't think he'd ever neatly tuck away the terror he had felt when that bomb went off with Maggie right there.

"I believe you."

She darted him an incredulous look. "But your boss said—"

"I know what she said, and I know from the evidence she has that it makes sense. But there's a reasonable, likely *nefarious* reason—" He turned to her smiling, ready to tease.

Tears were streaming down her cheeks as she gripped the steering wheel.

"*Maggie?*"

She swiped at her cheek. "I don't hurt people or try to extort money. I'm not like my parents."

"You thought I put you in the same category as your parents?"

"Didn't you?"

"*Hell*, no." Jesus, no wonder she had been upset.

"You were just doing your job. I get it. I do. It just stung." Her voice was so reasonable like she expected to be shit on and accepted that was how life went.

If Stone had been doing his job instead of doggedly fighting his attraction to Maggie, he would have considered Teague Alans had set Maggie up to be a person of interest. Which meant Teague Alans knew enough about the task force to set her up.

And that Maggie was in his crosshairs.

Pissed at himself, Stone pulled the quickest card he thought might work to keep Maggie safe. "So you've never tried to control your ability to read energy?"

She gave her eyes a final swipe, sniffling. "No."

"Do you want to?"

"Not really. It just happens."

Stone sat forward. "What am I thinking right now?"

Maggie rubbed her forehead with her free hand. "I'm not some party game."

"Of course not. I just want to try something." He hesitated. "Can you trust me for this? I promise I'll shut up if you want me to."

She cracked a smile at that. "Sure."

"Okay, what am I thinking?"

She drove, eyes on the road. After a few moments, she shrugged. "I got nothing."

"What about now? What am I thinking?"

Maggie swerved, narrowly missing a low-slung sports car moving as fast as a bullet train. Stone grabbed the dashboard.

She kept to the center of their lane and exhaled. Her face and neck had flushed a brilliant shade of red.

He released the dash. "Picked up on that one, did you?"

She kept her gaze straight ahead. She pulled in a slow, deep inhale before letting it out. "If you were remembering that kiss we shared in the airport, then yes."

Stone suddenly felt like he was underwater and shooting through the air at the same time. He held up his hands.

The air between his face and hands looked different. Almost … sparkly.

"Wait!" Maggie pointed at him, her voice laced with wonder. "I feel that. What is that? What are you thinking right now?"

"Uh … the kiss." It had been an explosion of his senses Stone wouldn't soon forget, not that he wanted to admit that.

"What else?" She sounded exasperated.

Embarrassed, Stone added, "I worried it was a dick move, seeing if you could pick up the energy of that kiss. Then the air got weird. Now I'm worried I'm hallucinating."

Stone turned his hands back and forth, watching as the air caught the light on edges it wasn't supposed to have.

It was unnerving as all hell.

Stone dragged his gaze away from his hands. "You said it seemed to be connected to emotion. At the airport, when you disappeared, I thought I had lost you. Then you appeared, and I was so damn *relieved*, I kissed you. Aw, hell, was it creepy?"

Maggie slipped her hand around his. "You're not creepy. Often infuriating, annoying as hell sometimes, way too good a kisser for my own good, but never creepy."

Stone tried to discreetly adjust in his seat. "You think I'm a good kisser?"

Maggie gave his hand a brief squeeze before pulling hers away. "Back to the weird air."

"How about not." He had just seen air with edges.

When she had pointed her finger, excited and asking what he was seeing, it felt like a goddamn bolt of electricity had arced from her to him, that she'd *shared* energy with him.

Science—and bodies—weren't supposed to work that way, were they?

"To be continued." Maggie tapped the steering wheel. "Huh."

"What?"

"I've never gotten a saucy memo." She tossed him a charged look. "I liked it, besides the almost crashing part."

Stone had to shift in his seat again.

Maggie darted him a glance. "You are freaked out!"

"I'm fine." He wasn't. Stone was trying not to get a full-on boner.

"You're not saying anything." Maggie gripped the wheel tighter.

"Trust me. You don't want to hear what I'm thinking."

Maggie's brow furrowed before a grin lit up her face. "*Oh.*"

"Now you're getting it."

She darted a look at his lap. "You sure I don't want to hear about that?"

CHAPTER THIRTY-FOUR

Heat bloomed on Maggie's cheeks, and she adjusted her grip on the steering wheel. She had never been so forward in her life.

That happened to her a lot when Stone was around.

He sat in the passenger seat next to her and started rubbing his jaw.

"Just say it, whatever you're thinking." She could handle it. She hoped.

He hesitated so long Maggie wondered if she should apologize. She had no idea flirting was such a minefield and chastised herself for breaking her own rule: no men.

It was experiences like *this* that she knew her sense of knowing, if she could even call it that, was untested at best or just plain faulty.

Finally, Stone spoke. "My mom's into crystal healing, or maybe it's past life regression meditations—" he broke off.

Maggie blanched.

A dousing in ice water couldn't have cooled her overripe hormones any faster. Nothing like a man bringing up his mother to put a woman in her place. Maggie didn't know if she was coming or going with this guy. Neutrally, she said, "You know those are completely different things, right?"

"Are they?"

She gave him a quick side eye but only asked, "Are you and your mom close?"

Stone's energy seemed to pull in, and he was suddenly fixated on the patches of water visible through the trees. "We used to be."

Something in his voice tripped her. "What happened?"

"I grew up."

Curious, she asked, "What does that mean?"

In a quiet voice, he said, "I didn't like the answers to the questions I finally started asking."

Maggie repositioned her hands on the steering wheel, eyes on the road. "I've never asked those questions."

Stone's gaze swung around. "Want to talk about it?"

"Nope." She hesitated. "Do you?"

"Someday, I probably should." Stone's voice held so much unprocessed grief that Maggie wanted to hug him until all the pressure valves he had holding in all those emotions so tight broke.

Instead, she kept her eyes on the road. "I can make that work in my schedule."

He stared at her, incredulous, before bursting out laughing. "God, you're good to be around." His voice was lighter than it had been. Maggie felt something bloom inside of her. In her own small, temporary way, she had helped this man lighten his burden.

"I've been around energy philosophies my whole life," Stone started. "My mom is into all that. I didn't really pay attention, but I think what you're describing is one of the *clairs*." He snapped his fingers. "Claircognizance? Maybe it's clairvoyance? I can't remember, but it's a thing. At least, for some people, it is. The ones that accept the magic woven within us."

Something tickled at the edge of Maggie's memory. She had heard that before.

The ones that accept the magic woven within us.

More pressing, though, was Stone's unexpected knowledge of the esoteric—and seeming acceptance. "You don't think I'm a freak?"

Stone turned in his seat, facing her. She could feel the intensity of his gaze.

"What?" Maggie asked, uncomfortable with his scrutiny.

"You don't let many people see you, do you?"

Maggie sucked in a breath.

Stone pressed, "You let me see you. Why?"

Maggie shook her head. She wasn't ready for this.

"Why me?"

She couldn't answer him.

Stone sat back in his seat and crossed his arms. "You're enough."

"Excuse me?"

"I said, 'You're enough.'"

Maggie adjusted her grip on the steering wheel. "What are you talking about?"

"You. You're like sunshine and fire, literally the energy of the planet. You're a goddamn queen." He paused. "High priestess? Anyway, you're elemental power personified. Whatever the fucktard adults in your life did to make you dim that extraordinary light makes me really fucking angry."

Shit. Stone was no longer one of those safe crushes that didn't go anywhere. They were skirting dangerously close to a shocking level of emotional intimacy.

Maggie turned on the blinker, taking the exit. "I need a coffee."

Fifteen minutes later, they were merging back onto the highway, lattes in hand.

"I'm sorry if I was too much back there," Stone said, opening the lid on his coffee.

Maggie smiled. She had only ever heard women apologize for being too much. "It's safer that way."

Stone turned his head to look at her. She could feel the wheels in his mind turning. "It's safer for no one to really see you?"

Maggie finished her sip. "You do catch on quick."

He sat up straighter in the passenger seat at her praise, and she melted a little more where Tanner Stone was concerned.

"And you weren't too much." His passion for her well-being felt like a strong, protective hug. Now, let's see how he would take this. "Can I meet your mom?"

Stone sputtered on his coffee.

Maggie laughed. "Not *that* kind of meet your mom. Christ, we barely know each other. I wondered if she might be able to help me with understanding the clairgonizance stuff."

"Yeah, she'd love that. She's written books on … different esoteric streams." Stone finished cryptically.

Maggie gasped. *"The ones that accept the magic woven within us."*

Stone turned his head sharply. "You know her work?"

"Oh my god, your mom is *the* Doris Stone."

Stone actually squirmed, which made no sense.

"You should be proud." Doris Stone had been one of the authors whose work Maggie had really connected with.

"Having a mom who self-identifies as a witch comes with some baggage," Stone said dryly.

Maggie laughed so hard she wondered if she should pull over.

"What's so funny?" Stone's tone was unimpressed.

When Maggie finally got herself under control, she reminded Stone, "Dude, my mom's in jail. I'd go for happy witch that helps people over psycho criminal who terrorizes her own children any day."

"Me, too. Jesus, especially when you put it that way." He turned. "You really don't mind she's a practicing witch?"

"No." Doris Stone's books were wise advice from a loving matriarch. Maggie adored them.

A comfortable silence descended as Maggie wondered about what Stone had said. After several minutes she finally asked, "It was hard, having a mom out of the broom closet?"

"It had its moments, that's for sure."

"Is that why you're upset with her?"

"Heck no!" Stone set his now empty coffee cup in the drink holder. "She had an affair with a married man. A dangerous, married ass. Then she went and named me after him." Stone turned to Maggie. "How could she do that? I mean, she knew he wasn't leaving his first wife for her, for us. Why in the hell would she saddle me with the constant reminder of the guy who never claimed me?"

Maggie's chest tightened. She put her near-empty coffee cup in the other drink holder and rubbed her chest one-handed, feeling Stone's hurt viscerally. He noticed. "You feel me, my hurt."

She nodded.

"Shit, I'm sorry. How do I make it stop?"

"You're enough." Maggie's quietly spoken words boomed in the suddenly silent SUV.

Finally, Stone answered, "It's not the same thing."

Maggie waited.

"It's not the same," Stone pressed.

Maggie reached across the console and picked up Stone's hand. She was half surprised when after a moment's hesitation, he held her hand back. "I'm enough."

She repeated the words back to him.

Stone looked at her. "Maybe if we say it enough, we'll believe it."

"I'm game if you are."

Stone squeezed her hand.

"Would you help me practice some more energy stuff? Probably a good idea to *not* when we're driving."

"Absolutely, though I don't know if I'll be any help."

Maggie drew in a sharp breath. *"Ohmygod."*

Stone pulled out a handgun, scanning the traffic and mirrors.

"Jesus, where the hell did you get that?"

When he found no danger lurking in the thinning traffic, Stone tucked the gun away again. "Forget it's even here."

"Stone."

"I'm *working.* Comes with the job. Why did you shriek?"

"I thought you said you would let the task force find Teague Alans?"

"I am." He was telling her a half-truth. Maggie let it drop for now. "I just realized if I could harness my … awareness, maybe I can find Sebastian."

Stone wiped his hands on the tops of his pants. "You scared the shit out of me."

"Says the guy holding a gun. Do you think that is even possible?"

Stone had no idea and said so.

Another thought sparked. "Do you think I could help you track down Teague Alans, too?"

"I don't want you anywhere near Teague Alans, literally or energetically."

"But if finding him can help me find my brother, I have to risk it."

"No, Maggie, you don't."

Maggie felt Stone's energy. This time, it was fear. He was genuinely scared she would get hurt. A shutter went through her. "What do you know that you're not telling me?"

Stone paused, and she knew he was weighing his words. "Teague Alans is dangerous. Promise me you won't try to energetically read him, or whatever you call it. I don't want you anywhere near him or energetically connected or whatever the fuck happens with what you do."

"What about Sebastian?"

"I told you, if he's alive, I'll find him."

CHAPTER THIRTY-FIVE

Sebastian waited until the hallway was empty before he let himself back into his and Phoebe's apartment. She wouldn't discover him. Since he disappeared, she hadn't slept in their bed, and several days ago, right before Maggie showed up, Phoebe had left the apartment and never come back. Sebastian was desperate to see her, hold her, wipe away her tears, and tell her it was going to be okay. But he couldn't, not yet. As long as Teague Alans was still out there, it was safer if Phoebe thought Sebastian was dead.

The apartment felt cold without her laughter, without her touch. Sebastian shoved the longing and love down and crossed through their room to his office beyond. Out of habit, he shut the closet door and kept the office lights off. A single small lamp illuminated the space barely past dim. He pulled out the folded sheaf.

Sebastian monitored three phone numbers and several email accounts, all routed through different places around the globe. Being kidnapped as a child by your own family to extort your extended family had given him some serious trust issues. The news of his murder must be getting around. He clicked through only a handful of messages. His Alberta number had two messages on it. He replayed the saved message first.

"Sebastian, it's me. I miss you so much. If you get this, please, just, just stay safe. If you're still alive, I'll find you."

Pain squeezed his chest. Maggie. He listened to it three more times before saving it. She had found the scribbled note in the cuckoo clock, and it had taken everything he could not to run to her when she had been in his apartment again. She was out of France and safe for now. He scrubbed his hand over his face before pressing the second message. It was Beaumont Correctional. "Christ, what did you do now, Mom?"

He replayed the message and swore.

His mom was out of prison.

Again.

This time on a technicality.

"Sebastian?"

Sebastian spun around.

Phoebe stood in the doorway. Light from the closet haloed around her. She was trembling. "Mon Dieu, it really is you!" She sprinted toward him. Sebastian met her halfway. He gathered her up in his arms as she wound hers tight around him. For long moments they just held each other as tears streamed down both their cheeks. Until their lips met. The soft, exploratory kiss reached a flash point and ignited. Frantic, they stripped off their suddenly confining clothes. Their lovemaking was raw, elemental, and over way too fast. Phoebe collapsed on top of him, coming down from her climax like he had remembered over and over in his mind.

She rolled off him, and they lay facing each other. She traced his face. There were scars there, as there were over his entire body now. "What they must have done to you," she whispered, her gaze scanning his body. "They tortured you and thought they had dumped your dead body, didn't they?"

Sebastian closed his eyes, nodding, and wrestled the memories down. Someday he would tell her everything if she asked.

But not right now. Sebastian took Phoebe's hand in his. "I survived. I can't stay, though. It wouldn't be safe. I have to keep you safe."

She started to protest.

"It's too dangerous. I have to find Teague Alans and put a stop to this once and for all. I can't have him hurting you or Maggie."

"I met your sister."

Sebastian stilled. He hadn't told Maggie about Phoebe.

"Where?"

"She and her man followed me to our spot." Phoebe cupped his face with her hand. "Our bench by the pond."

Sebastian pulled Phoebe's hand away, though held it. "My sister doesn't date."

"She was with an Australian operative, and if they're not dating yet, they will be."

"How did you know he was an operative."

Phoebe avoided his gaze. "She said you had to be alive, that you didn't feel dead." Fresh tears fell down Phoebe's cheeks. "I thought I just couldn't accept it that you were gone. You didn't feel dead. Sometimes I swore I could still smell you, that you were here, with me. You were, weren't you?"

The niggling questions fled in the wake of her tears, and Sebastian apologized over and over. "I didn't mean to get you tangled up in this, in me."

Phoebe pressed kisses across his brow. "You didn't, my love, you didn't. You didn't do anything wrong."

Sebastian pulled back. "What's that supposed to mean?"

Phoebe looked down, and louder alarm bells went off. Sebastian repeated, "How did you know the guy she was with was an Australian operative?"

Phoebe sat up, and fear crawled up Sebastian's spine. He pulled his clothes back on. "Tell me. All of it."

Phoebe slowly donned her clothing, too. Finally, she faced him. "Us falling in love was by chance."

"I know." Sebastian still couldn't believe Phoebe had chosen him.

"Us meeting … wasn't."

Sebastian felt like he was suddenly looking down the track of an oncoming train. "I don't understand."

"I know your sister's man is an Australian operative because … we work on the same task force. I was assigned to watch you."

Sebastian didn't move.

Teague Alans.

His beloved Phoebe had been assigned to him because of their connection.

Pain deeper than any torture lanced through him. "Is this a sick joke?"

Phoebe shook her head.

"You said you never introduced me to your co-workers, other officers, or inspectors because you thought I'd be *bored* by them. But that's not true, is it?" Sebastian's heart shattered. Suddenly, he looked down and was seeing his body from above. And Phoebe. And his ridiculously messy office.

He pressed his hand to his chest and closed his eyes, focusing on the one person in the world he could trust. His sister's bright, cautious smile played on the movie screen behind his eyelids. He had kept Maggie at arm's length, not wanting to poison her optimism with the darkness that always felt just under the surface of him, until he had met Phoebe in a carefully orchestrated sting.

When he opened his eyes, he was back in his body.

Phoebe looked like she had seen a ghost and clutched his arms. "Are you all right? What just happened? It's like you weren't here."

"You don't get to ask me that."

"*Sebastian*, darling, we'll get through this. We're to be married—"

He laughed. It hurt too much to cry. "Our relationship was all lies. It was all bullshit. I swore to myself *never again*. I won't be some pawn, not even for you."

Was that why he had never told Maggie about Phoebe? Maggie, who noticed everything, would have seen Phoebe for who she really was, a gorgeous investigator whose only interest in Sebastian was to use him for a fucking task force. At least his parents' and brother's treachery had been in character. Phoebe's betrayal cut on an entirely different level.

Enough. Sebastian would not be a pawn again. Phoebe had played him—it might even be for some worthy, higher good. But toying with someone like that, *fucking* someone like you cared, even a fake engagement, was not okay.

"Sebastian, please—"

Sebastian looked at the woman he had asked to be his wife, seeing the truth he had been too afraid to: his beloved Phoebe, who had always whispered her undying love to him, had never cared at all.

He looked at the woman who would have been his wife. "I will never marry you."

CHAPTER THIRTY-SIX

"They landed in Toronto." Teague Alans's new mercenary crew was proving resourceful. *Almost* worth what he was paying them.

"Sebastian's sister and Tanner's bastard are in Canada?"

The head mercenary nodded.

Satisfaction rolled through Teague. Bruce's bastard son was right on schedule. "I presume they went on to Alberta?"

"My sources did not track them on any connecting flights or car rentals."

"If you want to play with the big boys, you better deliver," Teague snapped.

The mercenary leveled him a dangerous look. "You should take your own advice."

The beast in front of him outweighed Teague by at least eighty pounds. Teague held his ground, refusing to step back. He wasn't weak, not like the others. Their consortium, all hand-picked by Bruce Tanner, had wielded power and unspeakable influence. And one by one, each and every one of them had died.

Teague was the last man standing. He knew not to bring a knife to a gunfight.

The mercenary did, too. Teague eyed the man, suddenly

wary he had deviated too far from his usual choice of pliable thug. He cleared his throat. "Anything else?"

"Sebastian's brother called the sister."

"What are you talking about? Sebastian doesn't have a brother." None that he had mentioned anyway.

The mercenary's eyes were cold. "He has an older brother, Lawrence. He did time for kidnapping and extortion."

"Who?"

"Kidnapped Sebastian, tried to extort the rich grandparents."

Teague perked up at the unexpected luck. "Go on."

"The parents were in on it." The mercenary's face twitched. Interesting. He didn't approve.

"Anything else?"

"Dad's been out awhile. Mom was just re-released." The mercenary hesitated briefly. "The parents have been most helpful."

Teague's smile was cruel.

This was better news than he had thought.

The mercenary continued, "It won't take long for us to find the location. Whether she has what's yours with her is another matter."

"Do it," Teague demanded. "I want you to find what's mine."

He wanted this finished once and for all.

CHAPTER THIRTY-SEVEN

"This is Meredith's *cottage*?" Stone stared at the massive structure. There was nothing cozy or quaint about the spectacle jutting out of the forest in front of him.

"They use the term loosely here." Maggie opened her door and climbed out of the driver's seat. She tugged her carry-on out of the back. Stone got out, too, retrieving his backpack before slinging it over his shoulder and walking around to the front of the SUV. Manicured gardens coexisted with prominent rock outcroppings. "Lots of rock here."

"Canadian Shield," Maggie answered, distracted. She was looking at her phone again.

"If you say so." Stone eyed the intricate display, not sure he appreciated the tamed gardens amid such elemental rocks and forest.

A tired grin flickered. "It's a thing here. Come on, let's get inside."

He saw glimpses of sparkling water beyond, and a pang of longing rose swiftly. Maybe it was the conversation on the drive, maybe it was his and Maggie's pact that they were enough, but Stone missed home ... he missed his mom. Stone hadn't been back to Australia in months, though that wasn't unusual, and usually, he was too busy working to notice.

He followed Maggie as she led the way up a wide flagstone walkway to the front porch before turning around, swearing, and started retracing their steps along the walkway. "Meredith likes to keep her vehicles in the garage."

"Let me," Stone offered.

She handed him the keys. "Thanks," she murmured, blinking her eyes closed where she stood.

He tried not to skip, finally able to help this woman who was categorically opposed to accepting help.

"Garage door opener should be on the visor," she called from the porch stairs. Eyes still closed, and face upturned toward the dappled sunlight filtering through the forest. Stone stopped, remembering another porch months ago, where Maggie had turned her face up to welcome the feel of winter sunlight on her skin. He hurried to put the SUV away.

The inside of the three-car garage was tidy. A few gardening implements were against the back wall, and a handful of pedal bikes hung from hooks out of the way. Besides that, there wasn't much. If Meredith spent any time here, she didn't dawdle in the garage or collect home maintenance gear.

He hustled out, pressing the garage door closed on the key panel hanging on the outside wall.

"My birthday's the code. In case you need it." Maggie's eyes were still closed.

"When's your birthday?"

"Tomorrow." She turned and led the way inside the cottage. Stone made a mental note of the key code she rattled off before realizing what she had said. "Tomorrow? Happy birthday."

She looked over her shoulder, giving him a sad smile.

Oh shit. "It's Sebastian's birthday, too."

She nodded.

"I'm sorry, Maggie. I'll do what I can to help you find him."

They had passed a grocery store in the small town they had

driven through on their way in. It wouldn't bring her brother back, but maybe the small shop sold birthday cakes.

He followed her through the front door and stopped in the cavernous doorway, staring. Massive wooden beams framed the elegant, open-concept design of the central corridor of the main floor. He closed the door behind him, a pronounced click sounding. Across the wide expanse of living space, floor-to-ceiling windows revealed the sparkling lake fringed by forest. His gaze aimed upward. A loft ringed three sides, with several doors opening off each wing.

Maggie hung her purse on an iron hook in the shape of a mermaid by the door and kicked off her shoes. She padded into the oversized kitchen, heading directly to the wine rack.

She held up a bottle. "I'm having American Cab Sav. You?"

"That's fine." Stone wasn't driving anywhere the rest of the day.

She grabbed a bottle opener from a drawer and pulled down two wine glasses from the cupboard. At his glance, Maggie handed him the bottle. Stone opened it with a few twists and poured two glasses.

Maggie accepted the glass he offered, as well as the bottle. "Come on."

Stone followed her to a large wrap-around porch overlooking the lake. The main floor, from the front, was the second floor of the rear, and the elevated porch afforded a stunning view of the sparkling lake and dense forest.

Maggie settled in one of the oversized cushioned chairs, and Stone did the same. She let out a gusty sigh before holding her glass up to his. "Cheers."

He clinked his glass to hers.

They both took long sips.

Maggie gently swirled the wine in her glass. "I love this tradition. We put what needs to go in the fridge or freezer away, but everything else waits until after we've had a drink—tea or harder—on the back deck." She took a long sip of wine and settled deeper into the plush chair, her legs tucked under her.

The day was bright and warm, and Stone thought the water looked damn inviting. That was another thing he missed about Australia, the water.

A loud splash sounded. Children's laughter could be heard drifting up from the lake and through the forest before two more loud splashes followed.

Maggie smiled, her eyes closed, and her face tilted toward the sun. "That's probably the Stoll kids."

Stone could see three kids playing in the water a few cottages down the lake. The rambunctious children swam like fish and splashed with wild abandon. One of the children dove underwater. He waited, expecting the tween to pop back up within moments.

Nothing happened. The other two climbed up an inflatable island before launching themselves off the attached inflatable slide.

Stone's sat forward. Still no sign of the kid that had gone underwater. "Uh, Maggie—"

Maggie opened her eyes, shielding them with her hand in the bright sun. "What's wrong?"

Stone stood. "I think one of those kids needs help." He started to cross the deck, heading for the long sets of stairs winding down to the water.

Maggie sprang up, following him.

He had descended to the second landing before he saw the third head pop up, sputtering and laughing. *"How long was that?"*

From the lower vantage point, he saw a woman standing on the kids' dock. She clapped her hands. *"Forty-two seconds, that's your new best!"*

Relief washed over Stone. The kid had simply been practicing holding her breath and was supervised by an adult. He ran a hand through his hair. "She's okay."

Maggie stood at the landing's railing, her hand against her chest. "That's Lori. I swear that kid's part dolphin."

Said kid spun in the water, arm outstretched, sending an arc of water around her. Her siblings complained she was too close to the bottom of the slide. She drifted out of the way, spotting them. The kid squealed in delight and waved both of her arms out of the water, yelling, *"Maggie, hi, it's me, Lori! Did you see that? Forty-two seconds."*

The other two kids and woman turned before waving at them, too.

Maggie called back, "I did. You did amazing!"

Lori smiled and dove underwater before popping up next to the inflatable island ladder. She climbed up and joined her siblings as they took turns rocketing down.

Maggie waved to the woman on the dock. "Hi, Karleen."

The woman waved back, giving Maggie a bright smile.

Maggie turned to head back up the stairs, and Stone followed her. "They're fun. Nice kids and normal parents."

Stone laughed. "Normal's not … *normal* here?"

Maggie snorted. "Not even close. Need a refill?"

Stone shook his head. He still had half a glass.

Maggie sighed as she resettled into her chair, eyes closed again. "That was sweet."

"What?"

She smiled. "You flew out of your chair, ready to rescue her. You really are a good guy."

"You sound surprised." And damn, if that didn't sting a little.

"Not surprised." She hesitated. "You're always ready to help."

"You were right there with me."

She went back to swirling her wine, not meeting his eyes. "Takes a village and all that."

Stone frowned. There hadn't been a village cocooned around them when Maggie and Sebastian had needed one.

"Don't," she said. "I've made peace with it, of a sort."

Maggie's head shot up. "Ah hell, I did it again." She covered her hand with her face. "I never thought of it as reading minds before, but with you, it feels like I'm in your head."

Stone clinked his glass to hers. "Relax." He was trying to. "Let's just enjoy the peace and the view. It's been a hell of a week." Crows cawed at each other from treetops ringing the deck, and they could just make out the soft sound of water lapping against the dock down below. The lake was massive, with numerous islands, bays, and irregular shorelines outlining the deep blue waters. Cottages lined those shorelines and most of the islands. This was Toronto's *cottage country*. Suddenly, Maggie placed her hand on his arm and mouthed *look*.

He turned as a hummingbird darted forward, then back, then forward again. Its feathers shimmered blue and green in the sunlight. It was nearly as pretty as watching Maggie beam, stock still, as she looked at it, watching it dart to and fro.

A deafening boom sounded, followed by the choking gurgle of an oversized engine whining.

"What the hell is that?"

The hummingbird shot off, and Maggie sat back in her seat again. "Wake boat."

Awful music blared across the bay before it zigzagged back, competing only with the sound of its oversized engine. Back and forth, it circuited the small bay in repeating passes of wince-worthy music and whining combustion engine.

"Are they always that loud?" Stone knew wake boats, though he had always preferred surfing or sailing.

"Welcome to Muskoka. Besides, it's the long weekend. There will be more."

She had no sooner said it than the whine of another power boat thundered past. Distant engines could be heard firing up, with equally awful music. The two boats jockeyed for position in the small bay.

"I could make peace with the supersized engines. It's the

spastic music, sketchy captaining, and pulverizing the shorelines that make them hard to root for."

Stone agreed. A shouting match exploded in the bay between two of the wake boats. "And that?"

Maggie shrugged. "Assholes need to escape the city as much as normal folk."

Stone snickered.

"I get it. It's a shared space. The water should be for everyone. But I've lost count of how many times I've nearly gotten run over by them when I'm kayaking or by jet skis, mind you. And just once, I'd like to be here for my birthday when it's quiet. Maybe if we're lucky, it'll rain—I know that's blasphemy on the long weekend."

Stone cocked his head. "And tomorrow is your birthday."

"It is." She tilted her face to the sky. "Any chance we could get a good and proper storm whip up overnight and settle in?"

"Do you always talk to the sky?"

She shrugged. "When the moment moves me. Don't you?"

"Hard pass on that one, but you'll love my mom." An idea started forming, it wasn't a thunderstorm, but it might get the job done.

Maggie was looking at him weirdly. She covered it by stretching and pulling herself out of the chair. "I think that wine just hit me, and I'm beat. I know that with jet lag, you're supposed to stay up on the new schedule, but I'm going to take a shower and have a nap. If I sleep through the night, so be it."

Stone stood, too. "I'll follow you in."

Maggie's eyelids were drooping, and she stifled a yawn. When they were inside again, she waved in the general direction of the kitchen. "Eat whatever you want. The cupboards and fridge should be stocked, but check expiry dates. The water is lake water, so only drink or cook with the jugged water. Feel free to claim a room."

Stone swung his gaze around the kitchen, his attention landing on a framed picture hanging on the wall. His half-brother, Gabe, stood with his arms around Savannah, Maggie's best friend. The happy couple was smiling as Maggie photo-bombed them in the background.

Maggie stopped next to him, giving a tired smile. "That was taken late last summer."

He turned, grabbing her bag. "I can carry your bag up."

"Do you really hate him that much?"

"It's complicated, and you're tired." He crossed the expansive living room and started taking the stairs to the second floor before she could argue.

She trailed after him. "Then uncomplicate it."

"You sound like Colt." Gabe, Colt, Tucker, and Becca were his half-siblings, and whole complications.

"I think he got it from Clint."

Stone looked over his shoulder. "How well do you know their family?"

"They're your family," she said quietly.

"Family is more than blood."

"Don't I know it."

They had crested the stairs, and Stone stopped. "Sorry, that was—I'm an ass."

"No, you're not. You're hurting."

Stone stood up straighter. "I most certainly am not."

Maggie cackled. "Pull my other leg." She headed down the hall. When Stone didn't follow her, she walked back to him. "Wow, you're really pissed." She reached for her bag. "I can take that."

He kept his hold on her bag. "I'm not pissed. I barely know them. What's to be hurt about?"

"Got it in one."

He actually staggered back at her simple assessment. "It's not like that."

"Okay." She held out her hand. "Can I have my bag back?"

"Maggie—I'm sorry. Years ago, when I found out I had half-siblings was trippy enough. That most of them want me in their life, it's hard to wrap my head around."

"Or heart."

"We're not going there." He held up her bag. "Which one's your room?"

"Second door on the right."

A few steps later, Stone set her luggage just inside the door. Something had shifted between them again. "You'll be okay?"

"I'll be fine. A long, hot shower and solid sleep will do me wonders. What about you?"

He inhaled deeply through his nose. "I said we're not going there."

She took a step closer. "Ever?"

He ran both hands through his hair, not wanting to leave her but not wanting to touch what she had just unearthed in him.

She slid past him and into her room. "Goodnight, Stone." She turned around, pausing. "Are we good?"

"Yeah." He didn't move.

She held his gaze. "Need anything else?"

"No." What he *wanted* was another story.

Electricity simmered between them.

When he didn't say anything further, she did. "I'll see you later." She slowly closed the door, not quite on his face.

Would it have been so hard to tell her his half-siblings and their tight-knit bond scared the shit out of him? That, yes, he did hate Gabe for his role in keeping him from them all these years. Or that he was crazy proud of her, worried, and hoped her twin brother was still alive.

But Stone hadn't said any of those things.

He didn't now, either. Instead, he gave the closed door a final long look before he jogged down the stairs, heading straight to the kitchen. He pulled out his phone and called one of his half-brothers, the closet chef. "Tucker, it's Stone. How do you make a birthday cake?"

CHAPTER THIRTY-EIGHT

Maggie waited silently against the closed door. When she heard Stone's retreating steps, she slid down the door. Sitting on the floor, with her back against the door, she wrapped her arms around her legs and let the tears come. Worst week ever.

She tugged her purse closer and slid her hand inside to pull out her phone. Her fingers brushed against card stock.

Maggie slid the postcard out. She had forgotten she had purchased it at Charles de Gaulle before their flight back to Canada. She studied the quaint watercolor image of a couple walking in a snuggled embrace down a tree-lined boulevard, the Eiffel Tower in the background. It was the Paris of postcards. Literally. The man in the image reminded her of Stone, with his tall, strong physique and gallant air. It was the only reason she had purchased it.

He was Paris to her.

She slid it back safely into her purse before pulling out her phone, swallowing down panic and fear. The caller ID of the unheard message terrified her. Prisons called family members when incarcerated relatives were being released and at risk for re-offending.

It wasn't the first time she had received such a call.

Maggie keyed in her pin and listened to her voicemail. Her mom had been re-released. She had broken parole but got out on a technicality.

Familiar fear threatened to swamp her, and Maggie fought hard against it. She wasn't the scared kid anymore. She had grown up and changed her name. She had a career and a few really good friends.

So why was she shaking like a damn leaf?

She went to listen to the message again and nearly shrieked when her phone rang.

No caller ID.

What if it was Sebastian? She answered. "Hello?"

"Oh, thank God. You are a hard person to find."

It wasn't Sebastian.

Fear chilled her veins. She had a death grip on her phone. "Who is this?"

"*Who is this?* It's your brother," the voice snapped.

Lawrence.

Maggie swallowed. "How did you get this number?"

He hesitated. "A prison guard."

"Prison guards don't hand out phone numbers of family members."

"They do if you bribe them."

Of course, he did. "What do you want?" She was proud of herself. Her voice sounded controlled. Inside, she felt like she was going to be sick.

"Mom's out."

Maggie now understood Stone's harsh words with brutal clarity. *Don't call him that, ever. He's not my dad.*

"And you think that makes it okay for you to call?" She wanted to scream in anger and fear.

"I just thought—"

"What?" Maggie snapped. "That I should know to now look

triple over my shoulder? Because that's what I do. The third monster is back out of jail. Let's terrorize Maggie."

"Maggie, it's not like that—"

"Then what is it like? Enlighten me."

"I didn't mean to upset you. I just thought you should know. Do you know how I can reach Sebastian? He hasn't returned any of my calls."

Maggie felt the blood drain from her face. "Are you fucking with me?"

"What? No."

"Sebastian's dead." She hated herself for saying the words.

Silence met her declaration.

"Did you hear me, you piece of shit? He's dead," she hissed into the phone.

"No … no way. He can't be dead."

"Really? And why's that? You weren't there when he wanted to end his life because he never got over the pain of your betrayal—" A sound very much like a sob rang through the phone, but Maggie ruthlessly pressed on. "You didn't get the call from the police department in another country saying your twin was tortured and murdered."

"Maggie, I'm so sorry—"

"He's been haunted since you guys did what you did, abuse a child to extort money. You're a piece of shit, just like them."

Lawrence broke down. Through shuttering sobs, he apologized. "I'm so sorry, Maggie … please, believe me. What I did was unconscionable."

Maggie's head started spinning. What the fuck was happening?

Her oldest brother pressed on, "I don't blame you for being unable to forgive me, but know I am sorry for my role in the whole mess. I hurt you both, and I'm sorry."

Maggie cupped her forehead in her hand.

"I've been trying to find you two for years—"

"We hid for a reason, asshole."

"Maggie—"

"Don't call me again." With shaking hands, Maggie disconnected the call.

If Lawrence had tracked her down, their parents could, too.

She stumbled to stand, grateful her room had an en suite. She made it into the bathroom. It took her four tries to pull her T-shirt off and the water was on before she realized she was still in her underwear and didn't really care.

She turned up the temperature and stepped into the stream. Hot water sluiced over her body, and she bowed her head, letting the torrent of water rain down on her. A sob escaped, and she pressed her fisted hand to her mouth. Tears mixed with the shower spray as more sobs wracked her body. Maggie dropped to the oversized soaker tub floor, curling into a ball, and tried to quietly release the powder keg of pressure that was her life.

Too late, she realized footsteps were thundering up the stairs. The bathroom door flung open, and Stone stood hand gripping the door handle. "Are you hurt? What's wrong?"

Maggie slid the steamed glass door open. "Stone?"

He came forward, crouching low. She slid her hand out of the shower and grasped his.

"You cried out." Stone squeezed her hand. "I've never heard a sound like that—Christ, Maggie, I thought you were being mauled."

Just on the inside.

For long moments they held hands as tears streamed down her face, and shower spray ran down his arm.

Stone took in her soaked underwear. "Maggie, has something else happened?"

She didn't answer him.

He ran his thumb across the back of her hand. "It's been a hell of a week—"

"My brother called."

Shock registered on his face. "Sebastian's alive."

Miserably, she shook her head. "Lawrence called to tell me

the woman who gave birth to me is out of prison." She met Stone's beautiful gaze. "He found me. And if he can, our parents can. He … he asked how to reach Sebastian."

Stone squeezed her hand. Maggie dropped her forehead to where their hands held each other.

"Did you tell him?"

She nodded against his hand.

Stone leaned forward, pressing his lips against the top of her head.

He shifted. "Uh … I don't want to flood Meredith's bathroom. I can join you in there—with my clothes on," he clarified, "or leave you alone to finish your shower and hold you later. What do you need?"

"You."

Stone shed the cargo shorts he was wearing and stepped into the shower wearing his T-shirt and boxer briefs. She scooted forward to make room as he leaned against the tub's back, and Maggie leaned against him. She had always thought the tub's size ridiculous, but now she was grateful for its wide, deep dimensions.

Stone's arms slid under hers and wrapped around her body. She leaned heavily against his wet shirt. Stone traced a finger across her wrists, the gesture soothing. Maggie tilted her face up. She closed her eyes and let the water pelt her face.

They sat with Stone's strong body wrapped around her, until the water ran cold. She didn't want to move, but her teeth started chattering.

"You're freezing. Let's get you dried off."

Maggie stood and turned off the taps. Stone got out first, finding a towel, and held it out for her. Carefully, she stepped out of the shower, and he wrapped the plush cotton around her.

He grabbed one for himself. "I'll just go lock up. Want me to grab you food or something to drink?"

She smiled, grateful. "There's a knob lock and deadbolt for

the front deck doors, and could you grab the pastry box in the care package?"

He grinned. "Absolutely."

Stone disappeared downstairs, and Maggie peeled off her soaked underthings, toweled the worst of the dampness from her hair, and pulled on a fresh cotton skirt and a tank top in record time.

She slid under the covers and reached for the remote. She rarely used the television in her room at the cottage, but tonight it would be perfect, and she started browsing streaming options. A crack of thunder sounded, making her jump. The wind picked up then, and a pelt of rain splattered against the windows. Soon a steady downpour was tap-dancing against the windows. Maggie couldn't help smiling. She had hoped for a birthday storm.

Stone appeared in the doorway. "Heck of a storm just blew in."

He had changed clothes, too, and was wearing a pair of basketball shorts and a long sleeve T-shirt. He had found one of Meredith's entertaining trays and had covered it in goodies—the pastry box, a bag of red licorice, sparkling water, a couple of oranges, and he had popped microwave popcorn.

Maggie's eyes widened in delight. "Ohmygod, remind me to fall apart near you more often. This looks brilliant!" She waved him over. "We're watching a movie and forgetting how effing tired we are and how bullshit families can be."

"I'll snack to that. There are pizza things in the freezer if you want."

She waved him off. "Let's start with this. If we're still hungry, we know where they are."

He stepped forward but hesitated. "I should stay on top of the covers."

"Fuck that. I heard your teeth chattering, too. You can come in—only because you brought epic snacks." It was a bald-faced lie. She would have curled into him in a heartbeat, snacks or not.

He handed her the tray and slid under the covers, propping pillows behind his back like she had. Maggie positioned the tray between them and popped a few kernels of popcorn in her mouth. "Man, sometimes it's the little things." She reached over and opened the pastry box lid. A Chelsea bun glistened inside. She waggled her fingers. "Don't mind if I do." She looked up. "What do Australians call Chelsea buns?"

Stone leaned over and ripped off a piece. "Chelsea buns."

"Right."

He popped a piece of the sticky treat into his mouth. "What do you want to watch?"

Maggie rattled off a handful of titles.

Stone made a slicing motion with his hands. "No global espionage or international crime syndicates."

"Too close to home?" Maggie teased. "Fine. I can go rom-com —ooh, how about a dark one? Wait, wait, I got it, a Jane Austin remake?"

Stone dove for the remote, nearly upending the tray of snacks. Maggie dodged just at the last minute. "Not a chance."

Stone pushed the tray farther down the bed before launching himself to grab the remote out of her far hand. He landed, half-sprawled across her.

"Are you quite done?" She laughed between gasping breaths, still holding the remote out of reach. It was a welcome lightness, and she was enjoying this revelry immensely.

She held up her index finger. "It's all fun and games until the snacks tip over."

"Good point." Stone resettled his hand in the bag of red licorice.

They finally settled on *Thor: Ragnarok*. Stone had never seen it, and Maggie got a kick out of hearing his fully-bellied laughter. As the credits rolled, the popcorn was long gone, the oranges still sat on the tray, and the package of licorice and Chelsea bun had serious dents in them. Sometime during the movie, Maggie had curled into Stone, her head on his shoulder and her arm wrapped around his deliciously chiseled torso. "Thank you, I needed that."

His arm draped across her shoulders tightened around her, and he dropped a kiss on the top of her head.

"It wasn't always awful," she whispered.

She felt him still but was glad he didn't move his arm wrapped around her shoulders.

"I mean, it wasn't ideal, but it got progressively worse until …" she trailed off. What could she say?

"Is Lawrence like your parents?" Stone's gentle voice gave Maggie an unexpected strength. "He apologized," she whispered. "I think he meant it. He didn't know about Sebastian."

Stone pressed himself closer to her. She didn't think he realized that he even did it. "Did you think Lawrence had something to do with what happened to Sebastian?"

She shrugged. "Maybe. I mean, it definitely crossed my mind. With those three, nothing surprises me anymore. Lawrence was part of the extortion plan. His job was to lure Sebastian and gaslight me." Her stomach did its familiar flop—it physically hurt when she thought about how stupid she had been, ten-year-old or not. What if she would have guessed sooner what they were about? Could she have saved Sebastian from that trauma? And what about Lawrence? "In my more generous moments, I've wondered if Lawrence had a choice. Sebastian and I were always a team, but Lawrence, who was eight years older than us, was alone with them for so long. There was no one else to weather those storms with. No wonder he turned out the way he had. Sebastian and I at least had each other." Maggie tilted her head back, looking at Stone. "Am I an idiot to think he's sorry?"

Stone's smile was sad. "I'm the wrong person to ask."

Maggie straightened, shifting to look at him. "But I am asking you. Do you think people can change?"

CHAPTER THIRTY-NINE

Maggie's gaze pinned Stone in place. *Could people change?*

"God, I hope so." He uttered the words with matching intensity, wishing like hell they were true.

"Me, too." Her smile slipped. "Maybe it's too big an ask. What Lawrence did, what he was part of … it was pretty bad."

Familiar anger bubbled in Stone. "Bruce never changed."

"He was always that bad?"

"After he died, a bunch of cold cases were solved. Bruce had been murdering sex trafficked women for years. The trophies and pictures were discovered after he died."

"What happened to him?"

Adrenaline, mixed with something a little too close to shame, filled him. "Why do you ask?"

"Stone?"

A bead of sweat rolled down the inside of his arm. Christ, his first assignment had gone better than this. "I mean, what do you mean?"

Stone had never second-guessed his decision. However, the thought of Maggie knowing what he had done—or rather *hadn't* done, deeply shamed him. There was no way she could understand.

"You all right?"

"What do you want from me?" Stone held his hands wide. "The monster's dead. He overdosed."

Maggie was eying him. "Yes, but—"

Stone interrupted, "There is no 'but.'"

She placed a gentle hand on his arm. He winced when she started rubbing his skin with the pad of her thumb.

"Stone, what's wrong?"

He just shook his head. There was no way he was telling Maggie he watched his biological father overdose when he held a Naloxone kit in his hands.

She ducked her head, trying to catch his gaze. He turned his head away. Indecision warred within him. She gave his arm a tender shake. "I've been through hell and came out the other side. Whatever it is, I can handle it."

"Don't say that. You don't know what I'm capable of."

She leaned back. "You're trying to scare me." The space between them felt like a widening chasm. Good. She was too good for him, and the sooner she realized that the better off she'd be. He had been a selfish idiot each time he had kissed her. "Gabe's right, I'm no good—"

"He said that?" Her voice was sharp, defensive on Stone's behalf.

Stone gave a cold laugh. "Not to my face. I overheard him talking to his brothers."

"They're your brothers, too."

"No, Maggie, they're not. There is no way I can ever belong to the Tanners. Becca can invite me for every holiday, but it can't erase where I came from. What I am."

"Don't fucking say it—"

"*Bastard.*"

Her hand shot up so fast he registered the sting on his cheek before he realized she had slapped him. Instinctively, he brought his hand up to his smarting cheek. "What the hell was that for?"

"You're being a dick—"

"I'm trying to protect you." Stone scooted to the edge of the bed, glaring at her over his shoulder. Maggie scrambled to her knees, following him across the bed in her long cotton skirt, nearly upending the tray. She pushed at his shoulders, trying to turn him around to face her. "If you would have let me finish, you would know you're being a dick *to yourself.* Knock it off."

He stared at her, incredulous. "That's ridiculous."

"No, I'm making perfect sense. Your stubbornness is ridiculous." She was kneeling, pressing close. Stone gripped her shoulders, stopping her. "I'm not—just give it a rest. I shouldn't have kissed you." Even as he said it, he was staring at her mouth. "Just stop defending me. You don't know what I've done."

She lifted her hands, cupping his face. "So, tell me."

Her hands were so hot against his cheeks, her body so close. Fuck, he was going to start hyperventilating if she got any closer. He didn't want to talk. He wanted to be inside her. Instead, he used the truth to shield her from him. "I watched him die," Stone spat.

Her hands hesitated before dropping to her sides. "Who?"

He held her gaze, needing her to understand he really was a bastard. "I had a Naloxone kit in my hand, and I watched Bruce overdose in front of me. I let that fucker die when I could have saved him, so don't tell me I'm not a bastard, that I deserve to be part of their family. I let their dad die." When he was done, his breath came out in pants, and his heart was racing.

Maggie sat back on her heels. "Wow. That is really fucking heavy."

Stone waited for her to leave.

"I'm *so* sorry you had to experience that. That's, awful."

"Did you even hear me?" Stone had expected her disgust, had counted on it. Her compassion was undoing him. He stood up, putting space between them. "I'm not a good guy."

"You keep saying that."

"And I mean it." He was angry. "You shouldn't want anything to do with me." His own father hadn't.

"Yeah, you barged into my twin brother's apartment in Paris when I was getting my ass kicked by assassins. You saved my life."

"That was one time."

She laughed at him. "How many times do you want me to get my ass kicked?"

He sobered. "Never. Do you understand me? I want you safe and out of harm's way—"

Her gaze didn't leave his. "Put the tray on the floor, Stone."

"Maggie—"

"*Stone*," she retorted. Her tone demanded obedience while promising he'd *really* like it.

His hand moved of its own accord, pulling the tray over. He placed it on the floor, toeing it out of the way. When Maggie slipped her hands around her body and grasped the hem of her tank top, his dick stirred to life. With excruciating patience, she pulled the soft cotton up, revealing toned, soft skin. Stone let out a huff of air as her hands rose higher, revealing the most beautiful pair of breasts he had ever seen. She ducked her head out of the top, shy now.

He clamored closer, kneeling before her on the bed, his hands ready to cradle her waist. He hesitated. She put her hands over his and pressed his to her sides before scooting them upward, guiding his palms to her breasts. They both exhaled with a sigh.

With his hands busy kneading her breasts, she reached for the hem of his T-shirt before flattening her hands and sliding her palms under his shirt. He sucked in his breath. She slid her hands up his stomach. The basketball shorts he wore were tented fiercely. She pushed him to a sitting position against the headboard before hiking up her skirt enough to straddle him. She settled against his hardness, a couple of layers of fabric the only thing separating them.

Her hands gripped the headboard on either side of his head, and she dipped her head, pressing her mouth against his. He traced her upper lip with his tongue.

"I want to see you," she whispered, grabbing the hem of his T-shirt and pulling it up.

The front door opened downstairs.

Stone stilled Maggie's hands. "Are you expecting company?"

She shook her head before firing her tank top back over her head. "Follow me."

"Stay here—" Stone hissed, desperate to keep her safe.

"I know where the creaky floorboards are," she whispered back, already off the bed. Stone reached for her but missed. Maggie was already making a circuitous path to the door. She plucked a decorative glass sphere off the dresser by the door. From the way she was carrying it, it had some heft. Silently, he followed her route. The floorboards remained dutifully silent.

She stopped in the doorway, visibly rattled, when she saw the gun he was holding. In a voice barely louder than an exhale, she asked, "Where the hell was that?"

Stone had retrieved the gun from the side compartment of his backpack, though he only shook his head once. He went to pass her, but she grabbed his hand, pulling him down the hall, away from the stairs. At the end of the hall was a reading area. The second-story oversized windows would give the impression of sitting within the forest canopy in daylight.

Maggie ran her hand across the adjacent wall paneling, and a narrow panel swung open without a sound. Maggie slipped inside the blackness, disappearing. Christ, she was going to get herself killed. He didn't know any civilian who flung themselves into danger so readily. Stone followed, moving sideways to fit his wide shoulders into the narrow shaft. His feet found the rungs of a ladder, and he maneuvered the gun to negotiate the descent.

His feet found solid flooring. They were in a short narrow hallway of sorts. It looked like three access points converged, though it was too dark to be certain. Before he could whisper for her to stay put, Maggie pressed her finger to his lips. She must not have trusted he understood because she gripped his chin and gave it a firm shake. In other words, *shut the fuck up*.

He nodded. She still gripped his chin and felt his acquiescence.

Maggie let go before slipping silently through the second exit.

CHAPTER FORTY

Maggie's heart was beating fast, and her palms were sweating as she gripped the weighted glass sculpture tighter. She had managed the ladder with it. If she dropped it now, it might be the last mistake she made. She was sick to death of fighting for her life—she spun around, pressing her forefinger to Stone's lips. He had been going to say something, probably something sensible like *wait in the fucking secret passageway*. But she wasn't going to wait. She might not carry a gun, but she had taken years of training. She sure as shit would not let Stone fight her battles for her. The thought of him getting hurt because of her brought physical pain to her chest. So, she gripped his chin and willed him to keep quiet.

He followed her through the second exit into the walk-in kitchen pantry. The pantry door was closed and frosted with a thin, repeating design patterned in clear glass. Muffled voices could be heard. Carefully, Maggie tiptoed across the unnecessarily large space, stopping at the door. A low moan sounded. Maggie leaned forward, peeking through a narrow arc of clear glass, and caught herself before she gasped.

Two figures were in the kitchen. Suddenly the tone of the

moan made sense. She spun around, ushering Stone to back-track. He thankfully obliged without protest.

With record speed, they crept back upstairs the way they came.

"What is it?"

Maggie was fluttering her hand in front of her face, the image seared in her mind's eye. "I should have known. It's the long weekend."

"Known what?"

Embarrassment flooded her. She had gotten an eyeful. "Do I have to spell it out for you?"

"You haven't spelled anything out."

"Savannah and Gabe," she wailed.

"That's who was in the kitchen? Their timing sucks, but come on, we should let them know we're here." He started in the direction of the main staircase.

Maggie grabbed Stone's arm. "We can't."

"Why not?" His arm was warm under her palm.

"Because they're having sex on the island counter right now."

Stone blinked before barging past Maggie. "We can interrupt."

"Are you nuts?"

Stone eluded her grasp. "They interrupted us." He trotted down the main stairs, calling out. "Gabe, bro, is that you?"

Maggie chased after him. She caught up in the kitchen and winced. Her best friend was straddling Gabe as intimately as a woman could straddle a man on the oversized island counter. Neither had a stitch of clothing on.

"We didn't see anything," Maggie said, her gaze firmly on Stone. She locked her fingers around his biceps, as much as she could anyway, and pulled. "Sack of bricks, you're coming with me." She hauled Stone out of the kitchen and pushed him into the living room.

Stone hooked his thumb over his shoulder. "Did you see

that? Christ, that's a slate counter. Her knees must be killing her."

"Are you out of your fucking mind?" How could someone capable of such compassion have such a jerk side? "That's my best friend and the man she loves. Why in the world did you do that?"

Stone had the grace to bow his head. For a second, she thought he would apologize, but he ran both hands through his hair and straightened. She could see where a muscle ticked on his stubbled jaw. "You don't know Gabe like I do."

"You don't know Gabe at all," she countered. "And you sure as hell don't know Savannah. *Do not* disrespect her again. Is that clear?"

His eyes were defiant and hurt. "Crystal."

Gabe stormed into the living room, looking ready to murder his half-brother. "What the hell was that all about?" At least he was clothed. He wore an alternative band graphic T-shirt and cargo shorts. His feet were bare. Maggie had never noticed how big they were.

Savannah entered wearing a turquoise sundress, piling her hair in a knot at the back of her head, and fastening a clip around it. "Honey, you promised you'd use your inside voice."

Gabe grunted, arms folded across his massive chest.

Savannah's gaze found Maggie's. For a split second, fear lodged in Maggie's throat, but Savannah ran to her. Maggie met her halfway. They were wrapped in each other's arms, and Maggie held on tight. Tears started streaming down her face, and she ducked her head in shame. She should have confided in Savannah years ago.

Savannah pulled back but cupped her hands around Maggie's cheeks. "What is it? I thought you were in France."

"I was."

Savannah dropped her hands, looking between Maggie and Stone. "What's he doing here?"

Maggie swiped the tears from her eyes. "I went to my twin

brother's apartment in Paris and was attacked. Stone saved my life."

"Holy shit, are you all right?" Savannah's face was so stricken.

"I am, thanks to Stone. He took me to the Canadian embassy, and the vehicle we were in exploded."

"*What?*" Savannah turned to her man. Gabe might be an archaeologist now, but he had been a CSIS agent. Gabe rushed to Savannah's side, draping a strong arm around her shoulders. "Maggie's here and safe." But he looked at Stone, who gave a small shake of his head.

"You followed Teague Alans to Paris."

Stone nodded.

"Maggie's brother is connected to Teague Alans?" Christ, Gabe connected the dots fast. This time Maggie answered. "Teague Alans had my brother tortured and left for dead."

"Oh, Maggie." Savannah left Gabe's arms and wrapped her arms around Maggie again. Maggie hugged her back, whispering, "He's not dead."

Savannah pulled back. "Because you would feel it."

Maggie nodded. Savannah hugged her again tight, before asking. "Do you know where he is?"

"That's why we're here. He left a clue. He has a boat in the Venus Marina here."

Gabe frowned. "That won't be open until Tuesday."

Maggie fisted her hands and swore. Goddammit, she needed something to go right.

"It's the long weekend. You know how it can be up here," Savannah said apologetically.

"Right." Maggie swallowed the frustrated anger. "We'll go on Tuesday."

Stone looked at Gabe. "Want to check tomorrow?"

Gabe cracked his first smile. "Sure."

Maggie pressed her fingers to her temples. Her head was throbbing. "You just said it was closed."

"It is." Gabe looked at Savannah. "That good?"

She nodded, and Maggie was as confused as fuck. "You just said—*oh*." They were going to break in. "Shouldn't I go? I might be able to notice something you don't."

"I'll look tomorrow. If it's safe, I promise I'll take you when it's open." Stone turned to Savannah. "Gabe will just be lookout. He'll be safe." Gabe started to object, but Stone reasoned, "You've been out of the game, and you've got Savannah. The stakes are too high for you. I'll go in alone. I just need you to work your perimeter magic—or are the stories untrue?"

Gabe gave another of his grunt sounds. "They're true."

"Good."

Maggie swallowed hard. Stone would willingly walk into danger, alone, to keep Gabe—whom he hated—safe because he had Savannah. The man should come with a translation manual.

Savannah shot Maggie a look, and Maggie gave her a sad smile. "It's complicated. Stone's boss thinks I'm in conspiracy with that Teague Alans guy."

"What the fuck?"

Savannah didn't swear, and it spoke to just how alarming the whole damn situation was. She looked around. "Are we in danger here?"

Maggie looked to Stone. "None of our intel suggests this location has been compromised."

Gabe asked, "How long?"

Stone glanced at Maggie before answering, "Long enough."

A sick feeling crept in. "Have you been following me?" Was this whole thing a setup? He had asked her what she was doing in Sebastian's apartment, but what if Stone and all his covert colleagues had expected her? What if—

"Are you seriously asking me that?" The look on his face twisted her insides. Maggie answered, "I don't know what to think."

"Let me know when you do." He turned to Gabe and Savannah. "I apologize for walking in on you two. Now, if you'll excuse me, I'm going to bed." Stone headed upstairs. Maggie tracked his retreating form with her gaze. He didn't look back.

"What was that all about?" Savannah asked.

Maggie blinked back tears. Stone's icy retreat had cut her to the quick. "It's just been a shitty several days for all of us. I just want to find Sebastian safe, go back to Alberta, and put all this behind me." It wasn't the whole truth. She didn't want Stone to be something she left behind. Stubborn and grumpy though he was, Stone was an unexpected ray of sunshine in the darkness that had descended after Sebastian's murder case.

Savannah squeezed her hand. "We're here if you need us."

Maggie nodded her thanks and retreated upstairs. She heard Savannah and Gabe's murmuring voices continue. Their intimate closeness had never felt so acutely painful, and for a half second, Maggie missed how it used to be. Even with half a continent between them, she and Savannah had remained undeniable best friends. But life moved ever forward, and Gabe was Savannah's best friend now. Maggie didn't begrudge her friend's happiness. She just keenly felt the loss.

At the top of the stairs, Maggie hesitated, seeing the closed door next to hers. Stone. She wanted to barge in, make him talk to her, make him assure her they were okay.

But they weren't.

Instead of following her heart, she knew it would be best to retreat to her own room. Alone, like she always was.

It was better this way.

So why did she feel like her heart was breaking?

CHAPTER FORTY-ONE

S
tone paced the elegant cottage room. It had been a dick move, busting in on Gabe and his woman, but Maggie taking Gabe's side had made Stone go a little crazy. He stopped, rubbing his aching chest and breathing low.

With old practice, he hardened his heart and shut down. Better to know now where Maggie's loyalties were, and it wasn't with him. She might like his kisses, might want to fuck him, but he was disposable, just like his mom had been to Bruce Tanner. Maybe he should thank Maggie. Before, Stone hadn't even rated high enough to be used first. He'd simply been discarded by Bruce, then Gabe. Thrown away like yesterday's trash.

Floorboards creaked in the hall, and Stone stilled.

Maggie stood outside his closed door. He would know her footsteps anywhere.

In a rush, he crossed the distance and swung open his door.

Maggie gasped. "Uh—hi."

"What do you want?" God, he sounded as much as a bear as he felt.

She pushed past him and into his room, rushing out, "I'm sorry I slapped you."

Stone closed the door, not wanting the audience downstairs. "When?" He remembered.

She stared at him, incredulous. "In my room, before we almost—"

Stone took a step closer. "Before we what? Had sex? We both know it wouldn't have come to that, and that has nothing to do with my douche half-brother interrupting us."

Maggie held up both hands. "Woah, Gabe's awesome. Savannah dated a douche before. Gabe's not it. So drop whatever bullshit that is. I'm apologizing. As infuriating as you are, I shouldn't have done that. I was upset you were berating yourself, but I shouldn't have slapped you."

He took a step back, crossing his arms. "Fine. Apology accepted. Forget about it."

Her eyes narrowed. "What do you mean we wouldn't have had sex? We were halfway there."

"It's late. Go to bed, Maggie."

She put her hand on his arm. "Stone?"

Her touch was like a brand. He didn't like it. She had made her choice, and it wasn't him. Stone would wrap up this case and put Teague Alans behind bars or six feet under. It really didn't matter. If Sebastian were alive, it would be safe for him to come out of hiding if that was what he was doing. Stone would have no reason to ever see Maggie again, and he could lick his wounds in peace. "Don't touch me."

"I want to touch you."

More like shred him. "No."

She stepped closer. "Why not?"

He couldn't think when she was this close. He could smell her shampoo's earthy fragrance and fought the desire to bury his face in her hair and inhale all his hurts away. He turned away from her. It was a tactical error. The bed loomed in front of him. In disgust, he spun around, arms wide. "Because I'm not as disposable as everyone seems to think."

Her eyes widened. "When have I ever—"

"About twenty minutes ago was the last time, but since I've met you, you've made it clear your loyalties are with Gabe and Savannah. I'm the idiot who hasn't let it sink in. I'm just some ogre you make out with until I piss you off."

"Savannah and Gabe," she said quietly.

"That's what I said." But it wasn't. Maggie was loyal to Savannah, and it was Savannah's trust and loyalty to Gabe that looped Maggie into his orbit. When Stone finally met her gaze, she whispered, "You're not disposable. You're precious to me."

He flinched.

"You're precious," she repeated, sliding her arms up his crossed ones. She leaned forward, dropping soft kisses on his forearm, then the other. Her quiet words and gentle touches ripped him open.

Stone looked down, ashamed and unable to meet her eyes. "I have been my whole life. I can't anymore."

"Am I?"

Stone whipped his head up. "Of course not."

"My parents used Sebastian and me, and our grandparents purposely tore us apart, dumped us on separate continents. I'm asking you, does that make me trash? Undeserving of love or care or loyalty?"

Stone cupped Maggie's soft face, kissing away the falling tears. "Never."

She gripped his forearms, holding him close. "Neither are you." She stood on tiptoe and pressed her lips to his. Stone staggered backward, wrapping his arms around her as his tongue found hers. She pressed closer, trailing her mouth down his neck.

"*Maggie.*"

"God, I love how you say my name." She pressed closer still, her body tight against his erection. "*This* is sacred, what's between us. I had every intention of feeling you fill me before we had to ... pause."

Stone shuttered. He had never been so hard in his life. "Does that mean I can press play?"

She breathed into his ear. "Oh yeah."

His hands shot down to her middle sliding low before he stilled. "Is this all right?"

She laughed, guiding his hand deeper in answer.

Heaven and earth met inside her. "Christ, you're wet." He buried his face against her shoulder, overcome with the depth of feeling coursing through him. He teased and dipped. Her unabashed pleasure made him feel like he was soaring. He scooped her up and placed her on the end of the bed.

"What are you doing?"

"You said something about sacred. I want to worship you." Stone kneeled next to the end of the bed, hooking Maggie's legs over his shoulders. "This okay?"

She nodded, laying back enough to prop herself up on her elbows, watching him. Stone slid his hands up her legs, hiking up her long skirt—she wore nothing under it. His eyes snapped to hers, and she gave him Lilith's smile. "I wasn't kidding. I wanted you then, and I want you now."

Stone closed his eyes. His cock couldn't get any harder. He leaned forward, pressing his mouth to her. He nearly came at the sound she made. His lips and tongue worshiped her.

"Stone," she pleaded, bucking under his attention. "Now … now."

He moved, crawling on top of her before swearing graphically.

"What?" Maggie's voice was filled with alarm.

He was in physical pain. "I don't have a fucking condom."

"I do," she rasped.

He popped his head up. "Are you serious?"

She laughed, pointing to the en suite. "Our rooms share a bathroom. My shower bag. I stocked up after running into you in Paris."

Stone was halfway to the bathroom. "When? We were glued

to each other's hips." He found several foil packets in her red shower bag. Grabbing a handful, he hustled back to the bed.

"Charles de Gaulle," she answered. She was curled in his bed and held the covers out to him.

He sheathed himself and slowly crawled under the covers and over Maggie. "We were fighting at the airport."

"So? I was hoping for makeup sex." Her smile was shy, and it nearly undid him. He lowered his head, kissing her fiercely. She met his passion, wiggling under him until her thighs were on either side of his hips. She wrapped her heels behind him. "Stone, slide into me."

He did as she said.

CHAPTER FORTY-TWO

M aggie woke up smiling and stretched. She and Stone had spent as many hours talking as they had making love. Her body felt better than it had in days.

Maybe years.

Sunlight streamed in from tall windows, last night's storm long gone. She watched two sparrows flitter through the forest canopy. It was a beautiful birthday. "Happy birthday, Seb," Maggie whispered. She quickly washed up and got dressed before heading downstairs to the kitchen.

The kitchen radio, hanging under one of the cabinets, was playing quietly. Meredith always had the radio on when she was here, and Maggie smiled as nostalgia swept through her.

A birthday cake sat proudly on the kitchen island. It dipped a bit to one side, and the frosting looked more enthusiastic than tidy. She leaned closer. Chopped red licorice was sprinkled over the top like confetti. After the events of last night, Maggie was surprised Savannah had remembered. That her friend stayed up to make it made Maggie's heart feel warm and loved.

"Happy birthday!" Savannah's voice was overly bright.

"You made me birthday cake. Thank you!"

Savannah made a face behind her coffee mug. "It wasn't me."

Maggie stilled. "Stone did this?"

"It wasn't Gabe. I've seen his cakes, this one's standing. It's not his handiwork."

Maggie pressed her hands to her face, warmed by Stone's thoughtfulness and ingenuity. She was surprised Meredith would have had the ingredients to make a cake at the cottage.

She busied herself, pouring coffee, hiding her reaction. She had slept in. She didn't realize it had been *that* late. "Where are the guys?"

"Gabe's kayaking, and I haven't seen Stone."

Maggie quelled the panic rising in her stomach. He wouldn't have left her. She took her time doctoring her coffee, pulling herself together. When she turned around, Savannah was looking at her closely. "*Oh my god,* you had sex with him."

Maggie darted her gaze, making sure they were alone in the kitchen. "Keep your voice down."

"You don't even date. How did you two get to *sex* in less than a week … it was a week, right?"

The spacious kitchen suddenly felt claustrophobic. "Why are we cooped up inside on such a beautiful day? Let's go outside." Maggie led the way onto the back deck. The sun-warmed forest smelled of maple and pine, and birdsong filled the air. A few pine cones had dropped onto the deck. In a couple of months, the deck would be filled with fallen deciduous leaves.

Maggie sat in one of the plush oversized chairs, her legs curled to the side under her, with a death grip on her coffee mug.

Savannah settled herself on the deck's garden couch. "Okay, spill."

Maggie stared at her coffee. "It started on New Years."

Savannah's mouth dropped open. "You two have been banging since January? How did I not know this?"

Heat warmed Maggie's cheeks. "It's not like that!"

Savannah took a sip of her coffee before softly clearing her throat. "What's it like?"

Maggie rubbed her forehead. "Christmas was so great—I've thanked you for inviting me, right?"

"Like a million times, don't change the subject."

Maggie's lips quirked. "I'm not. Becca's eco-inn is so beautiful, and everything was so perfect. Friends and family who actually like each other, the food—*oh my god*, the food and wine were incredible, the mountains and horseback riding ... everything was just so *sensual*. Did you notice we were surrounded by beautiful people, like *everyone* was hot."

Savannah laughed. "Yes, and you, darling, fit right in."

Maggie rolled her eyes. "I'm a librarian, not an international spy, or scientist, or world-renowned journalist."

"Librarians should rule the world, but your point?"

Maggie shrugged. "Stone was so ... *male*. And single and leaving."

Savannah raised an eyebrow. "There were like five other smoking hot, single men that left after the holidays."

Maggie snapped her head up. "There were?"

Savannah laughed. "Yes. I'm surprised you missed them."

Maggie hadn't noticed. She had eyes only for Stone. She shrugged. "Everything was just so beautiful and perfect. New Years was so special, and he felt so safe—"

Savannah's face melted. "Oh, Maggie, that's wonderful!"

"Is it? I'm hooked on a man I know barely anything about. Besides, he's got a hate-on for my best friend's boyfriend."

"Fiancé," Savannah corrected, holding up her left hand. A Celtic knotted band of white gold held a brilliant emerald.

Maggie squealed in delight, bounding over to the couch for a hug and a closer look. "Anna! It's beautiful! Why didn't you tell me?"

"It just happened."

"When?"

"Last night."

Maggie blanched. "*Ohmygod*, and we interrupted."

Savannah splayed her hand over her eyes. "That was so embarrassing. I thought Gabe was going to kill Stone."

Maggie winced. None of the Tanner siblings realized the anger Stone carried over Gabe's role in his estrangement from them. She covered it by asking, "How did he propose?"

Savannah smiled. "In the rain, and that's all I'm sharing."

Maggie hooted with laughter. "Of *course*, he did." The wild storm last night would have been the perfect setting. It wasn't the first time rain would have brought them together. She sighed. "Congratulations, I'm thrilled for you two."

Savannah smiled, tracing her forefinger over the engagement ring. She hesitated. Finally, she looked up. "Why didn't you tell me you were coming to Ontario?"

Maggie's heart lurched. She wasn't sure she wanted to have this conversation. "Everything happened so fast."

"You also didn't tell me about Sebastian. Maggie, that must be awful for you to carry on your own. I could have—"

"Could have what?" Maggie gripped her coffee mug tighter. "It's different. Now that—" She broke off, unwilling to finally voice the distance she had been feeling since Gabe thundered into Savannah's life, usurping Maggie's role as best friend and confidant. Maggie lived in Calgary and Savannah in Toronto, but they had kept their friendship stronger than ever.

Until Gabe.

Savannah and Gabe were the first couple Maggie had ever met that completely loved each other, which was beautiful and also made her redundant. He was also better at being Savannah's best friend. Gabe had managed to help Savannah mend the disastrous rift she had with her parents. Maggie had never been able to stomach encouraging Savannah to try.

"It is different between us, and I'm sorry. I never meant for that to happen."

Maggie's smile was real. "Never apologize for being happy."

Savannah's eyes teared up, her voice a whisper when she

said, "I never knew I could be this happy or love someone this much. It's almost spooky."

Maggie launched herself onto the couch and wrapped Savannah in a fierce hug, keeping their coffees upright with acrobatic ingenuity. "Hang onto that. Hang onto him."

Savannah clutched Maggie tighter. Savannah hadn't had an easy go of things, and as much as Maggie missed her best friend, she would never begrudge her happiness and the love of a good man.

"I love you," Maggie murmured, giving Savannah another squeeze.

"I love you, too." They pulled apart, both wiping at their eyes. Savannah's eyes sparkled. "So, you and Stone."

Maggie shook her head. "It's not what you think. We fight like cats and dogs."

"Mmm hmm." Savannah took a sip of her coffee. "How, then, did his penis end up inside of you?"

Maggie's mouth dropped open. "Anna!"

She smiled like a Cheshire cat. "What? You've been celibate for like ever. How was he?"

Maggie felt her cheeks flush. "Really good."

A nagging feeling crept in. Maggie didn't want to want someone else, let alone someone like Stone. He was too potent, too virile, and he made her feel things she didn't want to feel.

Savannah paused. "*Why* was he?"

Maggie knew what her friend was asking. Maggie didn't do romantic relationships, never had—she didn't trust them. As a rule, she didn't count on others, and she had already leaned on Stone way more than she should. It was inexplicable. "He's different, and before you ask how—I don't know. He just *is*."

Savannah's face lit up. "Good."

"That's it?" Savannah usually had stronger opinions on everything.

"Not even close, but you'll figure it out." Savannah turned

her gaze away from Maggie and looked past the tree canopy to the water below. "Is it oddly quiet for a long weekend?"

Maggie followed her gaze. Sun sparkled on the water as two kayakers and a canoe hugged the shoreline. A few speedboats were making the run from town farther down. Puffy clouds dotted the western horizon, but clear skies were overhead. "There're no wake boats."

Savannah settled deeper into the couch, closing her eyes. "Don't jinx it. They'll be tearing it up soon enough. Let's just enjoy this magical peace now."

It wasn't magic. It was Stone.

Maggie was sure of it.

She had wished for rain to chase away the disruptive lake crowds, and that man had figured out how to give her the gift of peace. She settled deeper into the plush deck chair, smiling into her coffee. It was a beautiful start to her birthday.

A siren split through the air.

"I hate hearing that sound." Savannah shuddered. Maggie agreed. It likely wouldn't be the last one they heard over the long weekend.

Savannah adjusted her sunglasses. "What do you want to do for your birthday?"

Maggie wanted to break into the Venus Marina and her twin brother's boat to find any clues that would help her and Stone find Sebastian alive and safe.

And something to put Teague Alans away forever.

"Let's start with that Chelsea bun and more coffee and go from there?"

CHAPTER FORTY-THREE

S tone pulled himself out of the water, taking care with the dive pouch holding two fistfuls of spark plugs and the fins he had found in the boathouse that hung from his wrist as he climbed out. It was still early in the season, and the water was cool. He had been at his task for a few hours and would have preferred a wetsuit to the tight swim shorts he wore.

With relaxed ease, he climbed the angular boulders protecting the elevated bridge bank like he had every right to. Once on the single-lane bridge deck, he stood, taking in the overall splendor of trees, rocks, and water of this cottage country. The sun had long cleared the horizon, the sky shifting from the pinks and purples of early morning to a rosy, orange glow, and now the starting blue of a bright day.

Maggie would love this spot. She had blustered into his life as bright as a sunrise while masking the churning depths within. She was straightforward and complicated, bright while mysterious. *Sacred.* She had called him that when she had welcomed him into her body. The woman was next level on everything.

Stone had awoken to the feel of her pressed against the length of his body, making his whole self feel a completeness he had never experienced. He had imprinted the moment in his mind like a treasured still frame.

Happy birthday, Maggie.

"Good morning."

Stone spun around at the unexpected greeting. Two older women were walking toward him. They wore stylized yoga pants and designer windbreakers. Stone smiled politely and inclined his head, cringing when they stopped.

"We haven't seen you before. Did you buy the Sweet's place?" the one with the orange jacket asked.

The other one in pink nudged her, whispering, "He's staying at Meredith's."

"*Oh.*" The other one perked up considerably. "Are you one of Ruth's friends, dear?"

Stone kept his face blank. He had never had senior citizens looking at him with such steamy speculation. He suddenly felt very naked in his wet shorts and bare torso and crossed his arms. He started to back away. "If you'll excuse me, ladies."

A kayak was gliding through the water below, just approaching the bridge. The soft dip of the paddle was rhythmic and peaceful until he recognized it was Gabe. He knew the second his half-brother recognized him. Gabe's massive shoulders looked ready to snap the paddle in half. Their gazes locked as the sound of an outboard engine could be heard in the distance. Damn, he should have included all outboards in his morning activities.

Orange Jacket pointed, "That's that nice young man, Savannah's fella."

Pink Jacket waved. "Hi, Gabe!"

Gabe dutifully waved back, bobbing behind the middle bridge pilings. "Hi Mrs. Kademan, Mrs. Pohlkamp."

Mrs. Pohlkamp leaned forward. "He's such a nice young man, so well-mannered." She had to raise her voice to be heard over the whine of the incoming engine.

Stone had a different take on Gabe but only nodded sagely to the older women.

Mrs. Kademan eyed the incoming powerboat. "He's not slowing down." A second engine sounded. A personal watercraft was overtaking the speedboat.

Mrs. Pohlkamp's eyes widened. "It's not enough they race on the four hundred. Now we have to put up with it on the lake?"

Stone's belly started to churn in foreboding. The two watercraft were arcing at top speed toward the bridge. He spun around, waving his arms, shouting to Gabe in warning.

Gabe had nowhere to go.

The full-sized boat thundered under the bridge on the deeper side of the piling as the jet ski raced through the shallow side. Gabe had nosed the kayak against the center piling and leaned forward, but the jet ski cut the turn short, trying to cut off the speed boat, and instead, rammed the kayak. Gabe's big body slammed against the racing speedboat.

Stone jumped over the bridge, feet first, aiming for the deepest froth. His body slipped through the leaping waves, ricocheting inside the tight space between the bridge piling and shore. His bare feet found the channel's bottom. From the sting, his left one had sliced open. He opened his eyes underwater, arcing his arms to spin himself around, looking for Gabe. The visibility was nil through the kicked-up sediment and chop. Stone popped up treading water and frantically scanning the surface.

From the bridge deck, Mrs. Kademan pointed. "There!"

Stone dove where she pointed. Kicking his feet and splaying his arms, desperate to find his half-brother. He kicked deeper, lungs screaming. Finally, his sweeping fingers brushed against something solid. Gabe wasn't moving. Stone ran his hands until he found Gabe's armpits and looped his arms through and across Gabe's chest, kicking off the bottom.

They broke the surface of the water, Gabe hanging lifeless from Stone's arm. The shallow side had a narrow strip of sand,

and Stone side-armed Gabe to it, dragged him up the miniature beach and started CPR.

Mrs. Pohlkamp and Mrs. Kademan appeared at his side.

Mrs. Kademan held up her phone. "We've called 911. They're on the phone now." Mrs. Pohlkamp flung off her jacket and bunched it up, pressing the soft cotton liner to a nasty laceration on Gabe's leg. He was losing a lot of blood fast, but it wouldn't matter if he didn't start breathing.

"You do the chest compressions. I'll breathe for him." Mrs. Kademan commanded. She had already handed Mrs. Pohlkamp her phone and positioned herself at Gabe's head, chin held, nose plugged. She breathed into him. Once. Twice. "*Go.*" Stone pumped his half-brother's chest.

"*Me,*" Mrs. Kademan breathed into Gabe, two full, solid breaths. "Go."

Over and over, they repeated compressions and breaths.

Stone winced as he felt Gabe's rib or sternum crack under his palms. Even knowing he needed to press that hard to circulate blood and oxygen until Gabe would, on his own, he shuddered at causing him pain.

Mrs. Kademan finished the breath. "Go!"

Stone pumped his brother's chest.

"Come on, Gabe. Come back."

Please, come back.

CHAPTER FORTY-FOUR

"Seriously, why can't you get these across the country?" Maggie popped the last morsel of Chelsea bun in her mouth. Meredith had thoughtfully included the favorite sweet breakfast treat in the care package. Maggie and Savannah were on their second French press of coffee and just finished a very large piece of Chelsea bun each.

"Right? These are great, but it's the fresh butter tarts I miss the most when we go west. If we do move back to Alberta, I need to scour the bakeries or learn how to make them." Savannah wiped her sticky fingers on a cloth napkin.

"You guys might move to Alberta?"

Savannah looked up swiftly, a guilty look on her face. "I wasn't supposed to say anything."

Maggie waited, daring to hope.

Savannah hedged. "Nothing is decided or guaranteed, but we've both applied for a few positions closer to home." She paused. "We miss everyone."

Maggie's heart leaped. "Really?"

"Since Gabe helped me and my dad reconnect, I don't know. I guess I let myself miss him now." She stopped, looked at her hands. "And I do. All the time." She met Maggie's gaze. "I spent

a long time away, didn't want to come home or have anything to do with my parents, really."

"That's changed?" Maggie asked, curious.

"I'm not angry anymore. I'm willing to listen, probably because I feel heard."

"Your dad has changed a lot." Dallas MacIntyre had fit the stereotype of a downtown oil baron until nearly dying from a heart attack had reshuffled his sense of self and priorities. Now he was a downtown oil baron in sandals and patchouli whose companies had strong renewables portfolios and community investments in sustainable practices. "What about your mom?"

Savannah smiled. "My mom's hairdresser is now in Toronto."

"What? That's insane." Catching a four-hour flight to get your hair done would never cross Maggie's mind.

"Yes. Well, she usually books several days at a spa, and I try and join her for one of them if my schedule allows."

"You hate spas."

"Yes, but my mom loves them. See, I'm learning to compromise."

Maggie laughed out loud. She had tried—unsuccessfully—to get Savannah to join her for any number of girly traditions. "You're a good daughter."

"I'm trying." Her voice lightened. "Though if I go to Milan or Paris, it's sure as hell not going to be for the shopping. God, I can't believe she can't find *anything* to wear on this continent."

Maggie was laughing so hard she almost spilled her coffee. "Noted."

"It wasn't that funny."

"It really was," Maggie assured her. Over the years, Maggie and Meredith had tried to introduce some glam into Savannah's wardrobe, to no avail. "Gabe's okay moving back?"

"Heck yeah. He only moved to Toronto because he didn't want to ask me to quit my job as a professor, but I know he misses his siblings. He spent so many years keeping them at arm's length because he had to keep the secret of Tanner—"

"He goes by Stone," Maggie corrected automatically.

"So he does." Savannah gave Maggie a considering smile. "Anyway, Gabe's trying to make up for lost time, but it's hard from two thousand miles away."

Maggie shook her head at the awfulness of everything. "Bruce Tanner really was a monster."

"Understatement of the century," Savannah murmured. "If Doris Stone hadn't moved them to Australia, Gabe and Stone would have been in the same class."

Maggie frowned. Kids being forced to weather the sexual indiscretions of adults was not cool.

Savannah made a face. "God, that would have been a disaster them finding out by accident at school or something. People can be cruel—adults or kids."

Maggie hesitated. "Or Stone's siblings may have stood up for him, protected him."

Savannah's eyes widened. "You can't seriously think that's how it would have gone down?"

"Why not? The Tanner siblings turned out to be incredible human beings, despite their parents. You don't think Gabe, Colt, Tucker, and Becca would have accepted Stone as an inno-cent kid caught up in the choices the adults around them made?"

Maggie's stomach squeezed when Savannah looked at her like she had grown a second head. "No. I think they would have seen Stone as a threat to their family. Why do you think Gabe kept the secret as long as he did? His father terrorized him, said if Gabe told anyone, Gabe would be the one responsible for breaking up the family, that it would be all his fault. He alien-ated himself from his siblings so he wouldn't accidentally rip the family apart. I can't believe you don't see that."

"And I can't believe you're defending Gabe's decision. Even as an adult, he kept quiet. Bruce and Samantha Tanner had been divorced for years, and still, he never said a damn thing. Never acknowledged that Stone existed. He never would have, either.

Lillian found out. She told Colt. That's why Stone's in their life at all." Or hers.

Savannah's voice softened. "You just don't understand family, Maggie. Family is … messy. Complicated. Often painful, but also beautiful."

Maggie swallowed. It was on the tip of her tongue to tell Savannah her past. Savannah mistook her silence. She placed her hand on Maggie's arm. "It's not your fault. You grew up in a boarding school."

Maggie resisted the urge to shrug off Savannah's hand. "Anna, I have to tell you something I never told you before." As soon as the words were out, she thought perhaps she understood a tiny bit of Gabe's reticence. "It's not pretty."

Savannah straightened. "You can tell me anything."

Maggie stared at her, unsure. It felt like the walls were closing in on her. Her breath came in ragged pants.

"Maggie?"

Maggie sucked in a long breath. "Never mind. I'm sorry for what I said about Gabe. I shouldn't have judged him for keeping quiet. He had his reasons." She was angry on Stone's behalf, protective, just as Savannah was protective of Gabe. They could agree to disagree.

"Please," Savannah pleaded. "I'm here. Let me in."

Maggie shrugged, feeling helpless. "It was a shitty situation all around."

Savannah was silent. Her eyes sparked with concern and hurt.

Maggie was sick of so much hurt, and finally blurted, "When I was ten, my parents and oldest brother kidnapped my twin brother and tried to extort our grandparents into paying his ransom."

"Holy shit."

Maggie pressed on. "It's not that I don't *have* a family. It's that they were all in prison when I met you. As much as I've pretended they don't exist, they do. And yes, Sebastian and I grew up in boarding schools on different continents, but he *is* my family. He's as much my family as I count you and Meredith as my found family."

And Stone.

They had found each other.

Savannah's face paled. "*Ohmygod*. That's why you never trusted romantic relationships. You never explained, and I always assumed you had been raped or assaulted."

"What? No." Maggie's hands fisted. "Reasonable guess. The stats on that shit is fucking dark."

Savannah burst into tears.

"Woah." Maggie gathered Savannah in her arms. "It's okay. I'm okay." A darker thought popped into her head. Before she could think of a sensitive way to ask, Savannah pulled back. "You're always so happy and bright." Savannah motioned to Maggie's bright attire. "I mean, look at you. You're so damn cheerful. You're always smiling. And kind. How the fuck did you come from such … awful?"

Maggie swallowed, forcing herself not to turn into a crying mess. "This?" She motioned to her colorful shorts and T-shirt, waggling her manicured hands. "This is armor. As above, so below." She'd been honing it for years.

"Cheerful on the outside supports cheerful on the inside?"

"It works." Mostly. Maggie consciously chose to be happy on the outside to heal the terrified kid on the inside.

"I'm sorry I didn't tell you sooner."

Savannah squeezed her hand. "I'm sorry I've been different."

They sat quietly for several moments. "I know Gabe really is a good guy, and I couldn't imagine you two without each other. I miss you, but God, you two are magic."

Savannah gave a watery smile. "That means a lot, thank you."

It had been seeing Savannah and Gabe together that had opened Maggie to the possibility that real love and real relationships existed. Meeting the rest of the Tanner siblings and their significant others reinforced it.

For some, love was very much real.

Savannah cleared her throat. "So, you and Stone—"

Maggie held up her hands. "I think I've shared enough for the morning."

"Fine, birthday girl. What do you want to do?"

"Can I use your eReader? There's a book I want to download."

"Of course." Savannah snagged her purse from the back of a kitchen stool and retrieved it. "Here you go. What are you looking for?"

Maggie accepted the eReader and hit the search icon. "Stone's mom writes metaphysical books on energy. I want to read one." Maggie's chest suddenly felt tight, and she absently rubbed her sternum.

"You're getting more of them, aren't you?" Concern laced Savannah's voice.

Maggie looked up. "Weird feelings and impressions? Yeah. Stone actually thought I could read his mind."

Savannah grimaced. "Ouch—oh wait, that could be sexy in bed."

Maggie rolled her eyes before looking at the screen. "Woah, Doris Stone has seven books out." Maggie rattled off the list of titles.

"Does the library carry any of them?"

"Just one of them." Maggie skimmed a few blurbs. "She makes picking up feelings from energy sound normal. I'm so in."

"Buy it. You can pay me back in wine."

"Deal." Maggie downloaded the purchase. Her hand found her sternum again as a wave of nervous energy passed through her. Savannah didn't notice. She retrieved a thick book from the kitchen's catch-all shelf. "I'll read this." Maggie recognized the latest Susanna Kearsley novel. Meredith had introduced Savannah and Maggie to the author years ago.

The two women curled up on the deck overlooking the lake. A few minutes passed, but the nervous energy was intensifying. Maggie put the eReader down in her lap. A siren could be heard in the distance, though with the water, it was always hard to tell from which direction.

Was this what panic attacks felt like?

Savannah looked up from her book. "You okay?"

Maggie sprang to her feet, nearly dropping the eReader. She grasped her arms around herself, letting her hands cup her elbows.

"What's wrong?" Savannah's voice was laced with concern.

Maggie started to pace the oversized deck, wringing her hands. "I'm agitated like I don't know what to do with my body." It felt like electricity was racing through her insides in a danger-is-afoot, not a yay-exciting kind of way.

Was she finally cracking?

An image filled her mind.

This wasn't a panic attack. Maggie shoved her hand into her shorts pocket and pulled out her phone. Her hands shook as she tried calling Stone.

Ringing could be heard coming from an open second-story window. "Are you shitting me? He didn't take his phone." Maggie stopped. She pitched her voice to a normal decibel. "Can you please try calling Gabe?"

Savannah's eyes widened. She jumped up and ran into the cottage. Maggie followed at her heels.

"He's not answering." Savannah had a death grip on her phone pressed tight against her ear.

Maggie took a hand and held her gaze. "We don't know that anything is wrong."

The song that had been playing on the kitchen radio ended, and the DJ's bold voice came on. "I've got a long weekend mystery for you. From Bala to Mortimer's Point, the wake boats are silent, like all of them folks. A mysterious malady, a Bermuda Triangle, something in the water? This long weekend just got a lot quieter for that end of

Muskoka, so turn it up because the next hour is uninterrupted." A fast rock ballad came on.

"Car," Savannah said, grabbing her keys. The women scooped up their purses and fled the cottage. In the passenger seat, Maggie said, "Just drive. We'll know where to go."

Savannah drove the winding cottage road at a speed Maggie had never dared before.

The agitation had been replaced by stark fear.

Something was very wrong.

CHAPTER FORTY-FIVE

S tone didn't know how long they kept up that rhythm, forcing blood and oxygen through Gabe's lifeless body, willing him to live, willing Gabe to breathe, to yell at Stone. Or ignore him. It didn't matter as long as Gabe lived.

A siren wailed in the distance. Stone kept pumping Gabe's chest between Mrs. Kademan's breathing into him.

"Here! We're down here." Mrs. Pohlkamp's voice rang clear. An ambulance had parked on the road above the small beach. In seconds, paramedics were scrambling down the steep bank.

Gabe's body spasmed, and Stone froze. Gabe coughed, and a torrent of water poured from his mouth. He sputtered on it as Stone and Mrs. Kademan rolled him to his side, where he wheezed, sucking in mouthfuls of air before vomiting out more water. He was curled in a ball, his big shoulders shaking. Stone squeezed his shoulder and got out of the paramedics' way.

He stood off to the side. Mrs. Pohlkamp and Mrs. Kademan recounted what had happened as good as any field doctors, while the paramedics attended to Gabe, made notes, and called it in.

Stone stared, silent.

Mrs. Pohlkamp walked over. "You know him."

Stone nodded.

"Your foot," she exclaimed and waved one of the paramedics over.

Stone looked down. Blood pooled at his left foot. He lifted it to take a look. "Shit."

"Come on. You hop into that ambulance and get sorted out. I'll call Savannah."

Stone didn't bother asking how. Mrs. Pohlkamp and Mrs. Kademan were clearly forces to be reckoned with. He hobbled over to the ambulance.

Mrs. Kademan held up his dive pouch. "Do you want us to drop this at Meredith's for you?"

Stone stilled, reaching for his empty side. He must have flung it off before jumping in after Gabe. "I'll take it." There was no way he was putting someone else in danger of being caught.

She tossed him the dive pouch. "Take care of Gabe."

Stone refitted the pouch. "Yes, ma'am." He looked past the bridge. "Where's the boat and jet ski?"

"Hit and run. I called it in."

Stone nodded his thanks and climbed into the ambulance.

The ride to the hospital was brutal.

Gabe was coherent but lay prone, strapped to the stretcher as paramedics worked on him. Stone remembered another time, six years ago. Gabe had been ambushed while on the job with CSIS. Stone hadn't been there, but he'd been tracking Gabe's career. After, Stone found intel that strongly suggested Bruce Tanner had supplied the information that had compromised Gabe on a mission. His half-brother had nearly died.

With an unsteady hand, Stone picked up Gabe's. It was cool to the touch, but Gabe squeezed his hand back. The paramedics had stabilized Gabe. He was alert, his heart and lungs working of their own accord, but he wasn't safe yet. Stone knew a drowning patient could die days later.

One of the paramedics noticed the pool of blood under Stone's barefoot. "You're bleeding."

Stone looked down. He had forgotten. His body had blocked sending pain cues. His sudden attention brought pain searing up. The paramedic moved into action, cleaning the four-inch wound on the bottom of his foot. Stone welcomed the pain, holding himself silent and still as the man did his job. When the paramedic checked the depth of the laceration, the pain was a thousand times easier than the tangle of emotions Stone was drowning in.

It shouldn't be this complicated.

He hated Gabe. But the helpless terror Stone had felt seeing his half-brother pinballed between a jet ski and powerboat before sinking beneath that choppy water had nearly dropped Stone to his knees. He might hate the guy, but the thought of him being hurt or dead, he hated more.

Stone's instincts had been to keep Gabe safe. In a word, complicated.

"Butterflies might do."

Stone blinked. "Right. Sure, mate." But the paramedic wasn't waiting for his approval and was already affixing four adhesive sutures to the bottom of Stone's foot. He rolled a thick medical sock over Stone's left foot.

The ambulance pulled to a stop. A hospital crew was waiting outside, and Gabe was rushed in. Stone stayed out of their way, jumping out of the back of the ambulance only when it was clear to do so. When he looked up, Maggie and Savannah were running across the small parking lot, fear on both their faces.

Stone motioned to Savannah. "Gabe. Go." She blanched but sprinted into the building. Before Stone and Maggie could follow, an Ontario Provincial Police officer intercepted Stone. Stone waved Maggie in. "I'll find you."

"You're okay?" She took in his soaked appearance and single medical sock.

He nodded, a lump in his throat.

She pressed a fierce kiss to his lips. "Find me."

"I will," he promised.

Thirty minutes later, he was hobbling through hallways like he owned the place. No one stopped him. They usually didn't when he had that look on his face. He turned another corner. When he glanced into the third room, he froze.

Gabe.

His half-brother looked up. "Nice outfit. I didn't realize hospitals had a no shoes, no shirt, no service policy."

Stone looked down, smirking, but his throat was suddenly tight, and his eyes stinging with unshed tears.

Gabe was going to be okay.

Stone cleared his throat. "Something like that. The officer had an extra T-shirt, and these foam rubber sandal things are from the lost and found." He stopped babbling and looked up. "You're going to be all right?"

"I'm only being kept to ensure pulmonary edema doesn't set in." His gaze found Stone's, and Stone had to force himself not to look away. "It could have been a lot worse. It wasn't, thanks to you."

Stone shifted his weight. Both men were equally uncomfortable with the conversation. "Want me to sink those assholes?"

"How about we just sink the boat and jet ski?" Gabe reasoned.

"Fine, but I'm not okay with hit and runs. Someone needs to teach those assholes a lesson."

Gabe's face changed. "Neither stopped?"

Stone shook his head.

"Did Mrs. Pohlkamp and Mrs. Kademan witness it?"

"Yeah, they helped me do CPR on you and keep that gash on your leg compressed until the ambulance arrived."

Gabe smiled, then winced, his hand flying to his chest, and Stone rushed forward. "Fuck, broken ribs and a broken sternum suck."

Stone started breathing again. "Sorry about that."

"I know the drill. I'll roll with broken bones over brain dead any day." Gabe slowly breathed out, his face relaxing. "That's better. Anyway, Mrs. Pohlkamp and Mrs. Kademan are retired lawyers."

Stone smiled, guessing where this was headed.

"Hell hath no fury like women with time, skills, resources, and a hell of a protective streak. They don't start fights, but they finish them." He gave Stone a pointed look. "Legally."

Stone had different ideas but would defer to the two wise women. For now. "Where are Maggie and Savannah?"

"Calling everyone."

Stone lifted an eyebrow.

Gabe actually sighed. "You know, Becca. If one of us got hurt and she finds out later we didn't tell her, she loses her mind—seriously, she goes ballistic."

Neutrally, Stone agreed. "She has some Momma Bear tendencies." Stone didn't mind getting caught in Becca's orbit. She wrapped everyone in her own style of nurturing cocoon. Instead of feeling strangled or guilty, like he often did with his mom, Stone felt the unexpected safety of being included.

Gabe snorted. "Throw in an emergency room, and she will move heaven and earth. Anna will keep her posted. Becca won't feel obligated to fly out. Everyone wins."

Stone nodded, like he knew what that would feel like.

"She'd do it for you, too."

Stone suddenly found the pattern on the tiled floor fascinating.

"Look, I know you and I—" Gabe paused. "As far as Becca is concerned, you're a Tanner—"

"I hate that fucking name." The words were out before Stone realized how shitty it must have sounded, but Gabe was laughing. "And that's why you go by Stone. I would, too."

Stone ran both hands through his hair. "What was my mom thinking?"

Both men were quiet. The question was bigger than either wanted to broach. Finally, Stone muttered, "Congratulations on getting engaged."

Gabe held Stone's gaze, a lifetime of pain between them.

"Thanks for not letting me drown," Gabe said, his voice gruff.

"I would never hear the end of it—" Stone stopped. The lump in his throat back. He hadn't realized until almost losing Gabe how much he wanted to put the past behind them. "Glad you didn't get dead."

"Yeah, well, Savannah would have killed me."

"That's my line."

Gabe looked at him sharply.

Stone stared. "Come on. Your fiancée is as protective as your siblings and their partners. What the hell do you think would have happened if anything happened to you on my watch?"

"What's that supposed to mean?" Gabe's voice had gone low. "Are you my keeper, now?"

Stone took a step back, not wanting to have this conversation. "Forget it, man."

Gabe's eyes flashed. "No. What the fuck did you mean?"

Stone crossed his arms. "What the fuck do you think your family or fiancée would have done to me if you would have died? My membership to this family isn't exactly solid."

Gabe stared at him. "You had nothing to do with those assholes racing. *They* nearly drowned me, not you. Why would anyone think it was your fault?"

Stone felt like he had been sucker punched. "Do you fucking hear yourself? I spent my whole life being blamed for what others did." Stone pressed his fist to his lips, willing himself to shut the hell up. A cold laugh escaped, paving the way to hell. "You spent decades helping your father hide that I even existed, so don't you dare say it's not my fault. Everything's my fault in your family."

The golden boy was silent. Stone felt sick at his outburst. He should have kept his mouth shut. Gabe was recovering from nearly drowning. Period. When push came to shove, no Tanner would give a fuck about Stone—not over Gabe.

He turned to go but froze. Savannah and Maggie blocked the doorway. "Excuse me," he said.

"Stone—" Gabe started.

He ignored his half-brother. "Excuse me," he repeated, squeezing past the two surprised women.

Maggie trailed after him, calling his name. Stone's heart was pounding. He had to get the hell out of here before he either broke something or broke down. He walked as fast as civility would allow, watching the signs hanging from the ceiling for a way out.

Maggie looped her arm through his and tugged. "The car is this way."

"Maggie, don't." He disentangled his arm from hers, maneuvering around her.

"Where are you going?"

"Anywhere but here."

"Then let me take you. You shouldn't be walking on that foot."

"I'll get a cab or a ride-share." Hell, he'd hitchhike. Stone had to get the fuck out of there, and he simply could not deal with her chastising him about Gabe. Not right now.

"You told me to find you." Maggie's hushed voice shook with emotion.

Stone caught up to her in two strides. "Hey," he said softly. "It's okay. Gabe's going to be okay."

"I thought it was you," Maggie whispered. The fear was etched across her beautiful face, and he circled her around, wrapping one arm around her back while the other hand cradled her head against his shoulder. "I'm safe. I'm okay."

She held herself tense, and Stone feared he had fucked it up again. After the longest pause of his life, Maggie pressed her forehead against his shoulder as hers shook. Stone held her, letting her cry for both of them.

"I almost drowned." Her words were whispered, barely audible, and Stone wasn't sure he had heard correctly. "Honey?"

She pulled back. "At boarding school. I almost drowned—*did* drown, technically."

"What happened?"

"Mean girls and a shitty gym teacher." She shuddered but didn't add anything further.

"Want to get out of here?" Stone asked.

She nodded. For the first time, she really looked at him. "What are you wearing?"

Stone glanced down at the too-small T-shirt, boxer brief-style swimming trunks, and foam rubber sandals. "It's a long story. Gabe asked the same thing." Stone looked down, ashamed. "Then I totally blasted him."

"About time."

Stone stared at her. "I thought you would be angry. I just lashed out at Gabe, and he's in a fucking hospital bed. I was way out of line. I'm the bad guy."

"Saying how you feel does not make you a bad guy. No one kidnapped, extorted, or tried to murder anyone. You guys are finally talking. Yelling counts."

"But—"

He allowed her to tug him out a door that said *parking lot*. "Can we please finish this conversation in the car? Gabe's fine, the doctors said so, and I don't want to have another breakdown in public."

Stone could relate and hustled after her.

Maggie unlocked the SUV with a double click. "You and Gabe finally ripping off your uneasy truce isn't pretty, but it will be. Now get in the car, Stone." She eyed the dive pouch at his side. "It's my birthday, and I'm going to enjoy what's left of this *quiet*, peaceful day."

Stone wasn't sure how to respond. "What do you want to do?"

She pulled out of the hospital parking space.

"Break into my brother's boat."

CHAPTER FORTY-SIX

Sebastian didn't realize a body could hurt this much. After all he'd endured, Phoebe's betrayal may just be his breaking point. He hadn't been this low in a long time. It scared him. He swiped at his eyes, ashamed he cared so much and focused on the task at hand. He needed to get to Canada without the hassle of a damn task force.

The café he sat in was adjacent to the Australian embassy. It had been a while since he had to hack anything, and it was taking him longer than he would have liked, but it couldn't be helped. Phoebe was at their apartment, and his not-so-secret lab was likely compromised by Teague Alans's crew.

Sebastian keyed in several more commands and waited, taking another swig of his café au lait.

He made a face. It was cold like Phoebe's black heart.

If he kept up a litany of her faults, he wouldn't be tempted to beg her for forgiveness, tell her he didn't care how they met, tell her he still wanted to be her husband.

Sebastian keyed in the next set of instructions with more force than necessary. His laptop made a satisfying ping—finally, something went right.

He was in.

Working quickly, he created enough space for him to fly commercially unmolested. Hopefully, the trail of breadcrumbs he had left Maggie would be enough to at least start to clear his name while Sebastian figured out how to neutralize Teague Alans. The psycho cared about Sebastian's research, and the stupid land Bruce Tanner left him. If he figured out what was so precious about that land, he could figure out how to deal with Teague.

After that, he had no idea.

How many times could someone reasonably expect to pick up the pieces of their life? Not wanting to burden Maggie had given him the courage to keep fighting another day, every day. That's what those long dark days of his life had been like. He had clawed out from that despair for Maggie and for his work, only to be duped by Teague Alans. Then Phoebe had been his light. Sebastian had clawed his way back from the brink of death so he could reunite with Phoebe when it was safe and when he could keep her and Maggie safe.

Except Phoebe was a false light. A player in a game he didn't even know he had been unwillingly thrust into.

Enough.

Sebastian checked his watch. He had just enough time to catch the shuttle to Paris CDG. By this time tomorrow, he would be in Alberta.

Sebastian was going to Hearthstone Ranch.

CHAPTER FORTY-SEVEN

"Gabe's not the asshole you think he is." Maggie pulled onto the highway, avoiding eye contact with Stone in the passenger seat when she checked her blind spot.

"He kind of is."

"Gabe knows your relationship is fucked and that he's as much to blame as you and your impossible hard-on for staying mad."

Stone gaped at her. Maggie flagged her fingers up from the top of the steering wheel. "Not that I'm complaining about your hard-ons." She knew it was risky, but if the last week had taught her anything, it was that if you waited to clear shit up, it might not ever come.

"How can you joke? I'm seriously an asshole."

"Yeah, assholes always make birthday cakes in the middle of the night."

Pink tinged his cheeks. "That's different."

"What about the wake boats?" Maggie prodded.

"What about them?"

"None of them are running."

This time he squirmed. "Sounds like some asshole must have tampered with them."

"Yeah, what a jerk." She scoffed. "Face it, Stone, you're a good guy, well, unless you're a wake boat owner. Accept it."

Stone stared out the SUV window instead. "Sorry you had to spend your birthday at the hospital." Something in his voice caught, and Maggie darted a glance at him. A storm of emotions chased across Stone's usually stoic face.

He was just as affected by everything as she was.

"Thanks for the birthday cake. And quiet morning," she said softly before tapping the radio on. Anything to give Stone a reprieve. The final chords of a rock ballad rang as the DJ came on. "*Still no word on our long weekend puzzle, but the mysterious rash of wake boat malady has prompted the Venus Marina to break their decades-long long weekend boycott. They are open for business.*"

Maggie and Stone turned to each other at the same time. Maggie swore. "I wanted to break in."

"What kind of librarian are you?"

She was quiet for a moment. "The kind that wants to fight for something she believes in instead of living life on the sidelines. And really, how unlawful would it be to tippy-toe into a closed marina simply to gain access to my twin brother's boat? I mean, it could practically be considered a scheduling mix-up."

He was staring at her. "You're kidding, right?"

She gripped the steering wheel tighter, grumbling, "Says the guy with a dive pouch full of spark plugs."

Stone opened his mouth, then closed it. "Do you have a plan?"

"Of course, I do." She didn't. Maggie had no idea how she would know which one was Sebastian's boat.

"I'm coming with you."

Maggie eyed what he was wearing. "Not dressed like that, you're not. That marina caters to a particular crowd." She checked the rearview. No one was behind her. She cranked the wheel, making a U-turn.

Stone put a hand on the SUV's dash, bracing himself. "Everyone wandering around town was in some variation of swim suit."

"We're playing a fancy couple."

"I'm not following."

"You will."

Forty minutes later, they pulled into the now-open tree-shrouded marina gate. The mermaid logo matching Sebastian's keychain was emblazoned on the large boat storages and marina shop.

Stone drove this time. He wore a tailored shirt with the cuffs rolled high on his forearms, linen pants, and a pair of deck shoes Maggie had found in the mudroom. He looked utterly European. Maggie wore a stylish oversized long-sleeved shirt over a sun dress, wedge sandals, an outrageous sunhat, and overly large sunglasses. A ginormous purse big enough to double as a beach bag completed her ensemble. Meredith's choice of luxury wheels paired perfectly with the vibe. She might not have grown up in the east, but she understood stereotypes. Wealthy patrons were a dime a dozen up here, and too often rubbed locals the wrong way. Maggie had witnessed class tensions in the cottage country paradise more often than not.

"Don't be nice. Don't speak to anyone who looks like a townie—"

"What the hell does that mean?"

"There are townies, and there's the cottage crowd. Nary, the two shall mix."

Stone shot her a look. "Canada has some weird ass rules."

"Australia's different?"

He paused for a second. "Not really. Why are we going for the upper-crusty crowd?"

"So they'll ignore us."

"I'm not following."

"You will." He still looked confused. Maggie added, "Would

you make someone wait who looked like a snotty, demanding client?"

Stone nodded. "Good point."

"I hope so—oh, and speak French."

"Seriously? That's frowned upon?"

"No." Maggie tossed him a heated look. "That's for me."

Stone gripped the steering wheel tighter. "*Comme tu veux, ma cherie.*"

"*Merci beaucoup.*" She smiled as her whole body sighed. "Now hang on, I want to try something." Maggie closed her eyes behind her overly large sunglasses. She inhaled slow and deep, like a gentle tide, before exhaling slow and long, just as Doris Stone suggested in her book. Maggie thought of Sebastian. Wishing moments, an undeniable sense of knowing blossomed inside of her.

She opened her eyes. "I know the way."

CHAPTER FORTY-EIGHT

No one questioned them. Long before Stone had become an agent, he had learned that the way a man moved set a tone. He set the tone he wanted as he exited the Range Rover.

Power, prestige, and impatience.

"Baby, baby, I swear this will just take a second." Maggie closed the passenger door of the SUV in full character.

Stone blinked, dazzled. She positively glittered in the sunlight.

"*Mon cœur*," he whispered, and she cast him a beautiful smile. She held out her hand, and he felt a jolt when he took her hand in his. He leaned down to her. "You look great."

Maggie gave him a very thorough once-over. "You're looking rather delicious yourself."

"*Careful*." Linen and boners were not a good combination.

They walked close, holding hands. Forest ringed the property, throwing dappled light onto the path until it forked. They took the boardwalk ringing the marina slips. Stone only counted two employees in uniform T-shirts, though neither bothered to acknowledge them.

"This way," Maggie said. Stone let her lead him down the boardwalk. At the end, she turned, heading down the largest dock. Halfway down the long, floating dock, Maggie froze. A beautiful Catalina bobbed in the slip. The name *Maggie* was artfully scripted on the white hull. Stone squeezed her hand.

"Do-do you have the key."

Stone nodded, helping her aboard as she deftly maneuvered the shifting deck in her wedge sandals. He so would have rolled an ankle by now. Stone pulled the boat keys out of his pocket and unlocked the cabin, and tried to ignore how great her legs looked. "Let me go first."

Maggie nodded.

Stone ducked through the companionway door and into the cabin. The interior was a work of art. He stepped to the side in the galley to make room for Maggie.

"It's beautiful," she breathed, making her way in.

Meticulously crafted, the mahogany woodwork was as elegant as it was functional. The galley was immediately to the left. It was an elegantly practical, if somewhat sparse—even for a boat—kitchen. Farther in, the salon had high-end furnishings, comfortable and durable. A flat-screen TV hung above the salon table. A rail-lined shelf edged the length of each side of the space.

It was a beautiful boat, but it was missing something. Stone turned around, looking. Then it dawned on him. It had none of the homey touches his parents' boat had: mismatched throw pillows, plants tucked here and there, and his mom's paintings hung on flat surfaces.

Maggie had stopped in the center of the salon, rubbing her bare arms.

"You okay?" Stone asked. She nodded. "I will be—" Maggie focused on the railed sideboard. She scrambled across the settee cushions and retrieved a waterproof case with a shoulder strap behind the rail. "Look."

Inside was a laptop.

It was dead.

Maggie spun around and sat at the compact table. Stone joined her. He rummaged in the case and found a power cord. He glanced around, found a power socket, and plugged it in.

Several moments later, the laptop sprang to life, demanding a password.

"Ah, hell." Maggie took off the floppy hat and stuck her fingers in her hair. "Not this again."

Stone sat down beside her. "Maybe try something with *Maggie* in it? The boat is named after you, after all."

Maggie rolled up her baggy sleeves before hesitating. "Sebastian is a tortured genius. The code to get into his apartment is a Nobel-winning physicist's birthday."

"So try *Maggie* in numeric code."

It didn't work.

She blew out a breath. Suddenly, a look of determination crossed her face. "Do you have that piece of paper from Sebastian's shirt?"

Stone pulled out his phone and found the photo he had taken of the crinkled slip of paper Maggie had found in her brother's shirt. He held it out to her. *One-three-four-zero-six-two-four-four-four-three.*

She punched in the code.

"Bingo," she said with satisfaction, and the laptop fluttered to life.

Impressed, Stone asked, "What is it?"

"One-three-four-zero plus my name in numerics."

"What's the first part?"

"The time I was born." Maggie was already scanning through the file finder. "What am I looking for?"

Stone leaned forward. "I'm hoping we'll know it when we see it." He pointed. "There. That was synced two days ago."

"Sebastian *is* alive!" Maggie clicked on it, fairly vibrating next to him.

Stone pressed his lips to the top of her head. "I hope so."

She angled into him as the video flickered to life. The camera angle was through a door, facing an elegant hotel suite where three men were speaking. Stone frowned. "The shorter one is Teague Alans."

"Who are the other two?"

"I don't know." Stone studied the scene, a feeling of dread building. He tried to shield her eyes. "You won't want to see this."

She swatted his hand away. "I can handle it—no, I can't." Maggie turned her head away from the horrific scene. The larger of the other two men was convulsing on the floor. Within moments, the second man was charging Teague, who promptly stabbed him in the gut, taking shocking delight. God, it was awful, and Stone had seen some sick shit in his day.

Maggie's eyes were still pinched shut. "Is it done, yet?"

"Not yet." Stone watched with an impassive face. Teague Alans was a sick son of a bitch.

Finally, the desecration of the bodies stopped. The sound of a shower running could be heard, then the video stopped.

Maggie wrapped her arms around herself. "That was disgusting."

Stone agreed. He pulled out a small device and plugged it into one of the laptop's ports before keying in a series of commands. The video started playing again. Maggie kept her gaze averted when she asked, "Are you copying the video?"

"I'm sending the video to the task force."

"Oh."

Stone hated when she used that simple, brief word. When she said it, it seemed to say, *you make dumb life choices*. When the file had been sent, Stone resumed searching the laptop. "It's safe to look now."

Maggie swung her gaze back to the screen. "Look for a folder that says *miscellaneous*."

Stone did a search. "There are twelve called *misc* with variations of dates attached."

"Only twelve. Not bad for Seb. Are any of them dated after the task force started tracking Sebastian?"

Stone scanned the list. "Four are."

"Check those first."

There were at least a hundred items in the folder. Several minutes passed, and Stone poured through the disorganized chaos as Maggie looked on over his shoulder. "What's that?"

Stone looked where she was pointing. It was a memorandum of understanding. He searched the technical jargon found within it, and a contract and deposit receipt pinged. Stone scanned the documents. "From these documents, at least, your twin brother looks legit—wait a minute."

"What?"

"They're all dated two weeks ago."

"So?"

"So, it looks incriminating."

Maggie glared at him. "You just can't imagine he's innocent, can you?"

Stone wanted to. He really did. It would make his life a hell of a lot easier, but he couldn't ignore the evidence. Nor could his boss, even if Stone's gut said otherwise. "Maggie—"

"I'm going to search the berth." She scooted the other way around the salon table before disappearing into the berth.

Stone watched her go before forcing himself to get back to work. He kept looking through the *miscellaneous* labeled files when a faint sound alerted him, and he turned his head. Through one of the long, narrow windows, he saw three men approaching the docks. They were all carrying.

"Maggie, time to go." Stone quickly gathered the laptop and cords, securing them in the waterproof case.

"Get bent," filtered in from somewhere in the berth.

Stone stood, looping the shoulder strap of the case across his torso. "Maggie, honey, be mad at me later. We need to go."

She popped her head from around the corner. "Stone—why are you holding your gun?" Her eyes were round. "Shit, what now?"

He checked the window. The three men were closing in fast.

There was nowhere to run.

CHAPTER FORTY-NINE

aggie followed Stone's gaze. Three dangerous-looking men were walking—more like stalking—down the long dock. "You got the laptop?"

Stone nodded. "But—"

Maggie kicked out of her heeled sandals and pulled off her hat, slipping everything into her bag and being careful not to damage the clue she had found. She tucked her arm tight against her body, sandwiching the ginormous bag, and grabbed his hand. "Come on."

She led them out through the companionway door and slid along the port side of the deck away from the dock. Her bare feet gripped the dry deck, and she hustled toward the bow, crouching low. Stone followed close behind.

Maggie glanced behind them. The three men were only a couple of slips away. They had to move *now*. She moved to scramble over the bow pulpit, but Stone held her hand. "We'll be sitting ducks in the water."

"You got a better idea?"

Stone hesitated, and Maggie knew he was weighing their options of him being able to fight them all off with a single sidearm. His answer was to tuck his sidearm into the laptop case and pick her up under her arms. She refrained from yelping, but just barely. From the bow pulpit, he lowered her soundlessly into the water.

"Keep to the bows. Head toward the parking lot."

Maggie nodded. In a lithe movement, Stone joined her, silently lowering himself into the water. She dove under, awkwardly swimming one-handed as she clutched her purse to her side. Stone paced her. He was a stronger swimmer than her, even weighed down with the bulky laptop case and still fully dressed, shoes and all. Maggie's sundress fluttered more in the water than weighed her down.

Adrenaline gave her courage.

They swam underwater, popping up on the starboard sides of bows, out of sight as they filled their lungs with air. Several minutes passed. Finally, they had made their way to the first dock. It was the only one with gas pumps on the end and sported a small shack. Several rows of slips held various styles and sizes of boats between them and Sebastian's Catalina.

A young woman wearing a Venus Marina T-shirt came out of the shack and rushed to the side of the dock, offering her hand to Maggie. Alarmed, she asked Maggie, "Are you all right?"

Between the woman's strong grip and Stone hoisting her, Maggie fairly levitated onto the dock. Stone braced his hands wide and pushed himself up.

Maggie and the young attendant stared.

Out of the water, Stone's wet shirt and trousers clung, outlining every muscled contour and ridge of him.

The young woman made an appreciative sound and leaned toward Maggie, "Well done."

Maggie drank in the steamy sight. Stone wet was hot as fuck.

"You okay?" Stone asked, dripping wet and oblivious.

Maggie nodded.

The attendant managed to pull her gaze from Stone's soaked body. "What happened?"

Maggie sluiced her hair back. "It's so embarrassing. I saw an ex, and I didn't want to ruin the day."

The young woman looked doubtful. "You swam across the marina to avoid an ex?"

Maggie gave her a conspiratorial grin, nodding toward Stone, and whispered, "Yes, but look at how it turned out."

Stone put his hand on Maggie's back, giving an indulgent smile. "*On devrait y alley, chérie.*"

Maggie nodded before giving the attendant a shy smile and a wave of thanks.

When Stone turned to go, the young woman pecked her forefinger in the air, pointing to Stone's butt. Maggie glanced down before sucking in a breath, remembering how he had felt in her hands last night.

The attendant winked and headed back to the shack.

Stone kept his hand lightly pressed against the center of her back as they quickly walked up the dock. "Want to tell me what that was all about?"

"Girl bonding," Maggie breezed, letting herself lean into Stone.

"You were checking out my ass, weren't you?" He scanned their surroundings as he spoke.

"Yes."

He glanced down at her honesty. "Good." They were almost to the marina sheds, with the parking lot beyond. "Do you know if Teague Alans knows what you look like?"

Maggie stiffened. "I have no idea."

Stone frowned. "Let's get you—" Suddenly, his arm snaked around her shoulders, and he ushered her behind a large speedboat on a trailer. The three men were on the boardwalk, seemingly empty-handed.

Maggie pressed close to Stone, their wet clothes clinging. He kept his arm around her shoulder. The three men got into a large, dark SUV. One had been on his phone.

Maggie remembered to breathe when they finally drove through the open gates.

"Who do you think that was?"

Stone was typing on his phone. "We'll know soon enough."

"Omran?"

Stone nodded. "Let's get you out of here."

Maggie slipped her sandals back on. "Want to search the boat better?" Stone hesitated but shook his head. "I want to get you out of here."

They made it back to the vehicle without incident. Maggie didn't object when Stone headed to the driver's side. Once they were on the road, she asked, "Those men were not part of your task force, were they."

Stone shook his head.

"Teague Alans's?"

"Likely." Stone paused. "We have no reason to believe Meredith's cottage has been compromised."

Maggie shuttered. She didn't like it when Stone used his work voice.

"What did you find in the berth?"

Maggie shot him a quick look. "What makes you think I found anything?"

"Because you would have told me if you didn't."

She frowned.

"Are you going to tell me what it is?"

"I don't know." Indecision warred within her.

"Maggie—"

She pressed her hand to her forehead. "Please, give me a chance to think."

Stone opened his mouth but closed it without saying anything.

Twenty minutes later, they walked into Meredith's cottage. Savannah met them at the door. "Gabe was released from the hospital."

Maggie gave her best friend a tight hug. "That's wonderful, Anna. That was so scary."

Savannah hugged her back just as tight. When she pulled back, Maggie stiffened. "What is it?"

"You're soaking wet," Savannah said.

"It's a long story." Maggie knew her best friend. Something was wrong. "What's going on?"

Savannah clutched her hands together. "Becca called. Sebastian was picked up at Hearthstone Ranch by Lillian's security detail."

CHAPTER FIFTY

"Did you find my property?" Teague roared, gripping his secure phone.

There was a burst of static. "Negative. No technology or files were located on the vessel."

Disbelief threatened to swamp Teague. Nothing was going to plan, *nothing*. He had buyers. Dangerous, impatient buyers willing to pay a premium for Sebastian's research. Teague wouldn't be able to hold them off much longer.

"What about the girl?" Teague demanded.

"No, sir." Static crackled.

"Where the fuck is she?" Rage flooded him, swift and violent. How he would have savored being able to permanently silence the man.

"We have reason to believe Sebastian Monroe is alive."

Teague stilled. "What did you say?"

"According to his parents, Sebastian Monroe is alive."

The irony was delicious. "You're still in contact with the parents?"

"Affirmative."

"Good—" A notification pinged on his cell phone. Bruce

Tanner's lawyer had an envelope for him to pick up at his earliest convenience. In Calgary.

"There's been a change of plans," Teague said.

"Boss?"

"Keep following the sister. And alert me immediately if you make contact with Sebastian. I've got something to take care of."

Teague disconnected the sat call.

Bruce Tanner had never been mysterious or particularly clever.

What could possibly be in the envelope Bruce had left him?

CHAPTER FIFTY-ONE

Hearthstone Ranch. Sebastian ducked low over the steering wheel of his rental car, eying the wrought iron lettering as he slowly drove under the stylized ranch sign. As he made his way down the drive, the Rocky Mountains loomed, a stunning backdrop to the sprawling two-story timber-framed ranch inn. The wrap-around porch was inviting, with several Muskoka—Adirondack—chairs grouped, and the deep windbreak of trees that lined the yard created a sense of privacy and ambiance. Solar panels adorned the large roof, and beyond, a trendy-looking barn was just visible. Saddle horses grazed in the adjacent paddock.

The place looked rugged and comfortable at the same time.

Sebastian hated that Teague Alans had any connection to this place.

He parked his rental, unsure what he was going to say.

Tap, tap, tap.

A tall man with a concerned, kind face stood next to the car. "You okay?"

Sebastian ran his hand down the front of his shirt and took a deep breath. He gave the man a weak smile before slowly opening his car door.

"Can I help you?" The man's voice was even, but he was assessing Sebastian with a new alertness.

Sebastian kept his hands visible at his sides. "I hope so. I believe my twin sister, Maggie Monroe, spent Christmas here—"

Four large black SUVs shot up the driveway, surrounding them. Armed men, weapons drawn but pointed downward, stormed out, circling Sebastian and the kind but wary, stranger. The stranger had a resigned look on his face. "Guys, is this really necessary?"

"You know the drill, sir," one of the commando types answered. "You've got thirty."

The stranger looked at Sebastian. After hesitating, he held out his hand. "Jason Chasseur."

Sebastian carefully shook the hand offered, keeping his other in clear sight. He didn't want to give the armed men a reason to aim at him.

"I remember Maggie. Let these guys do their thing. Once they clear you, we can get you sorted."

"Clear me—" Sebastian was swarmed before he had a chance to ask what the hell was going on. A tall, built man stepped forward. "Sebastian Monroe?"

"How did—" he pivoted, "am I under arrest?"

"You need to come with us." Two men stepped forward, gripping his upper arms. The tall man was still talking, but Sebastian didn't hear him. Fear had exploded. They were trying to lead him toward the waiting SUVs. He wouldn't be taken again.

Sebastian fought like a madman. Chasseur had his hands out, fervently talking, but Sebastian couldn't hear him. He couldn't hear anything.

Then everything went black.

CHAPTER FIFTY-TWO

S tone caught Maggie as she crumpled. One hand grabbed him, and the other shot up, covering her mouth. A wail escaped. *"He's alive. I knew he was alive."*

Savannah sprang into action. She held the door as Stone locked his arm around Maggie, helping her inside. Once through the door, he scooped Maggie into his arms. "What are you doing?"

"I'm getting you in dry clothes. Whatever news Savannah has, you'll feel better hearing it if you're not clammy."

Maggie dropped her head back a moment, before squirming. "I can walk up the stairs." Stone gently set her down. In ninety seconds, they were back downstairs.

Gabe had materialized and sat on one of the wide, plush living room chairs. Stone studied his half-brother. His color wasn't quite back to normal, and Gabe's face was even more drawn than it usually was. For the first time, Stone *saw* the weight of responsibility Gabe carried on his wide shoulders. Theirs hadn't been an easy path, and if they could get past their past, their future might find a better way. Stone followed his gut and asked, "You okay?"

Gabe turned, wary suspicion in his eyes. Stone didn't blame

him. He hadn't made Gabe's life easy since being introduced to the family, not to mention the disastrous way he had left things at the hospital.

"Don't worry about me." Savannah gave Gabe a sharp look, and Gabe added, "I'll be fine."

Stone looked between Savannah and Gabe. Grudging, he offered, "Good."

"You mean that?" Gabe's eyes were serious.

Maggie and Savannah seemed to hold their breath.

"I wouldn't have jumped in if I didn't." It was partially true. Stone had jumped in instinctively. His conscious mind had a harder time sorting out how he felt about Gabe. Hesitating only briefly, Stone walked forward and held out his hand. Gabe stared at it. They had never shaken hands before, neither willing to give. Finally, his half-brother clasped his hand. It was the shortest handshake in the history of the world.

Stone shoved his hands into the pockets of his cargo shorts. Gruffly, he said, "Glad you're home."

Gabe cleared his throat. "Good to be out of the hospital."

A look passed between them. Gabe's best friend, Andy, had nearly died in the hospital after a massive wreck while Savannah was being held at gunpoint, and in the months after, Colt, Tucker, Becca, and Jason had all been hospitalized after various attacks and shootings. It had been a hell of a year for the Tanner siblings and their partners.

"I don't like hospitals, either." Stone looked away first. His gaze found Maggie's. She had a small smile on her face like she was proud of him, and didn't he stand a bit straighter.

He motioned toward the couch, sitting down next to her. His entire right side was pressed flush against her left. When he put his arm around her, she snuggled closer. "Ready?" Stone asked her.

"I want to hear what Gabe was going to say," Maggie said.

The room went eerily silent.

Gabe finally asked, "How did you know—"

Savannah took a seat next to Gabe on the oversized chair, pulling her legs up. "She just does. Spill."

Gabe looked at Stone. "I think they're ganging up on us."

"I'm getting used to it."

Gabe hesitated. "For what it's worth, I am sorry how everything went down. When I was a kid, I was terrified to say anything. When I got older, I didn't know how to bring it up after so many years had passed. I was afraid of how my mom, Colt, Tucker, or Becca would react." He looked Stone in the eye. "I never saw you as someone to throw away. As far as I'm concerned, the definition of *bastard* is irrelevant. I mean, Christ, what century is it?"

Gabe's dry, righteous defense of Stone's birth circumstances gave Stone pause. "You didn't?"

"Honestly, I thought you were better off without us. In case you haven't noticed, we're pretty fucked. But that should have been your call to make, not mine. I'm sorry."

Stone blinked, before nodding. "Thank you for that."

The room absorbed the moment.

Gabe looked as shell-shocked as Stone felt.

Maggie picked up Stone's hand. "Now, I'm ready. Savannah, can you tell me what happened."

Stone couldn't believe they had spiraled into that rabbit hole while Maggie awaited details about her twin brother. It was unforgivable—suddenly, she pressed her forefinger to his lips, quieting his apology. "You're fine."

Savannah spoke. "Sebastian's alive and safe."

Maggie reached for her phone. "I should call him."

"He passed out," Savannah explained.

Maggie stopped. "Excuse me?"

"They didn't hurt him." Savannah was quick to explain.

"Do they usually?" Maggie asked sharply.

"No," Gabe answered before hesitating. "Sebastian is a person of interest for an international investigation."

"She knows," Stone offered.

Gabe eyed the two of them before continuing. "Lillian's security detail is state supplied. They were duty-bound to apprehend him. The detail had already identified him on the flights from Paris—"

"He was in Paris?" Maggie looked crushed. Stone gave her a squeeze. "He was probably trying to keep you and Phoebe safe."

She turned those bright eyes on him. "So you finally believe me? You don't think he's a bad guy?"

"I think I want to hear his side of the story." Stone also wanted to finish going through Sebastian's laptop. If there was evidence that could exonerate him, Stone wanted it found.

Maggie sat back, not quite as close as before.

Savannah continued. "When he showed up at Becca's, the security types stepped in. Jason was there at the time. Sebastian went nuts when they tried to bring him in."

Maggie raised her hand to her mouth. Tears streamed down her face. "Of course he did. He was taken when he was ten and then again several months ago. Christ, what's wrong with you people?"

Gabe looked thoughtful. "Jason said it was like Sebastian couldn't hear him. He just went ballistic. Then blacked out. Sounds like an extreme trauma response."

Maggie pulled a photo out of the pocket of her long skirt and handed it to him. "I found this in the berth."

Stone accepted the photo. It was a grainy image, likely taken from a CCTV. "I recognize Teague Alans. Who are the others?"

"Those are our parents. I think Sebastian was set up."

The cottage doorbell rang.

"Is anyone expecting company?" Stone asked the room, dropping the photo on the coffee table.

Three heads shook.

Bang, bang, bang, bang, bang.

Stone sprinted to the front door, gun drawn.

"Seriously, where do you hide that thing?" Maggie muttered, following close and swiping a wrought iron fire poker. He waved her back. Gabe had posted himself behind the front door, opposite Stone. Savannah gripped her phone, ready. Maggie was ready to crank whoever walked through the door.

Stone held his hand horizontal, motioning up and down, in the universal symbol for chill-the-fuck-out.

Bang, bang, bang, bang, bang. "Maggie, Stone, *es-tu là? C'est Phoebe.*"

Stone swung open the door.

Phoebe stood on the other side. Her hair was disheveled, her clothes looked like she had slept in them, and her eyes were red and bloodshot.

She looked like hell.

Maggie rushed forward, poker nowhere to be seen. "Phoebe, come in, come in."

Phoebe walked through the front door, hands wringing. "Sebastian's alive."

Maggie put her arm around the woman, leading her into the living room. "We just found out."

Phoebe sat on the edge of the couch. Savannah placed a glass of water in from of her.

Maggie picked up the glass, handing it to Phoebe. "You must be exhausted." Then she sat next to the Frenchwoman.

Phoebe allowed herself a sip before spilling the entire fight with Sebastian. "I swear, I didn't lie to him, not about loving him. *Mon Dieu*, what am I going to do? He's my whole world."

Maggie clasped her hands. "He's in Alberta. You'll come with us."

"*Merci, merci*—where did you get that?" Phoebe was pointing at the photo Stone had dropped on the coffee table.

Maggie picked it up, handing it to Phoebe. "It was on Sebastian's boat in the marina here."

Phoebe frowned. "These are the people that first approached Teague Alans, telling him about Sebastian's work."

Maggie glanced at Stone. "Did Sebastian know?"

Phoebe shook her head. "No, Teague told him he had been

following Sebastian's work in scientific journals. Sebastian had no reason to suspect differently. How did Sebastian get this?"

"It was on his boat. What do you know about them?" Maggie pointed to the picture.

"We got an anonymous tip they would be approaching Teague Alans. They did."

Maggie's face paled. "How anonymous?"

"I can't tell you that," Phoebe said apologetically.

"Was it Lawrence Plover?"

Phoebe straightened. "How did you know that?"

"Lawrence is our older brother." Maggie frowned. "I can't believe he'd want to protect Sebastian."

"That tipoff set the tone for the whole investigation."

"What do you mean?" Maggie asked.

"Teague went to a lot of trouble making Sebastian look dirty. Without that initial tip, Sebastian would have looked like any other of Teague's crews."

"Dirty?"

Phoebe nodded. She glanced at Stone briefly. "Bruce Tanner's criminal circle were taken out by authorities, as much as any in-fighting."

Stone kept his face expressionless.

"You said in-fighting." Maggie looked thoughtful. "Was there any angst between Bruce and Teague?"

"Some. Nothing that set off any specific red flags," Stone supplied. "Why?"

Maggie glanced between Gabe and Stone. "Bruce Tanner has been fucking with your family even after he died. He put a lot of wheels in motion that kept going when he was gone."

Gabe shrugged. "The guy was a sociopathic dick."

"Yeah," Stone agreed. "But would he screw his old partner, too?"

CHAPTER FIFTY-THREE

Sebastian came to in a rush.

"*Shhh*. It's okay. You're safe." A woman's voice he didn't recognize spoke, and he felt a gentle hand on his arm.

He blinked, finally able to focus his eyes. Alarmed, Sebastian realized he was in a bed and struggled to sit up. "Who are you? Was I taken again?"

The woman helped him up to a sitting position. "My name is Becca Tanner. You're in one of the rooms of my inn. You blacked out."

Sebastian pressed the heel of his hands to his brow. "You know my sister—"

"Maggie's on her way. Her flight arrives in a couple of hours."

His shoulders relaxed. Maggie was safe.

Phoebe.

Pain flooded him as he remembered everything.

He looked around the room, really seeing it. "This isn't a jail cell."

Becca shook her head. "No."

"I don't understand. There were armed agents—" He couldn't tell this nice woman he had expected to be arrested.

"As I understand it, your sister helped find significant evidence explaining your ... situation. The agents who approached you have been briefed."

"Are you serious?"

"Yes. I don't know the international legal hoops, but it's my understanding you're a person of interest in a considerably more favorable context now."

Sebastian sat back, scrubbing his face with his hands. He went to reach for his phone to call Phoebe. Then remembered. "This is such a nightmare."

Becca gave him a small smile. "Rest. I'll let you know when Maggie arrives." She stood. "Actually, are you hungry? I can bring something up."

Sebastian didn't have time to rest. "Bruce Tanner left land to Teague Alans."

Becca stilled. "Yes, that is correct." Her voice had changed dramatically. Gone was the gentleness. In its place, a steely suspicion. "Please understand, I mean you, your family, or your land, no harm. It's just that there is something valuable on or about that land. Do you have any idea what it is?"

The nice woman's frown was severe. "My father didn't give a damn about that land. The only value it had for him was leverage points."

"Leverage points? So, no coal or uranium deposits, no rare minerals? Nothing of significant monetary value?"

Becca shook her head. "Real estate isn't cheap out here, but as far as I understand, the natural resource development potential is minimal, particularly with the increasing public pushback. Pipelines have been proposed, of course, but after everything I've learned about my father, I doubt that would have generated enough money to tempt him or his business partners. If that land is valuable to him, my guess is that it would be something strategic for a bigger game."

"Could it be something with an election issue?"

Becca shrugged. "It wouldn't be the first time, but I have no idea what that could be."

"If I'm right, Teague Alans is coming to collect."

"Collect what?" Becca demanded. "It's *land*. What could he possibly want with it?" She stopped. "Sorry. I get a little nuts with anything related to that stretch of land or my father."

"I can relate."

From the look Becca just gave him, she had at least a passing knowledge of his and Maggie's less-than-nurturing parental units. She held up her hands. "Don't get me started. Anyway, maybe if we knew what loose ends my father left, we could figure out exactly what the hell he was thinking, leaving it to that psycho."

"Loose ends, you say." Sebastian turned the possibility over in his mind. For the first time, he felt his last-ditch effort just might work.

Becca shrugged again. "What else could it be?"

Indeed.

Sebastian had been looking in the wrong places.

It wasn't something valuable to Teague Alans. It was a loose end Bruce Tanner had wanted to cut.

CHAPTER FIFTY-FOUR

Maggie's stomach churned as Jason Chasseur, Becca's fiancé, pulled his truck into Becca's eco-inn. The RCMP officer hadn't asked questions, just offered his usual quiet, grounding presence. Maggie sat shoulder-to-shoulder in the front seat between Jason and Stone while Gabe, Savannah, and Phoebe had filed into the back of the extended cab. The ride from the airport had been snug, giving little breathing room for the anxiety that had been steadily building within her.

Through the windshield, the ranch eco-inn sprawled before them. It was just as beautiful as Maggie remembered. The windows were down, letting the sweet country air sooth across her tense nerves.

Sebastian was alive.

Whatever distance that had widened between them they would bridge. Maggie glanced in the rearview mirror at Phoebe. Her beautiful face had a decidedly ashen quality, and her shoulders were so tight they were nearly at her ears. She looked just as tense as Maggie felt.

Phoebe faced the mirror, catching Maggie's glance. Maggie gave her a small smile before looking away.

Sebastian stood on the front porch. As they got closer, he ran down the porch stairs.

As soon as Jason stopped the truck, Stone let her out, and Maggie flew into her twin brother's outstretched arms.

Sebastian's hug was fierce like hers. They held on, not saying anything for long moments.

She pulled back, aware of their audience. "You're shorter than I remembered," Maggie blurted.

He froze.

"I'm sorry, that was a dumb thing to say. I'm really nervous—"

Sebastian broke into a smile, and he slung his arm around her shoulders. "Still taller than you, sis."

She exhaled, her hand coming up to touch her brother's chest, like touching him would reassure her he was real. Tears burned behind her eyes. Sebastian was *alive*.

"Sebastian?" Her twin brother's fiancée closed the truck door and walked forward.

Sebastian turned his head swiftly, dropping his arm. "You brought *her*?" It came out like the accusation it was. "I don't want her anywhere near me. Or you."

Phoebe winced. Maggie held her ground. "Did you ask this woman to marry you?"

Pain crossed Sebastian's face. "I think it's been clearly established I'm an idiot with a piss-poor radar for appropriate partners." Even as he spoke the harsh words, his eyes sought Phoebe.

It gave Maggie hope. "Becca, is there somewhere these two can go to talk privately?"

Becca had been standing at the top of the porch steps. "Of course. I'll show you to my office. Please, come in."

"I'm not going anywhere with her." Sebastian's words were stubborn, his jaw clenched.

"Yes, you are. You just said you were an idiot." Maggie motioned to Phoebe. "That woman loves you. And how your

271

gaze has soaked up every heartbeat she's taken since stepping out of that truck, I'd say, so do you. You two might not work. But it sure as shit isn't going to be because of something as idiotic as stubbornness. Both of you, inside, now. Talk it out, makeup sex. I really don't care. Just figure your shit out." Maggie blew out a breath before adding, "*Please.*"

Sebastian glanced at Phoebe. "Just so you know, she's always been this bossy."

Phoebe stepped forward. "Is she right? Will you hear me out?" Phoebe bit her lip, waiting for Sebastian's response. He nodded, stoic. The two of them went up the porch steps and followed Becca inside.

Maggie bent over, her hands on her knees.

Stone was there, his hand making slow circles on her back as tears poured down her cheeks. She gulped in air. Everything felt too much, and not nearly enough.

Savannah had stepped toward her. "Maggie?"

Maggie straightened, letting a shudder tack down her body, before holding out her hand. "I'm okay. Just—I needed a moment. Everything's … it's all been a lot."

"What can we do?" Gabe asked.

Maggie had no idea. Before she could say so, Jason's phone buzzed. He looked up from it, frowning. "I just got a Red Notice from Interpol. Three known mercenary associates of Teague Alans's are assumed en route to Halifax with someone matching Teague Alans's description."

Savannah looked between the guys. "What's in Halifax?"

"My guess is fuel," Gabe said.

Stone nodded, typing into his phone. "Maggie and I nearly ran into another crew already at the marina in Muskoka. They knew which one was Sebastian's boat."

Fear iced Maggie's stomach. "They'll come here next, won't they?"

"I would," Stone said.

Jason's frown deepened. "Becca said Sebastian mentioned something about loose ends Bruce would want to cut."

Stone turned toward Maggie. "You called it."

Jason raised an eyebrow.

"Maggie wondered if Bruce would try to screw over his old partner. He left your and Becca's land to Teague." Stone motioned with his hand. "We all assumed it was to screw over you two. What if it was to get back at Teague for being the last man standing?"

Maggie's phone rang. Startled, she checked the caller ID. It was a number she didn't recognize. Her gut screamed for her to answer it. "Hello?"

"Maggie, please don't hang up! Seb's alive."

Lawrence.

Maggie put her phone on speaker and held it out. In unison, Stone, Jason, Gabe, and Savannah silently stepped into a circle around it.

"What is this about?" Maggie asked.

There was a long pause. "You knew he was alive? Why didn't you tell me?"

"If you have to ask that, this conversation is done."

"*Wait.* Don't hang up. I deserved that. I swear I'm trying to help." Lawrence took an audible breath. "Mom and Dad are using you and Seb again."

Fear congealed in Maggie's stomach. "What are you talking about?"

"They found out some psycho wanted Seb's work—did you know he's a fancy scientist now?"

With patience she didn't feel, Maggie answered, "Yes, Lawrence, I know Seb's a scientist."

"God, it's amazing how far he's come." Lawrence sounded starstruck, and Maggie kept the retort that wanted to thunder out to herself. "What are Mom and Dad about?"

"That's what I've been trying to tell you. They've been

tracking you and selling your location to some whack job named Teague Alans. Do you have a wheeled bag you've been using?"

Maggie was going to be sick. She swallowed thickly. "Yes."

Stone was already racing to the back of Jason's truck. He looked up after checking the bag, his face grim, and nodded.

"They know you're back in Alberta but lost your signal south of Calgary. I heard them reporting your location to him." Lawrence paused. "You and Seb be careful. This guy is a nut job."

A shiver iced up Maggie's arms. "We will. And Lawrence?"

"Yeah?"

She hesitated, hoping she wasn't being an idiot for caring. "Thanks."

"I was in a really bad place when I lost your and Seb's trust. Someday, I hope to make it up to you both." Lawrence hung up.

Slowly, Maggie pocketed her phone and looked around the ring of faces. "They're coming."

CHAPTER FIFTY-FIVE

"I can't even look at you." Sebastian tried not to shake when he said it. Becca had closed her French office doors behind her when she left, leaving him and Phoebe alone. The comfortable, inviting space was at odds with their ugly showdown.

Phoebe stood next to the floor-to-ceiling bookcase. "I didn't plan on falling in love with you. It just happened."

"Did you plan on sleeping with me?" His voice actually cracked. He stood on the opposite side of the spacious room in front of a cheery fireplace, empty in the summer heat. Becca's desk faced the room in front of the window. Beyond the desk chairs, a wingback chair and a loveseat filled the space between them.

Phoebe crossed her arms, looking down. "That was at my discretion."

"You *chose* to sleep with me, thinking me a horrific criminal?" Sebastian eyed the French doors, wondering how pissed his sister would be if he bailed right now. He wasn't sure how much more of this he could take. A heart could only break so many times.

Phoebe straightened from the bookshelf, moving toward him.

Sebastian rounded the end of the loveseat, putting the piece of furniture back between them. "What are you doing?"

Phoebe pursued him. "I need you to understand. I'm in love with you. That hasn't changed."

Sebastian kept the small couch between them. "And you think stalking is appropriate?"

Phoebe stopped. "No. You're right. It's not." She drew in a deep breath. "Sebastian, I had zero intention of falling in love with you. You, of all people. I didn't think it was possible, let alone with you. You're chaos. Messy. You've got this tortured, hot nerd vibe going on—*ohmygod*, I can't believe I just said that."

Sebastian was breathing hard, barely holding on as she completely disarmed him. "When I was being tortured, I dreamed of you," he whispered.

Phoebe grabbed the back of the loveseat. Hard sobs racked her body. "I looked so hard for you. I tried to find you. I-I'm so sorry I couldn't find you in time."

"Phoebe—"

"You were my responsibility." She was crying in earnest now, stuttering on her sobs. "I f-failed you. They h-hurt you. I s-should h-have s-stopped t-them."

Sebastian rounded the couch, standing an arm's length from her. "Did you order the attack?"

Phoebe stared at him. "No."

"Then how was it your fault?"

"I was a-assigned to watch you. If w-we hadn't been … i-intimate, I would have made d-different choices." She swallowed hard. "If I had kept to myself, I could have followed you without you k-knowing. Instead, we moved in together." The last part came out as a hiccupped wail.

Sebastian took a half step closer. "Remember when we first met, when you spilled your coffee on me? I couldn't take my eyes off of you."

Phoebe pressed her prayer hands against her face. "That was an accident! I felt so d-dumb, I k-knew I was in t-trouble the moment I laid eyes on you. You were never j-just an assignment, not to m-me." She hiccupped again. Phoebe—controlled, contained Phoebe—was a chaotic mess. It would have been adorable, except he had hurt her just as deeply as she him.

Sebastian took another step closer, inhaling deeper as he caught the intoxicating scent of her perfume, and let himself jump. "Phoebe … work this out with me. Please." Her shoulders shook as he continued. "I need you in my life. I-I love you. I couldn't stop."

She let him gather her up in his arms and buried her face in his shoulder. Her hot tears soaked the shoulder of his shirt, and he cradled her tighter. "Please, don't cry. I'm sorry I was so mad."

After long moments, Phoebe pulled back. "I'm so sorry."

Sebastian looked into the eyes of the woman he loved. She stood close, encircled in his arms. "I was really fucking hurt."

"I know. I'm so sorry."

Sebastian hugged her. "Remind me to thank my sister."

Phoebe's smile lit up her face, turning pain into joy. "Me, too."

He dipped his head, catching her mouth with his. Sebastian meant it as a gentle reassurance for Phoebe. She kissed him back, soft, tentative. Soon, they were learning how to re-stake the claims they had on each other. Tentative exploration of mouths and hands heated quickly, exploding into fiery passion. Clothes disappeared as Sebastian demonstrated to Phoebe just how sure of them he was, and Phoebe reiterated her devotion to him.

It was a long time before they relaxed into each other, their breath and heartbeats slowing back to a normal pace.

Sebastian leaned into Phoebe. "We should probably buy her a new couch."

Phoebe looked behind them before nodding. "Oh, yeah."

He threaded his fingers through hers. "I love you."

She brought their entwined hands to her lips. "I love you, too."

CHAPTER FIFTY-SIX

J ason walked into the kitchen from the back hallway where his fiancée's office was. His face was tinged pink. "Pretty sure they made up."

Becca looked up from the assortment of snacks she was laying out. "Good."

Maggie glanced at Stone. He simply nodded, envying the easy intimacy Jason and Becca shared, before returning to his task. Maggie's wheeled bag was in various pieces on the table in front of him.

"Did they know where we were in Paris?"

"My apartment in Paris is secure. I'm guessing the tracker your parents used isn't the latest technology, and why you were attacked at Sebastian's apartment but not mine." He poked at a wheel, looking for a lead.

"What about the SUV?" Maggie asked, reaching for a mini scone from the basket Becca had put out.

"The exploding SUV was an inside job. Teague blackmailed a junior agent." Stone rubbed his torso. "I would have been skewered full through, right here, if Maggie hadn't pushed me out of the way."

Becca and Savannah gasped. Gabe was pouring everyone coffee and stopped. "Dude."

Stone looked around the table. "What?"

"Bedside manner," Jason explained.

Stone winced. "Sorry." He spent nearly all of his time with other agents or law enforcement types.

Maggie asked, "What about the cottage?"

Stone checked another wheel. "I suspect they tracked us to Muskoka, that's why that crew showed up at the marina, but I'm guessing that steep rock wall on Meredith's property and the dense forest likely inhibited a solid signal."

"Gotta love Canadian Shield," Gabe said.

"That's the second time I've heard that. What is it?"

"A massive landform with a lot of dense rocks and boulders," Gabe answered, taking a sip of coffee. Becca's office doors opened, and a moment later, Sebastian and Phoebe emerged from the hallway behind the kitchen, looking rumpled and utterly pleased. Sebastian cleared his throat. "Uh, thanks, Maggie, for forcing us to … talk."

Phoebe smiled her thanks, cheeks flush.

Sebastian took in the debris spread out on the kitchen island everyone was seated around. "What's all this?"

Maggie stood, offering her brother her seat, which he declined. Maggie pressed, "No, seriously, you're going to want to sit down for this." Sebastian grudgingly sat, but only after Gabe had offered his seat to Phoebe and joined Jason leaning against the kitchen counter.

"I'm sitting. Now, what could be worse than what we've already gone through?" Sebastian asked.

Maggie steepled her hands. "Lawrence called me after you two went inside."

Sebastian's frown was fierce. "Why?"

"To warn me, he just found out Mom and Dad bugged my carry-on bag and have been feeding my locational data to

Teague Alans. Stone's looking for the bug. His sweeper thing beeped, but—"

"Found it." Stone pulled a black, narrow pin-shaded piece no longer than the width of his pinkie finger from the front pouch's fabric lining with tweezers. "Looks fancier than I was expecting." He looked up. "Do your parents know surveillance electronics?"

"Maybe that was extra credit in jail." Stone had never heard quite that tone of bitterness come out of Maggie before. She was staring at the offending piece. "How did they get near me? That bag's been glued to my hip ... ah, hell. Except when I stopped at work on my way to the airport." Maggie swallowed. "Ew. They know where I work."

Sebastian was watching Stone. "Aren't you worried about that tracker sending our location?"

Stone smiled. "We have a couple of sisters-in-law with very thorough security details. They swept the bag and jammed the frequency it was broadcasting on. We should be good." Tucker Tanner was engaged to HRH Princess Grace of Jordemorden. The small Northern European island nation trained elite agents, occasionally farming them out to high-profile political allies. Like Lillian Kensington, Colt Tanner's wife. Both women pulled elite agents, and both spent significant time at Hearthstone Ranch, which meant the eco-inn was one of the most protected places in Canada.

Sebastian looked around the kitchen, wary. "Who are you people?"

Maggie and Becca were both beaming at Stone, and even Gabe and Jason were smiling. Stone suddenly realized what he had said. Before he could try and cover up his blunder, Becca answered Sebastian, "We're normal, I swear." She held out the basket. "Snack?"

CHAPTER FIFTY-SEVEN

Maggie and Sebastian were the only two left in the kitchen. Savannah and Becca had retired to the living room after dinner, and Stone, Gabe, and Jason had headed to the front porch to consult with the ever-present security at *Hearthstone Ranch.*

Maggie folded, unfolded, then folded the corner of the tea towel again in front of her. Sebastian sat on the stool next to her, seemingly at a loss for what to say, too, and Maggie wondered if she should just beg off and go to bed. It was painful, this awkward distance between them.

Sebastian rested his forearms on the counter, his fingers loosely interlaced in front of him. "Remember when you tried to tell me over the phone about what happened when you almost drowned in gym class?"

Maggie stopped folding the tea towel. "I remember."

"I'm sorry I gave you a hard time when you tried to explain what had happened, what you had experienced."

"It's okay," Maggie said, wondering where this was coming from.

"No, it's not. I called you a crazy New Age witch."

She smiled, remembering. "You did. I think I called you a mis-programmed robot in return."

He grinned. "Oh, yeah. Not far off." He hesitated. "I'm sorry. I was terrified at the thought I had nearly lost you in stupid gym class, and I downplayed it."

Maggie gave his forearm a gentle squeeze. "It's okay." She moved to get a glass of water.

"I had an out-of-body experience," Sebastian blurted.

Maggie sat back down.

"When I was being … roughed up, it was like I floated above my body. I saw everything but from the air."

Maggie pushed down the fresh anger and fear that rose within her. "Sounds like a near-death experience." She was crazy proud that her voice was even.

He looked at her. "All I kept thinking was I had to survive. I had to keep you and Phoebe safe. I'm so sorry I haven't been there for you. All these years, I've stayed away. I didn't even tell you Phoebe and I had gotten engaged … I'm sorry."

Maggie blinked back the tears that had suddenly flooded her eyes. "We *both* stayed away."

They were silent for long moments.

Sebastian cleared his throat. "Sometimes, I don't want to be here."

Her heart started pounding, and Maggie sat up. "What?"

"Not like I was before. It's just … sometimes."

Maggie realized she had fisted the tea towel in her hand and hastily spread it flat in front of her. "I-I didn't know that."

"I've learned to manage it. Mostly. I'm getting better. I just—I thought you should know. I don't want to keep something like that from you again."

"Oh, Seb, that's … heavy." Maggie swallowed, unsure how to proceed. "Is there anything I can do to help?"

Her twin brother placed his hand over hers on the counter. "This. Let's just promise to be there for each other. I don't know what that looks like, but we'll figure it out." He gave a laugh. "You knew exactly what Phoebe and I needed to do."

"I thought I was going to puke after I pressed you two to figure it out," Maggie admitted. "What if I was wrong?"

Sebastian's smile was wide. "You weren't. Not on this, at least. The rest, we'll figure out."

A sob escaped Maggie, and she covered her face with her hands. "I missed you so much."

Sebastian wrapped his arms around her. "I missed you, too. We've got each other. Always. We just kind of forgot."

Maggie sniffed. "What about Lawrence?"

Sebastian stiffened and pulled his arms back, though he stayed close. "What about him?"

"Do you think it's possible he's changed? I mean, he sounded sincere, but I don't want to be burned again." Maggie frowned. "He burned us pretty bad."

"Possible? Yes. Probable?" Sebastian blew out a heavy breath. "I have no idea. How about we listen *if* he has anything to say? How's that?"

"I can roll with that." She dropped her head on his shoulder. "Together, we can roll with anything. Good to have you back."

CHAPTER FIFTY-EIGHT

"Teague Alans, I have an appointment." Teague stood at reception, glancing around the impeccable office. Vaulted ceilings and hushed music complemented the thick carpet under his feet and the smell of money. The law firm was one of the most distinguished in the country and had the flash Bruce Tanner was always so dazzled by.

"Yes, Mr. Alans, right this way." The pretty receptionist stood, leading him to a meeting room adjacent to reception.

His smile slipped as she motioned for him to have a seat. "Mr. Humphreys will be right with you. Can I get you anything while you wait?"

Teague eyed the uninspired art on the walls. The hallways boasted finer framed pieces. If he could have, he would have tasked someone on his payroll to pick up the letter Bruce Tanner had left for him. As it were, the lawyers would only release it to him, a stipulation Bruce had firmly outlined in writing.

The receptionist was still waiting for his reply. He simply gave her a disdainful glare. She sidestepped out of the room.

Twenty-three minutes later, a tall, fit man strode into the room, arm outstretched. "Mr. Alans, I'm Mr. Humphreys. Please take a seat."

The man was accustomed to having his orders followed.

Teague hated him on the spot.

The receptionist walked past the open door, and Teague glared at her. Mr. Humphreys leaned his tall frame toward the open door, closing it. The look he gave Teague was less than cordial.

"Why have you only now contacted me about this letter?" Teague demanded.

Mr. Humphreys opened the file folder he had placed on the table in front of him. "Because Mr. Tanner was quite clear on his schedule." Mr. Humphreys plucked a sealed envelope from the file and placed it just out of reach before he swung a piece of paper in Teague's direction. "If you'd sign here, please."

Impatient, Teague signed the release form. Mr. Humphreys handed him the envelope. "I trust you want to be on your way?"

Teague had never been so dismissed in his life. He filed the envelope in his inner suit pocket and stood. He didn't bother to shake the lawyer's hand. Once outside, he opened the mysterious envelope.

It wasn't a letter.

It was coordinates.

CHAPTER FIFTY-NINE

nock, knock, knock.

Stone sat bolt upright to the sound of loud knocking. Maggie murmured something intelligible next to him before snaking her arm around his hips, snuggling against him.

"Stone?" Becca's voice called. Pounding again.

Maggie's eyes flew open. Stone leaned over, giving her a quick kiss. "I'll find out what it is."

He was already grabbing his shorts when Becca called again, "Sebastian's missing."

Maggie launched herself out of bed, beating Stone to the door. He blinked. She was shoving her arms through the tank dress she had discarded on the floor long hours ago. Clothed, they joined Becca in the hall. She was wringing her hands. "Phoebe's in the kitchen talking to her bosses on the phone. When she woke up this morning, Sebastian was gone."

Maggie was halfway down the stairs before Stone caught up to her. "Maggie, stop."

She turned, eyes wild. "I have to find him." She headed down the stairs again.

"I mean, stop and think. Where would he have gone?"

That got her attention.

Stone reached her on the final stair. "You two had a long talk last night. What did he say?"

Maggie was wringing her hands. "We talked about our parents and our brother, Lawrence." Her face paled. "We talked about suicide—Sebastian's been suicidal."

Stone swore and ran back to their room to grab his phone. A knock sounded at the inn's front door. Stone ran out of his room and downstairs, unwilling to leave Maggie or Becca alone with whoever had arrived.

Becca was across the large foyer at the front door. A man Stone had never met stood just inside the doorway. He was medium build, in a T-shirt and jeans, and held a baseball cap in his hand. From the disarray of his hair, he had just pulled the cap off his head.

An armed agent stood next to him. "He's clean."

Stone had never appreciated his sisters-in-law more.

The unkempt man looked nervously over his shoulder before turning back to Becca. "My name is—Maggie? Thank god you're here." He was staring past Becca to Maggie at the bottom of the stairs.

Maggie stumbled on the last step, looking like she was seeing a ghost. "Lawrence, what are you doing here?" Sharper, she asked, "How did you know we were here?" Maggie had stopped at the bottom of the steps.

Stone stepped forward, putting himself between them.

Lawrence gave Stone an uneasy glance before turning his attention back to Maggie. "Mom and Dad met Teague Alans at the airport. They brought the quad and a side-by-side. I found a map on their shared drive." Lawrence held his phone out. "I think they're taking him close to here."

"How did you know we were here?" Maggie repeated.

Becca intercepted Lawrence's phone. Maggie's brother gladly relinquished it before answering, embarrassed. "Mom and Dad have kept tabs on you. They know you were here last Christmas.

They knew you went to Paris." Lawrence was looking a little green. If he was lying, he was good at it. Maggie's brother pressed on. "I swear I didn't know what they have been doing, what they are planning. After they left this morning, I snooped." Lawrence gave a helpless shrug. "I don't know what to do. I don't even know what to go to the police with, even if they would listen to a convicted felon. I have no idea what's so important about this map."

Becca looked up, angry. Her hand holding the phone shook. "This is Jason's ancestral land. This is the land Meredith bought for me that Bruce illegally willed to Teague Alans." Her face was a mask of anger and hurt when she asked, "What the fuck are they doing here?"

The agent looked at the phone. "We saw a few outdoors types with fishing gear crossing the land back there last week. It was outside your buffer zone, Becca, and we didn't notify you."

Becca frowned. "Legitimate outdoor types I'm cool with. It's the international criminal types that I want gone."

Lawrence stepped forward a half step. "From what I read, Bruce Tanner hired Mom and Dad to, and I quote, 'give Teague Alans his due.'"

"What does that even mean?" Maggie snapped. "And what does that have to do with Sebastian? Or the land?"

Stone glanced between Maggie, Becca, and Lawrence, hating what he had to do. "Can I see that phone?"

Becca handed it to him.

He pulled out his own phone.

"What are you doing?" Maggie asked, moving closer to him.

Stone stomped down the despair that crept up, knowing Maggie would be disappointed in him. "Finding Sebastian. I put a tracker on him."

Maggie stilled. "You still don't trust him."

"I'd have put a tracker on you, too, to keep you safe." Stone's phone beeped. "He's on the ridge above the coordinates Lawrence found."

Becca leaned over, pointing, her voice higher. "That rim isn't stable. That's where the avalanche was last winter, and we've gotten an insane amount of rain over the last few weeks. It could go at any time."

Phoebe ran down the hallway from the kitchen. She stopped, taking in the crowd. Slower, she walked up to Maggie and Stone, holding out a small piece of paper. "I just found this on the floor by the kitchen door."

Stone narrowed his eyes at the stylized cartoon duck with a kilt grinning up at him from the corner of the stationary. "May I?"

Phoebe handed him the small scrap of paper. It was the same kind that Maggie had found in Sebastian's plaid shirt pocket, and the folded paper packet the boat keys had been found in the cuckoo clock.

On the paper were numbers.

Maggie peered over his shoulder. "Are those map coordinates?"

Stone punched them into his phone before cross-referencing the map on Lawrence's phone. The map pin from the coordinates was less than a mile from where Sebastian's location was pinging.

He looked at the agent. "How fast can you get a helicopter here?"

"Thirty minutes if we're lucky, probably closer to forty-five."

Stone turned to his half-sister. "Becca, what's the quickest way to get here?"

She assessed the map. "Horseback. There's a single track that runs past there. You can take the quads, but it'll take longer, and I really don't trust that rim."

Stone turned to Lawrence. "Were your parents armed?"

Lawrence shook his head. "I don't know."

Gabe appeared at the top of the stairs. "What's going on?"

In moments he was brought up to speed. Stone turned to Maggie and Phoebe. "Can either of you ride?"

Phoebe shook her head.

Maggie's shoulders sank. "Not well enough. I'd hold you back."

Gabe trotted down the stairs. "I can. Becca, before you object, Jason would shoot me. You've been through more than seasoned agents, but Stone and I were trained for crap like this. Call Jason, Tucker, and Colt, and let them know what's happening."

Gabe turned to Stone.

"Let's end this bullshit once and for all."

CHAPTER SIXTY

"You sure you're okay to ride?" Stone eyed Gabe in the saddle. They rode two of Becca's best saddle horses, and Gabe rode tense as a board. "Relax in your seat, man."

Gabe made a sound suspiciously like a growl but did as Stone suggested. Stone kept an eye on him. The suggestion helped. Gabe didn't look quite as tense as he rode. "My siblings can all ride. I basically hang on, but what other option did we have?"

Stone agreed. He eyed his watch before the gathering clouds. "Are you good to pick up the pace?"

Gabe nodded. "I have to be."

Stone smiled. In this, they were in unison; there were times you simply had to step up.

Within fifteen minutes, Stone reined in his horse. He brought his forefinger to his lips. Gabe pulled up beside him. Stone pointed. Sebastian was on foot, winding his way along a steep single-track trail.

More of a breath than a whisper, Gabe asked, "Where's Alans?"

Stone scanned the forested landscape, answering just as hushed. "I don't know, but we need to intercept Sebastian."

They chose a higher trail, circling the rim. Becca wasn't kidding. The ground was an unstable mess. When they were nearly above him, Sebastian suddenly looked up. Stone motioned for him.

He shook his head, pointing ahead.

Gabe pointed at Sebastian, then spidered his fingers, pointing at the ground, before wiggling his fingers facing each other in explosive chaos. He finished by lolling his head to the side with his tongue draped out of his mouth. It was impressive charades pointing out certain death.

Sebastian frowned but scrambled up the broken terrain to the trail above. "I would have made—"

Boom!

An explosion sounded, and the ground shuddered. Stone held out his hand. Sebastian grabbed it. In a rush, Maggie's twin brother swung into the saddle behind Stone. Gabe didn't waste time leading them up the trail to the plateau above.

Once on stable ground, Sebastian slid off Stone's horse. "What the hell was that?"

Stone frowned. "What do you know about what's going down right now?"

Sebastian ran his hands through his hair. "My parents just rode up with Teague Alans. They disappeared into what looked like an old mine shaft. I—I don't think Bruce Tanner left the land for Teague Alans as a gesture of goodwill, or to screw over Becca. I think he set Alans up." Sebastian frowned. "I think Bruce Tanner paid my parents to do it, whatever *it* is."

"Why'd you come here?" Stone asked.

Sebastian's face was stark. "Maggie kept hoping they would change. I had to see for myself. From where I'm standing, it looks like they just bombed an old mine shaft to bury a guy for money."

Stone looked at Gabe. "We found Sebastian."

"That was the operation." Gabe eyed the valley. "With one explosion already," he pointed, "*that* looks like a suicide mission."

Sebastian's eyes rounded, just like Maggie's. "You can't be seriously considering going down there?"

Gently, Stone said, "They're your parents. What do you want to do?"

Sebastian didn't answer for a long time. Finally, he swiped quickly at his eyes. "I think I've got a hell of a lot to live for. I can't—I can't get sucked into their games."

Gabe gave Stone a curious look, and Stone shook his head. He'd fill his half-brother in later. Stone held out his hand to Sebastian. "Come on then, let's get you back. There's—"

Boom!

Another explosion rang before a terrible splitting sound tore through the air.

Both horses spooked.

All three of them were thrown from the saddles as the horses bolted.

Stone landed with a thud ... but kept moving.

The ground beneath him disappeared.

Stone tumbled off the side of the moving mountain. Frantic, he grasped for purchase but only clutched air. He heard Gabe and Sebastian yelling above him. Stone bounced off a rock face before snagging a tree with his elbows.

Abruptly, he was yanked to a stop, his feet dangling midair.

The spruce tree was no bigger than a Christmas tree. The plucky conifer was holding him. For now. How it had stopped his fall defied gravity.

"Stone!" Gabe yelled from above. "Hold on, man, we're coming."

Stone didn't dare move. He willed his arms to stay locked in place. His muscles screamed at him. He couldn't die yet; he hadn't told Maggie he loved her. It was a ridiculous thought, but it gave him focus.

Stone looked up. Gabe and Sebastian were shimmying toward him, and he yelled, "It's too dangerous!"

"Shut up, asshole. This is harder than it looks." Gabe was stretched upside-down as Sebastian held his legs. "Give me your hand."

"Are you nuts?" Stone asked, panting from the exertion. There was no way this was going to work.

"Probably. Now grab my fucking hand. Sebastian can't hold me all day."

Stone reached for his half-brother.

Gabe caught Stone's hand.

His grip was like a talon on Stone's forearm. "*Now,* Sebastian!"

Maggie's twin brother heaved. In grinding fits, Sebastian pulled them up. As soon as Stone's legs found purchase, he toed up. After a long, excruciating climb, they cleared the rim. Stone crawled several feet from the edge before flipping onto his back. Gabe and Sebastian were panting a few feet away.

No one spoke.

Boom!

All three of them sat up. "*Jesus,*" Gabe muttered, getting to his feet. "How dead do they want him?"

Sebastian's eyes widened.

"Dude," Stone chastised.

"What?" Gabe asked.

"Bedside manner," Stone answered.

Gabe laughed a deep, belly laugh. It was the first time Stone had heard it.

Sebastian was looking between the two. "Am I missing something?"

Stone slapped him on the shoulder. "We'll fill you in on the walk. Becca's horses are halfway back to the barn by now."

CHAPTER SIXTY-ONE

"They're here!" Maggie tore out of the eco-inn's kitchen door, running past the barn, stopping short of the worst of the helicopter's rotor wash.

Savannah and Phoebe had followed and stopped next to her, each averting their faces from the whirling debris of the landing aircraft. The helicopter touched down, and Stone, Sebastian, and Gabe filed out, crouching low as they cleared the spinning blades.

A safe distance away, the men turned and took a knee while Stone gave the pilot the thumbs up. The helicopter took off, heading back toward the backcountry.

Maggie reached the three men first. She didn't know who to hug first.

Stone wrapped her in his arms, whispering in her ear, "It's over."

Her legs wobbled in relief, and she hugged him back just as fiercely.

Sebastian had his arm around Phoebe, and Gabe and Savannah were tucked in close to each other.

Becca walked from the open barn door. "What took you so

long?" The words were light, but her voice was laden with concern. "My horses have been back for ages."

Gabe picked up his sister and spun her around. "Stone just had to step off a cliff."

In unison, Maggie and Becca cried, "*What?*"

Stone glared at Gabe. "Dude?"

Gabe put his sister down, grinning. Becca had a dazed look in her eyes. Gabe's overt rambunctiousness was at complete odds with his usual stoic reserve. He draped his arm around Savannah's shoulders. "Lillian and Grace's security are securing the scene. We'll fill you in on everything." He looked at Stone and Sebastian. "Is it too early for a beer?"

Sebastian smiled. "Not today." His smile slipped. "Lawrence?"

Maggie turned. Their older brother stood in the yard, on the periphery of the small group. His face was wet from shed tears. He took a step forward but stopped. "Sebastian, thank god you're safe."

Sebastian frowned. "Mom and Dad aren't."

Lawrence ran his hands through his hair. "Were they ever?"

Maggie watched her two brothers. Their mannerisms were more alike than she had ever realized.

"No," Sebastian answered quietly. "Those two lived on the edge. It's a wonder they didn't bring us down with them."

Lawrence looked down. "They almost did."

Something about the way he said it alerted Maggie. Sebastian was studying their brother, too. "You okay?"

Lawrence looked up, giving a half-hearted smile. "Sure."

Sebastian waited.

"Not really," Lawrence admitted, his small smile falling, and he shook his head. "No, I'm not."

Maggie froze, remembering Sebastian confided demons.

Sebastian nodded at Lawrence. "Me, neither. Come on, then, let's go inside. Maybe between the three of us, we can figure out how to be okay together."

Lawrence sprang to join the small group. "I'd like that."

Maggie's hugged Stone tight against her as she watched her brothers take the first steps toward reconciliation. She leaned her head against his shoulder. "Thank you."

"For what?"

"Keeping me alive so I could see this."

"*Maggie*—"

"No … you can't use that voice, not when we're surrounded by our relatives." Every feminine part of her was humming.

"Yes, I can." He dropped his head to hers. When their lips touched, she sighed … *sighed*, for heaven's sake. She didn't have time to worry. His lips were so soft and moving over hers. He cupped her jaw, deepening the kiss.

"Told you she would be good for you."

Maggie broke the kiss. "Tucker?"

Tucker Tanner stood on the back deck and spread his arms wide. "In the flesh. Happy to see Stone took my advice."

"What is he talking about?" Maggie asked the man in her arms.

Stone nuzzled her neck, whispering, "I'll tell you later."

She was looking forward to it.

Becca waved to her brother. "Did we get the all-clear?"

He nodded. "Grace got the thumbs up a few minutes ago. We were just at Colt and Lillian's. They're all on their way."

"Excellent. You're on food duty. We'll have a full house."

He gave her a thumbs-up and headed back inside.

Maggie turned to Stone. "What are they talking about? Do they mean the explosions?"

He was looking at his phone. "Grace and Lillian's security details just secured the scene. They found intel on scene …" He kept scrolling before he abruptly looked up. "I'm so sorry, Maggie. There were no survivors. Your parents, they didn't make it."

A surreal fusion of pain and surrender washed over her before a curious lightness—much like relief—filled her.

An hour later, Maggie leaned against Stone as they sat on the plush bench seat on Becca's back deck. Plush chairs and love seats were arranged to form a circle of family and friends. Sunlit mountains lay beyond the back pasture where Becca's horses grazed. Sebastian and Phoebe sat on Maggie's left and Lawrence beyond them. Sebastian and Lawrence had taken the news of their parents' death with as much relief as pain. They all had complicated relationships with their parents in life. It made sense their death would be just as complicated.

Gabe and Savannah sat to Stone's right. Maggie and Savannah kept exchanging happy glances as the two brothers talked instead of glaring and grunting.

Lillian and Colt had come with baby Emma. The little girl was currently bouncing in Maggie's lap, delighted at the circle of loving adults surrounding her.

"Yoo-hoo, we're here!" Maggie looked up as Samantha, Bruce Tanner's first wife, made a grand entrance, with Meredith, his second wife, laughing beside her. Samantha held a bouquet of flowers, and Meredith a large pastry box from a well-loved patisserie. "Darlings, I didn't know we were planning a party?"

"We weren't, Mom, just a spontaneous celebration of life." Becca had jumped up. "Those are lovely, Mom. Are they for Lillian?" Samantha leaned across the table and handed Colt's wife the lovely bouquet. "Thank you, Samantha. They are beautiful." Lillian's smile was ever gracious.

"Of course, they are. You will get flowers when you give me a grandchild."

"Who's giving you another grandchild?" Jason Chasseur had just walked in with his mom, Rose. He dropped a kiss on Becca's forehead, and she said, "Apparently us."

Jason's eyes widened, and Becca was quick to reassure him. "*If* I want flowers from my mom."

He pulled a bouquet from behind his back. "So do I give you these, or—"

Becca's smile could light up the room. "You do!" She

smacked a big kiss on his lips. "Thanks, honey." She admired the beautiful bouquet of sunflowers, mums, and roses. "They're gorgeous!"

Tucker walked through the back door, carrying two heaping trays of appetizers. He set them down with a flourish. "There's plenty more, don't be shy. Chris is grabbing an assortment of beverages, and Grace has the brownies." Maggie leaned over to Stone and asked, "Chris is Becca's sommelier that saved Meredith, Becca, and Jason's life, right?"

Stone nodded, whispering back, "Austin is his brother. I think I heard Tucker mention he's popping in tonight, too."

Maggie nodded, wishing she had a spreadsheet to keep all the Tanner family and their friends straight.

A collective bow started, and Maggie turned. Princess Grace had walked onto the deck with a massive platter of brownies. She looked horrified. "Guys, please!"

"Babe, they're bowing at my brownies." Tucker beamed as Grace planted a kiss on his cheek. "Well, in that case, do carry on. Your brother simply adores the attention."

"Hey!"

Becca nodded. "He does, doesn't he." Her voice dropped to a serious timbre. "So, what happened?"

Tucker and Gabe looked at Stone, who answered. "We tracked Bruce Tanner's final business partner, Teague Alans, to Paris. He had gotten a tip on Sebastian's hydrogen energy research and wanted to weaponize it for profit. Except Sebastian caught on and hid his research before Teague Alans's crew attempted to murder him. Teague Alans was getting frantic. Problem with selling arms is the buyers are less than understanding if you don't deliver."

Sebastian sat forward. "Enter our parents. They knew Bruce Tanner, and tipped Teague Alans off to my research in the first place, then tracked Maggie and fed him her locational data. Bruce also paid them a king's ransom to give Teague Alans 'what he deserved,' but I still don't know what that was."

Lawrence cleared his throat. "I think I can help with that. Bruce Tanner blamed Teague Alans for his drug addiction."

The whole deck went silent.

Tucker asked, "How's that?"

"Teague supplied him in the beginning, goading him. Bruce didn't want to appear weak, so he took it, not realizing Teague wasn't using. In days, he was addicted." Lawrence's shoulders sank. "Drugs are like that."

Becca frowned. "That's a cold move, even inflicted on a monster like Dad."

"Bruce got the last laugh," Gabe said. "Teague Alans died in that mountain, chasing the treasure he thought Bruce had left him."

Samantha scoffed. "Everlasting Hell? What a pair." She rarely spoke of her ex-husband. Theirs hadn't been a loving marriage.

Meredith placed her hand over Samantha's. "We survived."

Samantha's smile reached her eyes. "Damn straight."

Gabe's phone pinged. He looked at Savannah, his face dazed. "I got in."

Her eyes lit, and she wrapped her arms around her fiancé. "Oh, honey, congratulations, I knew you could!"

"Got in where?" Becca asked.

Savannah looked at Gabe. "Can I tell them?" He nodded, smiling. "Gabe just got into his Ph.D. program, and I got an incredible offer at the Hydrology Centre. We're moving back to Alberta!"

Becca squealed. In three seconds, raucous congratulations and laughter, and plans were bouncing around the deck. Maggie watched Stone soaking it all in. She covered his hand in hers. "This is your family."

He nodded, eyes damp. "They're your family, too."

CHAPTER SIXTY-TWO

S tone sat on Becca's front porch, watching the dappled sunlight in the trees.

The front screen door opened, and Gabe walked out holding two beers. "I figured we could use one of these."

Stone accepted the beer Gabe handed him as Gabe sat in the chair next to him. Wordlessly, each angled their beer bottles in, clinking them.

Gabe took a sip of his beer. "Well, that was one hell of a morning."

"That's one way to put it." Stone took a sip of his beer, gathering his courage. "How did you know Savannah was the one?"

Gabe gave him an assessing look. "If you have to ask, she's not."

Stone exhaled. "That's what I was afraid of." When Gabe's brow furrowed, Stone explained. "I can't breathe without her. It's terrifying." His voice caught. "I can't imagine life without her—don't want to imagine life without her. Seriously, she's like the air I breathe."

Gabe's face lit with a rare smile. "Right *there, that's* your answer."

Stone's heart felt like it was pulsating with hope. "I am so in love with that woman."

"You're a goner, for sure, but the good kind of gone." Gabe settled back and took a sip of his beer. "I can relate, man. Savannah's the best thing that ever happened to me."

"Falling in love?"

"It's not enough to fall in love. That's the easy part. It's having the balls to go for it. To say yes. To be all in. To make the choices that will support it and make it work. Falling in love is easy. Being in love can be hard. It takes care and attention. Work, but the good kind. Like the good kind of gone."

Stone took a sip of his beer. "*Good kind of gone*, I like that. Yeah, I can rock that." For Maggie, he'd do anything.

Gabe clinked his bottle against Stone's. "Welcome to the family."

They sat in companionable silence for a while. Sipping beer in the warm summer sun.

Gabe spoke. "I'm sorry I never said anything. About you. That wasn't fair."

Stone turned his head but remained quiet.

Gabe continued. "When I was a kid, I was terrified I'd break up the family if I said anything. When I was older, I honestly didn't know what the right thing to do was." He looked across the yard. "You had parents who loved you. We had ... chaos." Gabe ran a hand through his hair. "God, there was so much fighting. I wondered that if you didn't know about Bruce, that he was your biological father, would I be turning your life upside-down for no reason? I mean, Christ, the guy was a monster."

Stone had never considered that. "Thanks, Gabe. The whole mess ate me up for a lot of decades."

Gabe looked him in the eye. "Sorry, man."

Stone held out his hand and meant it. Gabe was quick to shake it.

"Thanks for saving my life this morning."

"Thanks for saving mine in Muskoka."

Stone was quiet. "I judged my mom pretty harshly for carrying on with a married man."

Gabe looked at him, listening.

"Why'd she have to name me after the guy, to boot?"

Gabe blew out a breath. "I'd go by Stone, too."

Stone took a sip of his beer.

An airport sedan pulled up.

"Is Becca expecting anyone?" Gabe asked.

"No idea," Stone said before watching in disbelief.

His mom stepped out.

CHAPTER SIXTY-THREE

S tone stood. "Mom? What are you doing here?" He hustled down the porch stairs and swept his mom up in a hug.

She hugged him back. "Tanner, what's wrong? This isn't like you."

Stone held her a second longer. "I just missed you, Mom."

Her eyes were damp when she pulled back. "I missed you, too."

Stone retrieved her bags from the sedan. "I'm happy to see you, but why are you here?"

She waved the sedan off before giving Stone one of her light-up-the-room smiles. "I had a feeling."

Stone smiled. "I just bet you did."

They walked up the porch steps where Gabe stood. Doris Stone immediately shook his hand. "Gabe Tanner, I presume. It's a pleasure to meet you."

Gabe glanced briefly at Stone as he shook Doris's hand. "Likewise, Ms. Stone. If you'll excuse me, I'll give you two some privacy."

"Thank you, dear," Doris said. Gabe gave Stone one more look before heading into the ranch inn.

Stone asked, "You must be exhausted. Do you want to rest for a bit? Or are you hungry?"

Doris marched to one of the porch chairs and sat down. "I'm fine." She patted the arm of the adjacent chair. "Come sit with me."

Stone felt like a child in trouble but did as she bid. He leaned back in the chair, his fingers interlocked and resting on his torso. "What's up?"

She gave him one of her *mother* looks, waiting.

Stone squirmed for long minutes. His mom sat quiet and calm, waiting. Now that the time was here, he didn't know what to do.

"Just ask," his mom suggested reasonably.

He had dreamed of this moment, of having the courage to confront his mom. It wasn't righteous anger he felt, though, as he had expected. It was an aching inferiority. Stone was ashamed. His voice shook when he asked, "Why'd you do it?"

Doris looked out across the ranch yard. Three mule deer grazed placidly on the velvety grass at the end of the drive. "Why did I have an affair with a married man, you mean?"

"Yes, Mom." Stone made himself exhale. "Why did you have an affair with a married man—why'd you do it?" He hated how his voice broke but wouldn't back down now. He'd wasted decades running from this conversation. Letting unanswered questions pull them further and further apart.

Doris was silent so long Stone realized she wasn't going to answer. Pain shredded him. Resigned, he started to get up. Her hand on his arm stayed him. "Sit down."

Feeling like a chastised child, Stone sank back into the deck chair, wishing he was anywhere but here.

"He wasn't always a monster." Doris paused. "Bruce was older, handsome, and charismatic. The attention he gave me felt … good, mostly. There was always an undercurrent I wasn't comfortable with, though I couldn't put my finger on what it was exactly. Though, I guess hindsight's twenty-twenty." His mom looked down at her hands. "I didn't realize he was married until after our affair had started."

"But why'd you let it go so far? Did you think he was going to leave his wife?"

His mom turned her head sharply. "Of course not. I would have never asked him to do that. Gabe was on the way."

"Are you fucking serious?" Stone felt sick. All these years, he had villainized Bruce for choosing Gabe over him. It had never occurred to him that his own mom had done the same thing.

"Language."

"Condom," Stone retorted.

Doris inhaled sharply, and Stone realized they balanced on a precipice. But he couldn't retreat, not to the way things were. The chasm between them had never been wider, and he was afraid that if they didn't sort it out now, they'd never be able to bridge it.

"I didn't realize how much you hated me." His mom's voice was quiet but in no way small.

Two of the deer had moved on. The third remained in place. Stone met his mom's gaze. "I don't hate you. I don't understand you. Never have."

Doris studied him for long moments. Stone sat in silence, letting himself be studied. She didn't know him. How could she? He had kept himself away so long.

He had also never dared be so blunt with her, never wanting to skirt such disrespect.

Finally, she spoke, "What do you feel about me?"

Trick question. Stone had sidestepped this minefield his entire life. Time to walk through and hope he didn't blow anything up. "Hurt, Mom. I feel hurt and shit on. You and Bruce made me a bastard. On purpose. *What* were you thinking?"

His mom went to wrap her arms around him, and Stone instinctively leaned away. "I don't want a hug. I want us to finally talk about this."

Doris looked at him like she was seeing him for the first time.

"I've never considered you a bastard. That's church dogma, not mine. As for the show, it was a different time then."

"What's that supposed to mean?"

"If a man didn't want to wear a condom, a man didn't wear a condom. Women were expected to oblige."

Stone saw red.

Doris put a staying hand on his arm again. "I'm not saying it was right. I'm saying what it was like."

"Why'd you keep me?" The question was out before Stone could stop himself. "You believe in reincarnation. I could have incarnated into another family." He didn't add *stable* or *loving*. He didn't have to. "Why did you keep me?"

His mom's shoulders started to shake, and Stone realized she was crying.

"*Mom?*" Stone stilled. He had pushed too far. "Stop. Please don't answer that."

She wiped at her eyes. "I didn't think I was going to."

Instead of feeling shredded at hearing his mom confirm his worst suspicions, Stone felt compassion. "That choice must have felt impossible."

She was looking at him like she never had before. "It was!" She looked down. "Bruce asked me to terminate my pregnancy." She swallowed before continuing. "I was alone and scared. I didn't want to, but I didn't know what else I could do. I had made the appointment and was trying to make peace with it. With the choices I had made—"

"You didn't conceive me by yourself," Stone stormed.

"It wasn't seen like that."

"It fucking was that. Is that why he never claimed me? I wasn't his responsibility because you two were never married?" The obnoxiousness of it all was suffocating. "Bruce sent that money over the years to keep you quiet, didn't he?"

"You knew about that?" He hadn't. Becca had told him it was how Gabe had found out as a child.

"Only this year."

"I claimed you." Doris's voice rang with stubborn conviction. "And you have a father. We *are* a loving family," she said, completely ignoring the fact that they were a family of secrets.

Stone sat back, wrung out. "That doesn't erase how I came into this world."

"You came into this world wanted."

"You said ..." Stone couldn't finish it. It hurt too much to think that his existence had caused his mom to have to make heartbreaking choices. "Wait, how did I end up here? I interrupted you."

A smile brightened Doris's serious face. "I saw your siblings."

Stone sat up. "Good God, do you have more kids I don't know about?" It was too much to process.

Doris laughed. "No. I saw the Tanners. Your siblings."

Half-siblings.

Stone crossed his arms. "What about them?"

"I *saw* them." The silver rings on his mom's fingers caught the fading sunlight as she straightened her broom skirt. "I've never told you this, but I *see* things."

Stone waved his hand, urging her to tell the rest. "I know."

Doris's head came up swiftly. "Oh."

It was so much like Maggie's *ohs*. Stone smiled despite himself. The thought of Maggie immediately brought him a grounded peace. More patiently, he asked, "What did you see, Mom?"

She smiled, her eyes looking somewhere far away. "You were with a roomful of Tanners and their loved ones. You were happy but didn't feel like you belonged." She looked at him. "That's why I named you Tanner, so you would know you belonged to them. You're one of them."

"You didn't name me after Bruce?"

Doris was plucking at her skirt when her head shot up again. "Heavens, no! I named you after the children he would have. They're lovely. I *felt* them. I wanted you to feel connected to them and know you belonged. Their energy felt so good each time I sensed them. I knew you all would be good for each other."

Stone was having a hard time processing and had to be clear. "You didn't name me after that monster?"

Doris leaned over, placing her hand over his. "No, darling. I did not name you after your biological father."

Stone wasn't quite sure what to say. He had judged his mom so harshly. "I'm sorry I didn't ask you all this sooner."

Doris gave him a teary smile. "I didn't know this was how you felt. Otherwise, I would have told you all of this sooner. I wasn't trying to keep it from you. I just didn't realize it mattered."

"So, not psychic?"

His mom scoffed. "I really don't like that word."

Stone smiled. "Mom, I have someone I want you to meet."

EPILOGUE

*P*aris
Fall leaves scuttled across the pavement as the sun dipped lower behind the Paris skyline. Fall was Maggie's favorite time of year. She and Stone were staying with Sebastian and Phoebe. Maggie had never seen Sebastian so happy, and Lawrence was doing well. Their reconciliation would take time, but for the first time, there was hope. They would all be at Hearthstone Ranch for Christmas, and Maggie knew miracles happened at that place, especially at Christmas time.

She leaned into Stone as they walked hand-in-hand on the tree-lined boulevard, and it suddenly dawned on her that they were holding hands as the Eiffel Tower stretched before them. She dug into her jacket pocket and handed him the card stock.

Stone accepted the postcard Maggie handed him. "What's this?"

"I got it when we flew out of Charles de Gaulle in the summer."

A warm smile lit Stone's handsome face. "It looks like us."

"That's what I thought!" Maggie beamed, snuggling tighter against Stone. He was smiling more than usual, and there was a definite spring in his step. "You're bouncy."

That drew a frown. "Hardly."

"You are. Paris suits you."

He gave her a long look. "I may be rethinking my previous opinion of the City of Lights."

They were now at the base of the Eiffel Tower, and Stone suggested, "Let's go up."

"What has gotten into you?" Maggie laughed as they stood in a short line to purchase tickets.

"You." His eyes were so serious when he said it Maggie's breath caught in her throat.

They took the elevator up and made their way to the west side. Maggie stood at the railing, and Stone stood at her back, his arms cradled around her. She leaned against him, and he pressed his cheek against hers as they looked across the Paris skyline. The view was exquisite. A full moon had risen in the east as the sun set in the west.

"This is magical," Maggie whispered.

Stone kissed her. The last several months had been the best of his life. "I like your fire."

She groaned. "You always say that."

"I always mean it." Stone pulled out a small box and flipped it open. He held it out in front so she could see it. "I saw this and thought of you."

Maggie gasped. It was a gold band with a deep red ruby, surrounded by yellow diamonds. "Stone, it's beautiful."

Stone smiled. The ring was stunning, just like Maggie.

She cupped the box in her hands. "I've never seen a piece of jewelry like this. It's like passion and fire but with such elemental grace." Suddenly she stiffened. "Stone, what does the ring mean?"

He moved to her side. "Maggie, I can't imagine my life without you. I tried to take this slow, to be rational and reasonable, but I can't wait another second. I love you." He took a knee. "I finally feel the sun with you. I'm asking you to marry me. I'll wait if this is all too soon, too much. But, I need you to know I love you and want to spend the rest of our lives together—"

Maggie launched herself at him, hugging him fiercely. "I love you, too," she whispered in his ear. "Yes!"

Stone kissed her. "I knew I was a goner when I met you."

She kissed him back. "Yeah, but it's the good kind of gone."

He laughed as he pulled out his phone.

"What are you doing?"

Stone looked up. "Texting the family group chat. We just got engaged." He stopped. "We did just get engaged, right?"

Laughter bubbled up as joy blossomed inside her. She cupped his face and kissed him soundly. "We most certainly did!" She held out her hand. "Will you do the honors?" Stone hustled to slip the ruby and yellow diamond ring on her finger. The dancing tower lights flicked on, dazzling them in their glittering glow. The moment was perfect. It felt so right. "I love you."

"I love you, too." They stared into each other's eyes for a long moment. Heat sparking between them like it always did.

"Come on."

"What are we doing?" Stone asked. Maggie wrapped her arm around him and held up her hand with the fiery ring. "We're sending them a pic."

Stone turned his head at the last second, kissing her as he snapped the selfie.

Maggie felt his love burning bright and strong.

It was as bright and nurturing as the sun.

She kissed him back. "This is definitely the good kind of gone."

The End.

AUTHOR'S NOTE

I want to let you in on a little secret. Sometimes authors and publishers have a working title for a project until the title of the book reveals itself. Early in this project, my publisher, Mark Leslie Lefebvre, and I landed on *Sunrise of Dreams* for this novel, the fifth and final book in the *Hearthstone Series*. Even though I had proposed it, the title never quite hit. I waved off my hesitation and wondered if I was simply being too fussy. From the get-go, though, the fiery shades of sunlight on the cover image, however, felt very right.

As the story unfolded and the characters pulled me deeper into their story, I realized how much that liminal sunlight on the cover fit. Readers could see dawn in it, the welcoming of a new day as the characters found each other. Or sunset, the closing of the different chapters in the characters' lives, as well as the series. The fiery shades also fit Maggie's unacknowledged passionate spirit and Stone's lingering familial anger.

As I progressed through writing the book, the characters also made it clear, in no uncertain terms, that the title was *Good Kind of Gone*. I hesitated and kept writing. Just because I saw *gone*, as in *goner*, as in totally smitten, and crazy in love, didn't mean readers would—gone can also be construed as a negative.

The characters persisted. Firmly. That's what writing is like, at least for me. The characters lead me on their merry adventure and let me know what's what. As I finished the last third of the book, they were delighted I had finally *heard* their title. That's another thing about writing. Sometimes it feels a lot like listening as the characters whisper their story. The more I sat with *Good Kind of Gone* as the title, the deeper it sank within me. Then I *felt* it; there can be good kinds of gone.

Point taken, my darling characters, point taken.

I immigrated to Canada for love.

The decision was not made lightly, but it was made promptly. The day before I immigrated, I was pulled over—shocking, I know. Dusk was setting, and I hadn't turned my lights on (yes, cars used to have manual headlights). The officer's eyes widened when he saw my tear-streaked face and asked if I was all right. In that hiccupped voice unique to crying, I told him I was moving to Canada the next day to live with my husband—which made me ecstatic—but that meant I would be moving away from my family—which was all rather crushing. He slowly backed away while telling me to turn my headlights on. Poor guy.

It's easy to move toward love, not so much to move away from it. It was the right choice, but it wasn't without consequences. I've been blessed to have a lot of love in my life, and each move I've made has been bittersweet. Perhaps, I am a *good kind of gone*—in love, and with each new adventure.

Thank you, dear readers, for coming on this adventure with me. The Tanners and their found families have filled me with so much light and happiness (okay, stress and freakouts, too) as I've navigated their stories. Thanks for coming along for the ride.

Sarah Kades
August 2023
35,000 feet, somewhere between Quebec City and Calgary

ACKNOWLEDGMENTS

Book five in this series—what a ride this experience has been! *Kiss Me in the Rain, Wild Not Broken, Not an Easy Truce, Loyal to You,* and now *Good Kind of Gone* ... I am humbled and dazzled at the path this journey has taken me on.

To my readers, thank you for making this career possible. I hope you love reading these stories as much as I have loved writing them. Mark Leslie Lefebvre, your ongoing support, wisdom, and tenacity are incredible gifts. Thank you for helping me share these characters and their stories with the world. Jonas Saul, great editors are a sacred thing. Thank you for giving a damn. Dave Sweet, thank you for your service to our community, for answering the cop craft questions, and for choosing me to co-write our first book. Writing the *Hearthstone Series* has been a beautiful way for me to process our writing *Skeleton in My Closet, Life Lessons from a Homicide Detective.* Paris and her people, thank you for captivating the world—myself included. Suzy Vadori, thanks for being the best conference roommate ever. Chris Humphrey for the Hamlet performance and Norse chats. Tania for the coffee breaks, virtual, and for realizes. Carmen, Karleen, and Kathy, for always asking how the writing is going. Thank you to the entire When Words Collide and Alberta Romance Writer Association communities for creating space for magic to happen.

Randy McCharles, your writing retreats are a godsend; thank you. Tracey Retallack, you have a great career ahead of you. I can't wait to see the beautiful places you will go. Rosanna Jackson, for sharing happy, and Erica Carrasco, for dragging my butt downtown. Rachel New, Kate Phillips, Stuart Martin, et al. re *Miss Scarlet and the Duke,* thank you for creating a binge-worthy TV series. As much as I adore reading and writing books—sometimes a glass of wine and the remote is pure bliss.

To my family, you all roll with my random character musings, plotline finessing, and deadline crunches (because no matter how fastidiously I plan, it ends up a crunch). I appreciate your patience, amusement, support, and love. Always.

To Momma Earth, this is quite an extraordinary planet you've got here. Thank you for sharing your magic with us and including us in your story.

BOOK CLUB QUESTIONS

Good Kind of Gone

By Sarah Kades

1. Though uncomfortable with the thought of having to use it, Maggie is well-skilled in hand-to-hand combat. She has spent years training with above-average instructors. What internal tension generated that drive? Has there been a time you chose to learn a new skill that was driven by necessity? What was it? How did it change your life?

2. Stone adamantly considered himself a bastard. What external messaging did he internalize, and from whom? How did that play out in his life and the choices he made? Has there been a time in your life you realized you had internalized messages others thought or said about you? What happened? Would you do things differently? How?

3. Gabe struggled with his past choices to keep quiet. Has there been a time in your life you were not sure what was the best path to take? Did you wait? If so, did you reach a point of no return where too much time had lapsed to change course? What would have helped you with your decision?

4. Savannah's loyalties to Gabe and Maggie were, at times, in conflict. Has there been a time in your life when you felt

compelled to choose between two (or more) people you care about? What happened? What advice would you give another experiencing a similar conflict? What would have helped you?

5. Maggie didn't realize the distance that had crept between her and her twin brother, Sebastian. She was surprised he hadn't shared meaningful life events with her. Has that ever happened to you? What happened? Were you able to strengthen your relationship again? If so, how? What advice would you give someone wanting to reconnect with another?

6. Stone is uneasy with his mom's past choices. Is there someone you love that has made choices that you don't agree with? What happened? How did you find common ground? Was forgiveness required? What was the biggest realization you came to?

7. Maggie and Stone dance around their attraction. Has there ever been someone in your life like that? What did they bring out in you? What did you bring out in them? Did you have a relationship with them? Do you still? Do you miss them? If you had anything to do over again, what would it be?

8. Maggie put off a trip to France in general, and Paris specifically, for years. Is there ever a "right time" for a trip of a lifetime? If so, when? If not, why not? Is there a trip you've dreamed about but never took? Why not?

9. Stone and Gabe have a combative relationship. The actions and choices of others put them in positions not of their making but that they had to respond to. Is there anyone in your life like that? Do you wish it was different? What would have to change to make a positive relationship be able to work? Explain.

10. Maggie catches herself while having an exquisite moment with her newfound family on Christmas Day. Has there been a time in your life you caught yourself in a moment? Was it good or bad? Who was there? What made it memorable? Explain.

11. Sebastian felt Phoebe's actions betrayed him deeply. Has there been a time in your life you were betrayed by someone you

loved? What happened? Did time give you more perspective? Explain.

12. Phoebe fell in love with Sebastian under challenging circumstances. Do you feel love conquers all? Has there been a time in your life love blossomed unexpectedly? What happened? Did you nurture it or not? Explain.

13. Stone's mom shared incredibly personal histories with her son. Has there been a time in your life you feel you would have benefitted from uncomfortable but important conversations? Has there been a time in your life when you found out misunderstandings had snowballed and caused significant damage? What happened?

14. The book's title, *Good Kind of Gone*, is a homage to not only falling in love, it's the recognition of the courage it takes to act on feelings that will completely upend your life—hopefully in the best possible ways, but with no guarantees. Has there been a time you've felt passionately about something and took the risk? What happened? Was it worth it? Would you do it again? Did you learn something about yourself? If so, what? Explain.

ABOUT THE AUTHOR

Sarah Kades writes eco-thrillers, and narrative non-fiction as Sarah Graham. Her writing is largely inspired by her previous career as an archaeologist where she routinely lived in tents, caught rides in helicopters and adored the awesomeness of the landscapes around her. Sarah is a two-time Energy Futures Lab Banff Summit storyteller, a recipient of the Calgary Arts Development individual artist grant, and has presented at the British Society of Criminology conference on the application of using arts-based approaches. When she's not writing you can find her running, bumping into her next adventure, or trying to figure out where in the garden to put the makeshift wood-fired pizza oven.

ALSO BY SARAH KADES

HEARTHSTONE SERIES

Kiss Me In The Rain

Wild Not Broken

Not an Easy Truce

Loyal to You

NON-FICTION

Skeletons in my Closet (with Dave Sweet)

www.ingramcontent.com/pod-product-compliance
Lightning Source LLC
Chambersburg PA
CBHW051330020726
47501CB00007B/2016